She was stunned by his declaration

Maybe none of what was happening was real. Perhaps she was dreaming. Or maybe her mind had finally snapped from all the strain. It was bound to happen sooner or later—she'd been functioning under tremendous pressure of late. He wasn't in her kitchen, professing his love and quoting Ecclesiastes by dawn's early light. It was just a figment of her overtaxed mind. In a moment she'd awaken to find herself alone, in her bed, a little confused but otherwise unaffected by these wild imaginings.

He took advantage of her dazed state, catching the front of her silky jersey and gently drawing her closer until their lips were but a breath apart.

"You can act like you don't care. You can tell me daily that I'm wasting my time. But I'm not giving up on you so long as there's that spark of hope whenever I kiss you," he solemnly vowed, claiming her mouth with a needy urgency that shook them both....

ABOUT THE AUTHOR

Compliments from one's colleagues are indicative of a masterful grasp of the skills required in one's profession. Ruth Alana Smith, a former Golden Medallion winner, regularly receives kudos from her fellow Superromance authors. They usually comment on her lively, intelligent writing style and her willingness to tackle interesting and unusual themes—such as reverse discrimination in *A Gentleman's Honor*. Ruth, who is married and has two grown children, makes her home in Texas.

Books by Ruth Alana Smith

HARLEQUIN SUPERROMANCE
158–THE WILD ROSE
208–FOR RICHER OR POORER
265–AFTER MIDNIGHT
311–THE SECOND TIME AROUND
356–SPELL BOUND

A Gentleman's Honor

RUTH ALANA SMITH

Harlequin Books

TORONTO • NEW YORK • LONDON
AMSTERDAM • PARIS • SYDNEY • HAMBURG
STOCKHOLM • ATHENS • TOKYO • MILAN

Published April 1990

ISBN 0-373-70400-3

Printed in U.S.A.

CHAPTER ONE

VIRGINIA VANDIVERE-RICE, Creative Director was the fancy signature penned across her formal correspondence. Interoffice memos were initialed VV-R in large florid script at the bottom.

The staff at the Madison Avenue advertising agency held two very separate views when it came to Virginia Vandivere-Rice, a.k.a. VV-R. One's opinion depended directly upon which side of the board table one sat. The agency's partners thought her bright, imaginative, capable and poised. Those who worked side by side with her on the agency's accounts agreed that she was all of those things, but they also knew her to be a high-strung workaholic, a demanding perfectionist.

Behind her back, co-workers joked among themselves about her manic tendencies. What amused and amazed them the most was the way Virginia managed to keep the volatile aspect of her personality in check around the head honchos. She never displayed anything but cool confidence in the presence of her superiors. Selling an image was her stock and trade and she was damned good at it. She packaged herself as a paragon of composed efficiency and the bigwigs bought it.

Her standard operating procedure was to assure the agency's partners that a presentation slated to be pitched to a client twenty-four hours hence would be delivered without a hitch. More often than not she was bluffing. Usually, the all-important strategy to sell the newest high-fiber food or the latest fashion craze was still no more than a germ of an idea on a storyboard. Yet somehow she and her creative crew always managed to pull off an eleventh-hour miracle. Most of the time, it was due to Virginia Vandivere-Rice's genius. What the partners didn't see was the sequence that occurred prior to a presentation: Virginia's proverbial fretting and pacing, her driving herself and everyone else to the limit, pushing harder and harder as the hours grew shorter and shorter.

The crazy part was that she seemed to thrive on crisis. She was at her best under the gun. And though her subordinates admired her talent and grit, they privately theorized about her methods. The general consensus was that Virginia Vandivere-Rice was a stress junkie—a human Chernobyl, as one seasoned adman so aptly put it. A meltdown looking for a place to happen.

Of course, no one made any such inferences to her face. Promotion was the name of the game, and the creative team was collectively respectful of the boss's position and clout within the agency. The snide remarks were saved for the watercooler. In between breaks, everyone was busy playing office politics and jockeying for a favorable notice from the stress junkie.

The newcomers at the agency called her Ms Vandivere, since after her divorce she preferred to be addressed by her maiden name. She simply hadn't gotten around to changing the letterhead. Those who had been around Hanks, Udell & Partners a number of years were on familiar enough footing to call her Virginia. But only one person at the firm presumed to call her Ginny: Rita Mundo, her personal assistant.

Rita had been with Virginia since she'd assumed the creative directorship and the two had grown very close over the past five years. Given their starkly different personalities, no one at the agency quite understood the camaraderie between the two women. Rita was Puerto Rican and, by virtue of her Latin ethos, was as fiery and flashy as Virginia was aloof and conservative. Rita was also much older than her boss and had packed a lot of living into her fifty-two years. Virginia at thirty-two seemed to have no social life at all, except for business mixers. She'd divorced shortly after joining the agency. Nobody really knew the reason for the breakup. There was, however, some speculation on the subject.

The most popular hypothesis was that her husband had placed a poor second to her ambition. Even the janitorial crew discussed the fact that Virginia Vandivere-Rice was married to her job. She routinely put in twelve and fourteen hour days. She'd also been know to spend weekends and holidays holed up at the agency. Most believed that it was the disgruntled hubby who had walked out on Ms Vandivere, not vice versa. Of course, no one could substantiate that, except maybe Rita, and she refused to make any personal disclosures about her boss.

Which was another strange thing. Rita was a very open person. She had no compunction about sharing intimate details of her life with total strangers, whereas Virginia never revealed anything personal—at least not to anyone likely to pass the privileged information on. The staff suspected that she confided in Rita, but the assistant was loyal in her allegiance to her boss. And that was the strange part. Rita was not above engaging in office gossip. She did so regularly. But when it came to the subject of Virginia Vandivere, she was fiercely protective. Her dark eyes would snap toward the guilty party, her red-painted lips clamp shut, and that was that; the conversation was ended.

One thing Rita and Virginia did have in common was their marital status. Rita, however, had the distinction of having three ex-husbands as opposed to Virginia's one. Rita claimed to still love them all. Virginia made no such disclosure regarding her ex. Rita was still very much interested in the opposite sex. Virginia's interests seemed more corporate than corporeal.

Indeed, the contrast between the two women was glaring, even in regard to their physical appearance. Rita was short, a bit hippy, darkly complected, with ebony hair and dark eyes. Virginia was tall, slender, fair skinned with strawberry-blond hair and blue, blue eyes. Rita liked to wear wild ensembles. She decked herself in bright splashes of color and adorned her ears, neck and wrists in lots of looping, dangling, jangling jewelry. Virginia's taste ran more toward a tailored look with only minimal accessories: a Liz Claiborne or Dior suit with a designer scarf draped over a padded shoulder and a pin or flower on the lapel—very proper, very professional.

As Rita sat guard at her desk outside Virginia's office, a phone propped between an ear and a shoulder, conversing while she typed, she motioned for Russell Keaton to go on in. He was late for the meeting and tried to slip into the inner office without drawing any attention to himself.

Virginia was sitting on the edge of her desk, talking strategy on an upcoming ad campaign with the six-member, minus one, creative team. She acknowledged Russell's tardy arrival with a circumspect look in his direction and then went on with what she was saying.

"It's catchy, but too glib for the image we want to convey. We've been over all of this before—the graphics, the market research, the general tone we want to establish from the onset." She stood, pushing back her jacket and putting a hand on her hip. "We're not focusing on the teen set this time. If we hook them in the process, fine and dandy. But they are not our main target. It's the twenty-five to thirty-five-year-old affluent yuppies we're zooming in on. They're not into fads per se. They're into style, status. There's a big difference," she reminded the group.

Russell smiled nervously at Julie Dobeckie as he pulled up a chair alongside of hers. She was new at the agency—a fresh face with fresh ideas and a great pair of legs. Virginia was not only her idol but her goal. She'd made it clear from the get-go that she fully intended to stand in the boss's high-heeled, high-powered shoes one day.

Noticing Russell's inspection of her legs, she shot him a "grow up" look and ventured an opinion on the topic under discussion. "The way I see it, it's the designer we have to hype. Name recognition is the crux of the campaign."

"Exactly," Virginia agreed. "We have to sell America on Don Sebastian. Our objective is to make his name as big in the States as Calvin Klein's. His Argentine essence gives us a great angle to work with. We need to offer him as something different from the same old homespun trends. What words come to mind at the mention of Argentina? Colorful, cultured, spicy and sumptuous are some.'' She walked to the big drawing board propped on an easel in the corner and scribbled the words in red marker. "Give me one-word, off-the-top-of-your-head impressions,'' she prompted, trying to stimulate their sluggish brains and get them to produce a skeleton theme from which to proceed.

"Tango, bolero!" Russell blurted, hoping to redeem himself for having committed the cardinal sin of arriving late.

"Real original, Keaton." Julie's critique of his contribution made everyone laugh, except for Virginia, who was busy jotting his impressions on the board.

"Okay, so it's a little elementary." Russell struggled to maintain a good-humored smile. Generally an easygoing sort, he was a bit touchy when it came to Dobeckie. Probably because she'd rejected his offers of lunch as flippantly as she had just ridiculed his suggestions. "I don't see *you* dazzling us with flashes of brilliance." He couldn't resist getting in a dig of his own.

Julie ignored him and concentrated on answering his challenge. "Actually I was just about to suggest that maybe we're on the wrong track. The smoldering Spanish approach is too obvious and way overdone. We need something more subtle, at least in the beginning. Something sophisticated. A class act or, more precisely, a class ad."

Russell tapped a pencil on his knee. "Great idea." His retort was more sarcastic than enthusiastic.

"Specifically, how do we go about creating this, uh, class ad?"

Accustomed to rivals...bantering among the troops, Virginia refrained from comment and let the two engage in one-upmanship. It had been her experience that creative people had colossal egos. Whenever the distinctive trait came into play, the creative sparks would fly, and quite often, the bit of inspiration with which to ignite a campaign came out of the heated parrying.

"Well..." Julie was stretching her intellect and searching deep within herself for an innovative follow-through. "What if, for instance, we identified Don Sebastian with Buenos Aires? Instead of the loud bolero stuff, we could go for steamy elegance. The city has a unique flavor, you have to admit."

The newcomer's idea struck a positive chord within the creative director. But something was still lacking. In order to develop a fresh approach, create a truly unique flavor, a blend of ingredients was necessary.

"Elegance is fine for promoting ladies' lingerie—which we are not," Russell argued. "We're talking jeans here, Dobeckie. A line of menswear. Men are *not* going to relate to some sissy in a gaucho hat and a pair of dungarees doing the party-hardy scene in festive Buenos Aires. Where's the machismo?"

An excited rush went through Virginia. The perfect angle, the necessary blend had crystallized in her head.

Being a confirmed feminist, Julie took issue with his attitude. "You're straight out of the fifties, you know that, Keaton? In case you haven't noticed, it's a new generation. Macho men are out. The refined and sensitive type is in."

"Is that a fact?" He shot her a caustic grin. "Well, I have news for you, lady. There's a vast contingency of macho men still around, and they happen to have big bucks to spend. And if we fail to appeal to that group, Don Sebastian might as well forget about stitching up jeans and go into the wine-making business."

The debate had taken on a decidedly personal note. Virginia exercised her authority and took control. "You two can carry on the fifties versus the nineties debate in private. For now, let's concentrate our energies on the campaign, shall we?"

Russell complied with a shrug of his shoulders.

Julie donned a stiff expression, turning slightly in her chair so that he was viewing her back, not her legs.

"Actually you both made valid points," Virginia said, donning her mediator hat. "I think perhaps the two of you have struck upon the heart of the Don Sebastian theme."

The two subordinates were equally baffled. What winning strategy had they introduced? They were thrilled at being given credit—even if it was shared credit—but they hadn't the vaguest notion what terrific idea they had come up with. As always, they waited for Virginia to enlighten them.

She assumed a relaxed posture, bracing her hips against the desk and slipping her hands into the deep pockets of her jacket. "The flavor of the campaign will most definitely be Argentine, but we will incorporate both the sophistication of Buenos Aires and the ruggedness of the pampas in our ads. Our Don Sebastian man will be multifaceted. He will be a man who bridges both elements, a man who is at ease with himself and comfortable in his Don Sebastian jeans in any setting, be it amid the polo set of Buenos Aires or the rugged splendor of the pampas. The subliminal message we'll get across to the buying public is that Don Sebastian encompasses both the casual and the elegant. His jeans are designed to fit the male body and most any occasion well.''

The creative crew grew excited at the premise. Most amazed by the concept were Russell and Julie. Had they suggested all of that? Hardly. It took the Vandivere touch to bring the concept into imaginative focus.

"Further," she continued, "we can take the idea of a split-focused theme a step beyond that. I agree with Russell's assessment of the potential risk of falling into an attitude gap. We certainly do not want to exclude any sect of dollar power.''

Russell looked pleased with himself.

The swing of Julie's leg became a bit more pronounced.

"But neither do we want to make the mistake of falling into a gender gap," Virginia went on.

A smug smile materialized on Julie's glossed lips.

Russell began tapping the pencil on his knee once more.

"In order to assure a broad appeal for the Don Sebastian line in America, we have to interest women as well as men. Girlfriends and wives exert a great deal of influence over the males in their lives. Many of them are the fashion consultants and the buyers. We'd be foolish to underestimate their importance. If they are convinced that their boyfriends and husbands will look sensational in a pair of Don Sebastian jeans, they'll pitch the line for us, swamp the stores and make our job generally easier. So, how do we secure their interest?'' She scanned the faces of her creative team.

"Let's be blunt, Virginia.'' Walter Miller, a seasoned adman, spoke up for the first time. "Securing female interest is just a polite way of saying that we want to seduce them into buying. Certain fundamental tactics apply. Women don't like to be rushed or pressured. Any guy will tell you the wham, bam, thank-you-ma'am approach won't work. You have to woo a woman along. Use a little artful persuasion. Tease and titillate.''

"Oh, pul-eeze!'' Julie rolled her eyes.

Virginia merely smiled. During working hours, she was wholly the professional. The fact that she was female was incidental. Walt's analogy triggered an idea. "Subtle teasers, huh?'' She stood and walked behind the desk as she mulled over the notion. "I think that approach would work beautifully, and not just on the female psyche. Picture it—we begin the campaign slowly, intrigue the public by building curiosity with fifteen-second spots on TV and radio. Yes, indeed—'' her eyes took on a glazed expression "—it might just be the answer. We could accomplish name recognition at the same time with just a flash across the screen or a one-liner over the airwaves. 'Don Sebastian is coming to America.''' She liked the sound of it. "Something along the lines of Hollywood hype but more clever and classy, more suave than slick.'' She was on a roll, hardly aware that others were present in the room.

"I get it! Sort of like previews to a coming attraction.'' Russell was high on the idea.

Virginia refocused with a blink. "Yes. We pace the campaign. Hold back on the main launch. We'll introduce Don Sebastian slowly, smoothly, *seductively*. Then, we'll pick up the tempo of the campaign as the launch date nears. I think it's a sound approach.''

Everyone seemed to agree, except for Spencer Gebhardt, the oldest member of the team. A thin and jaundiced-looking fellow, he tended to sit and bite his nails and say little until a campaign displayed signs of getting off the ground. He was not a motivator. The role he played within the group was that of moderator. He was a detail man, always on the alert for possible pitfalls, and he could usually be counted on to voice a concern or two.

''I see problems with it, Virginia,'' he interjected, instantly putting a damper on things. Everyone knew he was going to say something that would take the wind out of their sails. There were grumbles and sighs as the rest of the crew slouched back in their chairs and awaited his objections.

He pushed his glasses back up on the bridge of his nose. ''If you try to center this campaign on a one-liner, it had better be a gem. Because if it bombs, so does Don Sebastian. You're taking an awfully big gamble with an account that this agency sweated blood to get. Hanks and Udell have a lot riding on this one.''

So do I. You have no idea of the personal implications, Spencer, she thought to herself. ''I'm aware of that,'' was all she said.

''I was against the idea of focusing the campaign on a sole model, if you remember. I said in the beginning that it was too damn limiting to identify an entire line with one handsome face. And look what's happened. We've spent weeks looking at every male model in New York and we still haven't come up with the Don Sebastian man.''

His criticism was specifically directed toward her, since it had been she who had insisted upon the single image and she who had subsequently vetoed every applicant the top modeling agencies in town had sent over. There wasn't a male model in New York who wouldn't give his soul to land the choice assignment. Hundreds had presented their portfolios and been interviewed but none had possessed that certain charismatic quality Virginia was looking for. The staff was beginning to compare the manhunt for the perfect Don Sebastian image to that of the quest for the Holy Grail.

"We're running out of time, not to mention applicants." Spencer knew she disliked having her decisions questioned, especially after the fact and in front of others, but he was genuinely distressed about the snag they'd hit in the preliminary stages of the campaign. "I say we should reconsider our previous position and go with a more traditional approach—have various models represent the line. I also strongly suggest that you scrap the idea of hinging the campaign on a one-liner unless you want to risk running into the same kind of dead end as we did on the single model focus. We botch this account and we could all be filling out forms down at the unemployment office."

Virginia's tone when answering his concerns was measured and cool. "You don't get ahead in the ad business by playing it safe. There are more than a few laid-off admen who'd argue the merits of sticking with the traditional approach. I appreciate your reservations, Spencer, but my decision to go with one face to promote the line still stands. If time is growing short, get more aggressive in your search."

"But we've run the gamut of available models at all of the top agencies," he persisted.

"Then go to the smaller, less-known agencies. If that proves fruitless, then conduct our own screening. Run an ad. Scan the streets. Do what you have to, but come up with the face we need." She rested her arms on the high-backed leather chair and pinned him with a steely look.

"Hell, Virginia! I don't even know what it is you want. Everyone I thought was right, you thought was wrong."

Her smile was deceiving. "Just keep after it, Spencer. That's what you're paid to do. Me—I'm paid to take risks and make decisions. And as for the one-liner strategy, I never meant to imply that I would hinge the entire campaign on a single slogan. I may opt to use several one-liners. The point is, I want to keep each one short and provocative. Tease and titillate, as Walt said. That's the strategy. I expect each and every one of you to give the Don Sebastian account priority over everything else." She glanced down at her watch, noting that she had allowed the rap session to run beyond the allotted time. Her attendance was required at an executive board meeting already under way in an upstairs conference room. "That should do it. I want to hear your ideas by the end of the week."

Once the meeting was dismissed and her team had left for their respective particleboard and Plexiglas cubicles, more commonly referred to as bull pens, Virginia quickly ran a brush through her bobbed hair, retouched her lipstick and then hurried to the next matter of business on her busy agenda. Whenever she passed Rita's desk, it was generally on the run. Her assistant had to get in as much information as possible in the short space of sixty seconds or so. She handed Virginia her morning messages, which were organized in descending degree of importance—those requiring her immediate or special attention on top.

Rita talked quickly. "Your mother, she called again to remind you to bring Godiva chocolates when you come this weekend. She say your aunt will be heartbroken if you forgot."

Her Puerto Rican accent was noticeable only at certain times and with certain words. She indiscriminately exchanged vowel sounds, especially long *e*'s for short *i*'s, rolled her *r*'s and used incorrect verb tenses.

"Forget," Virginia automatically corrected her. "Chocolates for Aunt Caddie. Got it. What else?" She adopted an abbreviated speech pattern whenever she conversed with Rita.

"You have a four o'clock with your dentist today," her assistant continued.

"No can do. Reschedule." Virginia scanned her messages, slipping the ones that were important into her jacket pocket, tossing a few of the pink slips onto Rita's desk for her to handle and dropping the rest in the trash can.

Rita wondered why she bothered writing down phone numbers and requests that she knew Virginia would not answer. "You're expected at the cocktail party Mr. Udell ees giving tonight. A dressy affair. *Muchos* VIPs."

"Damn! I'd almost forgotten. What time?"

"Eight."

"How does my schedule look for tomorrow? I need to squeeze in a meeting with Jarvis Thedford about the new fitness center account. It may take some time. What can I shuffle around or table until later?"

Rita already knew the answer. Her bracelets jangled as she flipped the calendar to the next day's date. Her expression and voice became sulky as she replied, "Tomorrow ees full up, except for lunch."

"I'll see him then. Arrange it, okay? I'll be in with the heads until two or so." She made a motion to leave.

Rita muttered a few expletives in Spanish and began slinging papers around.

Virginia knew she'd made some gross faux pas. "What is it?" she asked, retracing her steps.

Rita kept her eyes averted as she rolled a fresh piece of stationery into the typewriter. "What ees what?" she returned, pouting.

"Come on, Rita. You don't cuss me in Spanish unless I've goofed up royally. What grievous offense have I committed this time?"

Rita's only reply was the clicking of the typewriter keys.

Virginia turned the calendar around and examined it. The next day's date had been circled and a notation made in the margin beside the one to three o'clock time slot. *Birthday lunch,* it read.

Virginia felt like a first-class ass. She'd forgotten a promise she'd made to a dear friend and loyal assistant. "Oh, Rita, I'm sorry. Your birthday lunch completely slipped my mind."

"Ees okay." Rita pretended to shrug off the importance of the occasion.

"No, it's not," Virginia insisted. "I'm a real screwup sometimes. You deserve to be treated better. Forgive me?" she begged.

Rita favored her with a toothy smile. "Sure. Ees no big deal."

"It most certainly is a big deal. Call and make reservations anywhere you'd like, then cancel the rest of my appointments after one tomorrow. We'll celebrate into the night if you want."

Rita's mood instantly soared. "I bought a new dress. Ees the color of melon and ssss-hot!" Her shoulders shimmied and she rotated her dark eyes from corner to corner.

Her clowning made Virginia laugh. "The heads are waiting. Have to go." She dashed down the jade-carpeted corridor. "Call for reservations. Don't forget," she hollered back over her shoulder.

Rita shook her head. Ginny never stopped. Work, work, work! No rest. No fun. No man. Rita suspected that the only thing even remotely close to the euphoria of an orgasm that she'd experienced in years was the mention of a junior partnership in the agency if she successfully pulled off the Don Sebastian campaign. Of course, no one knew about that except Rita. The stakes were the highest they'd ever been for Virginia Vandivere-Rice. Rita worried about what would happen to her if the ad campaign fell flat. She found it ironic that the pinnacle of Ginny's career depended on a man—the Don Sebastian man. A woman who had no time for and seemingly no great use for men was now suddenly in dire need of a hot-blooded, great-looking male.

Oh, well, such was the irony of life, was Rita's philosophical thought as she reached for the phone. At least for a few hours tomorrow Ginny could forget about the pressure while they celebrated her birthday. Fifty-three and still the *magnífico* Mundo could catch a man's eye. Not as often anymore, but often enough to assuage her ego and libido.

She smiled to herself and dialed to make the reservation.

CHAPTER TWO

A LOW WHISTLE ESCAPED J. D. Mahue's lips as he tilted his head and let his eyes climb the towering Chase Manhattan Bank Building. He'd never seen anything as impressive. New York was awesome. The descriptions in Cousin Mason's letters paled in comparison to standing in the shadow of the immensity, the complexity, the actuality that was New York City.

There was an excess of everything here—steel and glass, people and vehicles, motion and noise. The metropolitan milieu was certainly overwhelming to a cotton picker from Mississippi. When he'd left the Delta bound for New York on a Greyhound bus, he'd had no idea he would be traveling to a new dimension. Previous to his arrival, New York had been just a dot on a map, a city on the Eastern seaboard, a hope of a better life than the one he'd known on the levees of the Tallahatchie River.

New York was where his cousin had gone to seek his fortune three years earlier. A place he rambled on and on about in his letters home. A place where—according to Mason—there was plenty of opportunity, an abundance of pretty women and all sorts of fancy restaurants and shops.

Come on up and give it a try, Cousin Mason had urged him. Time and again he'd written about his important job at an investment bank. The granddaddy of 'em all. He was working his way up, becoming a whiz kid on Wall Street. He'd extended an open invitation to his Delta relations to venture beyond the Mason-Dixon line and share in the bounty. He had connections and would be happy to help any member of the family reestablish themselves in New York. After all, what was kin for, he'd written.

Being the most daring and discontented of the Mahue clan, J.D. had decided to take Mason up on his generous offer. He'd packed up his few belongings in a duffel bag and traveled north into Yankee territory. And now here he was in the Big Apple, standing at the tip of Broadway, in front of the building where Cousin Mason wheeled and dealed. The long journey was over. He'd finally arrived and was about to embark on a brand-new adventure. He felt invigorated and full of expectation. It didn't matter that he was toting the extent of his worldly possessions in a canvas bag and the sum total of his net worth in his back pocket. So what if he only had fifty-five dollars and some silver change to his name. Soon things would improve. Once Cousin Mason tapped his influential connections and got him work, his future prosperity would be assured.

He took a deep breath, shifted the duffel bag from one shoulder to the other and headed into the bank building. He smiled warmly as he held open the door for two stylishly dressed ladies. They both did a double take as he proceeded into the lobby.

"Is that not the best-looking man you've seen in a while?" one asked the other.

"In a while? Are you kidding me? Try *ever*!" The lavish compliment was followed by a sigh. "He's probably married, involved or gay. They always are."

THE RECEPTIONIST at the front desk was bent down, pretending to be searching for something in a bottom drawer while inspecting the cap job the dentist had completed that morning on her two front teeth. She was so engrossed in her own mirrored reflection that she was unaware of J.D.'s presence until he spoke up.

"Excuse me, ma'am. I'm looking for Mason Mahue," he explained in a thick Mississippi drawl. "Would you be kind enough to point the way to his office?"

She quickly slammed shut the drawer and sat up in her chair. "Mason Mahue is no longer in our employ," she informed him in a brusque tone. She was unhappy with the end result of her cap job. The damn dentist had overdone it. She looked more like Bucky beaver than Farah Fawcett. The color didn't even match the rest of her teeth.

J.D. was stunned by this unexpected bit of news. "Are you sure? Maybe we're talking about a different Mason Mahue. He's tall and lanky and—"

"—and terminated." She finished his sentence for him. Geez! The man talked like molasses poured—slow and syrupy. "He hasn't worked here in quite some time. He was let go shortly after Black Monday."

"Black Monday?" He hadn't the vaguest notion to what she was referring.

"October 19, 1987—the day the market crashed," she said in a voice that implied any well-informed person would know the date and its significance.

J.D. was more confused than ever. "That can't be possible. There must be some mistake. We get letters from him regularly and he's always talking about his fine position and the big deals he's making here." He

set down his duffel bag atop her desk and started to
unzip it. "I have a letter we got from him just a few
weeks ago." He fumbled amid the bag's contents to
find it. "The stationery has your company name on it.
You must have him mixed up with somebody else."

Neither his obvious bewilderment nor his striking
good looks had the slightest effect on the impatient
receptionist. She had worries of her own. Specifically, a bungled cap job and the thousand dollars it
had cost her. "I assure you, I am not confused. There
has been only one Mason Mahue at this firm. Thank
God!"

J.D. wondered why she found it necessary to add the
disapproving postscript.

"I wouldn't be at all surprised if he swiped the stationery from the supply room before he was let go.
The man was without scruples and obviously an im-
poster, too. If he presented himself as being some sort
of wheel around here, it was an out-and-out lie. He
was only a gofer." At his puzzled look, she put it in
plain English. "An errand boy. A flunky who delivered messages and went for lunches." She dismissed
the letter he held out for her inspection with a flick of
her hand. "I'm sorry if you believed differently but
I'm not surprised that he misrepresented himself.
Mahue had an attitude problem. He was a con artist
deluxe," was her unflattering appraisal of his cousin's character.

J.D.'s spirits sank as he dropped the letter inside his
duffel bag and rezipped it. His mind was numb. What
would he do now?

Thinking the matter of the masquerading Mahue
was settled, the receptionist picked up the phone and
directed her attention toward more pressing busi-

ness—threatening her dentist with legal action if he didn't redo the caps.

"I hate to be a bother, ma'am . . ."

She expelled a disgusted sigh and returned the receiver to its cradle.

". . . but I was wondering if perhaps you could provide me with a home address for him. You see, I'm new in town and—"

"This isn't the Visitors' Center," she snapped.

J.D.'s normally warm brown eyes grew icy. "I know that, ma'am. You do keep personnel records, don't you?"

Afraid she had gone too far and the hick might complain about her, the receptionist forced herself to be a bit more amiable. "We do. Just a moment, please, and I'll check."

She dialed an inner-office extension, asked for the information, then jotted it down on a memo pad and hung up the phone. "The address and phone number he gave us are in Brooklyn," she informed J.D. Handing him the piece of paper, she pointed out, "Of course, there's no guarantee that he's still living in the same place. He very well may have moved by now. I'd call before I made the trip."

"I appreciate your trouble." He tucked the memo into his shirt pocket, picked up his bag and marched out of the plush offices without a backward glance.

The receptionist stared after him as he walked away. The guy had his nerve. What did he think? That she was the local information bureau, maybe? He did fill out a pair of jeans nicely, though, she mused off-handedly as he stepped into the elevator. Long, lean, hard body types were usually great in the sack. "Are you crazy?" she muttered to herself, snapping from her reverie with a jerk. "The guy shares a genetic link with that mutant, Mason Mahue." She shivered at the thought.

J.D. PRESSED A FINGER to his ear in a futile attempt to better hear what the woman on the opposite end of the phone was saying. Between the traffic noise and her broken English he was having trouble understanding her.

"No live here anymore. Gone long time," the woman told him. Her accent was difficult to decipher.

"Do you have any idea where he went?" he shouted into the receiver.

"He owe me rent. Leave in the night and tell me nothing. You find him, you tell him I want money he owe," was the angry response.

"Yeah, I'll do that," he replied, hanging up and looking around bewilderedly. He hadn't the faintest idea what to do next. He didn't have enough money for a return ticket to Mississippi. He was stuck in New York with no place to go and precious little money to exist on while he searched for his missing cousin. Damn Mason for luring him to New York under false pretenses.

A rueful smile spread across J.D.'s lips as he raked a hand through his sun-streaked brown hair. He should have known better than to have believed Mason's glowing account of himself. Even when they were kids, he'd had a bad habit of stretching the truth, especially when it pertained to himself. He'd always been a braggart, constantly claiming to be the bravest and best arm wrestler, rock skipper, tree climber or lady-killer in the whole of Tallahatchie County. But whenever the true story of his cousin's latest escapade came to light, his awe-inspiring account of the great feat never quite matched the actual deed. J.D. had thought he'd outgrown being suckered by his cousin. Obviously not. Once again he'd been taken in by another of his cousin's whopper tales. Only this time Mason had cost him time and money he could ill afford to squander. The predicament in which he found himself was his own gullible fault, and as usual, he'd have to rely on his own resourcefulness to get himself out of yet another fine mess Mason had instigated.

First things first, he decided, reaching down to retrieve the duffel bag he'd dropped at his feet. He'd search for some cheap place to stay until he found work. Realizing he clasped only thin air, he glanced to the spot where he'd dropped the bag. It was gone. Disbelievingly, he pivoted and surveyed the immediate area. Nothing. Not a sign of it.

He looked around, hoping to catch the culprit who'd swiped his worldly possessions. Passersby were carrying briefcases and shopping bags, but none were toting the easily identifiable maroon canvas bag. He quickly slapped his back pocket to make sure his wallet was still there. It was, thank the Lord for small favors.

Swell, just swell. All he had left were the clothes on his back. Disheartened, he walked to the subway stairs he'd noticed earlier halfway up the block. He had no earthly notion where he was headed—somewhere less crowded and more hospitable, he hoped. He descended into the tunnel, dropped in the proper change at the turnstile and blended with the other commuters waiting on the platform. At the approach of the rail car, he stood back like a gallant Southern gentleman to let the ladies board first. Two young punks sporting spiked hair and psychedelic T-shirts under leather aviator jackets cut in front of him. Their crude talk and manners rubbed him the wrong way. He was strongly tempted to snatch the two of them up by their coat collars and deposit them at the end of the line. Deciding they weren't worth the trouble, he curbed the impulse and followed the pair to the rear of the car. They took the last available seats. J.D. stood in the aisle beside them and grabbed the overhead hand bar as the train moved to the next stop.

"So I said to myself, 'Hey! Who needs it?'" one of the punky characters told the other. "I don't have to take no crap from this joker. So I was a little later clocking in. So what!" He shrugged his shoulders. "So maybe it happened a time or two before. It ain't like I was stealing the silver!" He shrugged again. "The manager had no right to chew my butt out in front of the customers like he did." With an indignant stretch of his neck he stated, "Nobody talks to Frankie Garbelli like he's so much garbage."

"So what'd ya do?" the other asked.

"I told him where he could stick it. I walked outta the place in the middle of the lunch rush, but not before I caused a helluva commotion. Everyone in the joint was watching."

"But whaddaya gonna do for bread? Jobs ain't easy to come by," the sidekick with a bad case of zits pointed out.

"Something'll turn up. I'll work the streets before I clean tables again. I hated the whole scene since day one, man. Busing dishes ain't my style. I only took the job to tide me over until my uncle Vinnie can pull some strings and get me hired on permanent down at

the docks. Well, that and because of the fringe benefits. You wouldn't believe the rich babes that come in
there. Oozing money. Limos, furs, rocks the size of
golf balls on their fingers.''

''Yeah, I hear Le Bouves is the new hot spot for the
society bitches,'' the cohort concurred. ''So, how'd ya
make out? You score with any of 'em?''

''Once or twice,'' Frankie confided with a nasty
wink. ''But they're losers, man. No boobs and no fun.
They expect ya to scrape off their stinkin' leftovers and
kiss butt for a stinkin' tip. Not me, man. I don't want
no part of them or busing dishes no more. When that
swish of a day manager started riding me right in front
of everybody, I dropped a load of dishes on his foot,
threw in my apron and blew the ritzy joint. It gave me
a real rush, man, to tell 'em to kiss my butt for a
change.'' He demonstrated the kiss-off by puckering
his lips and making a loud smacking noise.

The pair shared a good laugh.

J.D. readied himself to disembark at the next stop.
He'd overheard all that was necessary. He planned to
hunt up the nearest phone book, look up the address
of Le Bouves and apply for the busboy position.
Cleaning off tables might be too lowly a job for the
abrasive kid with the spiked hair but not for a sharecropper's son who was accustomed to hard work and
hard times. So long as it was honest work, it wasn't
beneath the dignity of Joe Dillon Mahue.

CHAPTER THREE

THROUGHOUT LUNCH Rita was even more efferves-
cent than usual. She loved all the special attention
they'd been receiving since their arrival at the trendy
café. Of course, she didn't realize that the enormous
fuss being made over her was a direct result of the
fifty-dollar bill Virginia had slipped the maître d' as
they were being seated.

"Eesn't this great?" she enthused as the hovering
waiter topped off her champagne glass once more.
"We're really getting the royal treatment. I've been
dying to come here. Ees the hottest spot in town, you
know." Her eyes danced around the posh dining
room. "Oh, look who just came in. Can you believe
it? Donald Trump and his wife. We're dining with the
Trumps! Imagine me—Rita Mundo—sharing bread
with one of the richest couples in America."

"We're not exactly sharing a table with them."
Virginia couldn't help but grin. It amazed her sometimes how at the age of fifty-three Rita still retained a
childlike penchant for oversimplification. Life was one
big never-ending party to her.

Rita grinned back at her and shrugged. "We're
sharing the same air. Ees nearly the same thing," she
insisted.

"Close enough, I guess." Virginia decided it was
better to let Rita have it her way. After all, it was her

birthday bash. She tried to sneak a discreet peek at her watch.

Rita noticed. "Always in a rush to get back to business," she scolded her boss. "We're supposed to be having fun."

"We have been, but—"

"Correction. *Yo* have been. *You* have not. For the past hour you been itching to leave. What am I going to do with you?" She sighed and sipped from her champagne glass. "You act like a good time ees a sin."

"Sorry. You're absolutely right. I promised that we'd forget about the agency for one afternoon and we will." She reached across the table with her glass and clinked it against Rita's. "May the upcoming year be a fabulous one. I hope it brings you nothing but good fortune," she said by way of a toast.

"I'd settle for a semigood man to snuggle up with at night." Rita shot her a wicked wink.

Virginia shook her head amusedly. "You have a one-track mind. What would your grandchildren think if they knew your tawdry secret wish?"

"They'd thank God their grandmother Mundo ees living with someone other than them," she said flatly. "My son's house ees a zoo. Five kids, his wife's mother and only one bathroom. Ayyy!" She rolled her eyes. "I pray I snag a fourth husband before ees time for me to retire."

"You've a long time before then." Virginia was uncomfortable with the thought of Rita's eventual retirement.

The older woman sensed her concern. "You would miss me, no?"

"I would miss you, yes. I've come to rely on you a great deal, both personally and professionally."

"At the office ees okay, but you need to associate with others more. A woman friend ees fine, but a man friend would be better." Rita launched into yet another stanza of the same old song.

Virginia knew where the conversation was headed and wanted to sidestep the lecture. "Don't start, Rita. We've been over the same ground a hundred times before. I don't want to be involved. I tried cohabitation once, remember? The arrangement was a dismal failure. I'm perfectly happy on my own."

"You don seem so happy to me," Rita said pointedly. "All you theenk about ees work, work, work. You keep busy to avoid facing what ees really troubling you. I know and you know ees only your wounded pride that makes you antisocial."

"I am not antisocial. I just happen to like my privacy," she argued, wishing Rita would drop the subject.

"That ees a bunch of bunk. You make excuses on the outside for what ees wrong on the inside." She signified the exact area of her friend's malaise by pressing a hand to her heart. "You suffered a double dose of hurt and it makes you doubly wary of men."

"Nonsense," Virginia scoffed, careful to keep both her inflection and expression politely temperate. She had become very adept at masking her feelings. So good, she sometimes wondered herself what it was she really felt. Numbness mostly. "I went through a divorce. A lot of women do. It was unpleasant but not traumatic. I am not especially bitter and I certainly don't consider myself among the ranks of the walking wounded. I've always been somewhat of a loner. I simply prefer to devote my time and energy to something more productive than idle flirtations." It sounded good—quite convincing, in fact. But then, that was what she did best—convince, persuade, sway and impress on a grand scale.

Rita wasn't buying it. "Sure, okay, you're fine. Completely self-sufficient. An island." Her eyes narrowed and pinned Virginia. "I suppose you don have hard feelings toward your ex, even though while he was married to you he slept with any and every woman who could get him where he wanted to go."

"Ancient history." Virginia summed up past heartaches with a dismissing lift of the tulip-shaped glass to her lips.

Her attempt to skirt the touchy issue only made Rita more determined to discuss the many transgressions of her adulterous husband. "First he has a fling with his agent, next the script writer for the daytime soap and then the producer. A regular Don Juan, your ex," she said with a derisive snort. "I suppose it don bother you that you supported the bum while he was nothing more than a struggling, two-bit actor, and now that he's an afternoon sex idol and worth a mint, he don even mention a former wife. He don get any high ratings in my book!" Her bracelets jangled with every animated gesture.

Virginia opened her mouth to speak but Rita neither encouraged nor paused for a response.

"And it couldn't be a sore spot that the gossip sheets say he's having thees hot affair with his current leading lady. No, you're much too busy, too productive to be bitter," she needled her.

Virginia tried to get a word in, but Rita steamrollered on.

"You don watch him on TV because it interferes with daily business, not because it cuts like a knife every time you see him make love on the tube. You keep his identity a secret to protect your privacy, not because it would be too painful to answer the curious questions about why the marriage break up.''

Broke up, Virginia mentally edited. Her fingertips drummed the table.

''Explaining how you caught him again and again with other women and why you stayed in a bad marriage as long as you deed has nothing to do with wounded pride, eh?''

''No one but you knows those sordid details,'' Virginia managed to inject. Her features grew stony as she set aside her glass. ''My own mother is unaware of Rob's infidelity. I want to keep it that way. Rob Rice is a closed chapter—a foolish but certainly not fatal mistake. I lived a soap-opera-like existence the years we were married. Why would I want to watch reruns of it on TV? I'm glad he's doing well. I even hope he wins an Emmy. He's a better actor than he was a husband, that's for sure.'' She smiled at the backhanded compliment she'd extended her ex. Normally, the only thoughts she harbored about him were categorically negative ones.

''We're both doing great on our own. He sells the public on sex—I sell them on corn flakes. In a sense, Rob did me a favor. Finally facing and dealing with his indiscretions made me tougher. Our divorce freed me to pursue my own ambitions without feeling guilty. So you see, your amateur analysis is all wrong. I'm not bitter or wary when it comes to the opposite sex, just realistic. So could we please put an end to this ongoing pseudo therapy session we engage in periodically? I know you mean well, but—''

"You're sick of hearing it." Rita put it more bluntly than she would have.

Virginia nodded.

"Fine, ees okay," Rita agreed, capitulating. "I won say any more about the bum. Not today, at least," she qualified. "And I keep my opinion to myself about Saint Billy and the problem with your mother, except to beg you to talk to her about it. The stone wall between you two only grows stronger with silence. Ees a shame. A mother and daughter should be close."

"Please. Let's not spoil a pleasant lunch by discussing my family." At the mention of her dead brother and the ever-increasing emotional distance between her and her mother, Virginia's heart lurched in her chest. She was relieved to spy the waiter making his way toward their table with the birthday cake she'd requested in advance. It was a timely diversion.

Fifty-three candles flickered brightly. Rita was more animated than a Saturday-morning cartoon as the cake was set before them. "Oh, for me? So many candles. We should save them, maybe. In case of another city blackout, we could use them to light the expressway," she joked.

"You have to make a wish," Virginia pointed out.

Rita sucked in a breath, closed her eyes, made a wish and blew hard, snuffing out all the candles. "I deed it! I get my wish."

"You can't tell," Virginia cautioned her.

"Superstition." Rita began plucking the candles from the cake. "We both desire the same thing. You to fulfill your ambition and me to fill my empty bed. A man ees what we both desperately need."

"Poor choice of words. Never say you are desperate." To be desperate implied a lack of control, which was a state Virginia both irrationally feared and periodically fought. She forced herself to fend off the bottomless, floundering feelings she experienced intermittently; lately the condition was getting progressively worse.

"I'm not as prideful as you. I'm not ashamed to say what ees true. And the truth ees, I yearn for a serious lover and you must find the perfect male to push the Don Sebastian line. Time ees growing short for us both."

"I'm not ready to push the panic button just yet." She watched as the waiter cut two slices of cake, and she accepted the extended plate he offered her after serving Rita.

"My favorite—chocolate and more chocolate." Rita licked a dab of icing from her fingertip. "So..." She smacked her lips. "Now that you have stuck your neck out and said there can be only one face to sell the Argentine's jeans, what will you do if you can't deliver the goods?"

"I'll deliver him. Don't worry." She sounded more confident than she felt at the moment.

"I do worry." Rita's voice dropped to a confidential hush. "You are taking a great risk centering the campaign on a phantom man. Why do you gamble on something so important to your future?"

"Everything will fall into place, Rita," she assured her between bites of the rich dessert. "I always come up with the right angle in the nick of time. You have to trust your instincts in this business. And mine are telling me that we have yet to find that perfect someone to represent Don Sebastian. The male models I've interviewed so far just aren't the right type. They either look like male dancers at Chippendale's or the men you see in every mail-order catalog."

"But this ees no ordinary client and not just another campaign. What of the partnership offered you? There ees great pressure on you to produce," Rita persisted. "You must chooz someone soon."

Virginia sighed, lowered her fork to her plate and shoved it away. "I'll pull it off. If worse comes to worse, as a last resort I'll go with an unknown and create the necessary magnetism myself. It'd be a lot easier if the guy had natural charisma, but it's not absolutely essential. Images are made every day. Freeze-dried Madison Avenue commodities are becoming a trend in themselves. It would be nice if our guy had something a little different about him, but if not I'll manufacture it."

Rita scooped the last bite of cake from her fork and dabbed her ruby-painted lips with the napkin. Folding her arms on the table, she directed a sizing look in Virginia's direction. "Then why do you hesitate to do so? Ees it because you are bluffing again, maybe?"

For the first time, Virginia displayed a gut response. "The only reason I've delayed producing a synthetic image is because I'd like to come up with the genuine article for once," she answered a bit defensively. "You should know better than anyone that I don't make claims I can't back up. I could, here and now, pick most any reasonably attractive male and mold him into the larger-than-life Don Sebastian man."

"You are good, Ginny, but I theenk maybe you underestimate the difficulty of doing such a thing with so little time left."

Rita purposely baited her boss. She most certainly did know Virginia better than anyone else. And it was precisely for that reason that she worried. She was afraid Ginny had put herself in a compromising position by stubbornly persisting in focusing the campaign on a sole model. She was prideful to a fault. She would rather run the risk of losing a long-desired and much-deserved junior partnership in the firm than admit that perhaps her strategy was wrong this once. The big summit with Sebastian's American rep was only days off. The scuttlebutt around the office was that the magic worker of Madison Avenue was stymied on the Sebastian account but too damned stubborn to cry uncle. Rita felt a great responsibility to try to spring her boss from the trap her bullheadedness had caused. Knowing her as well as she did, she decided the best way to motivate Ginny was to imply that a feat was beyond her doing. Trick her into action.

"There remains only a few days until you must present a detailed version of the campaign to Don Sebastian's people. Where ees your image? Your *caballero*?" She feigned a resigned tone. "Bluffing ees not exactly the same as bragging but sometimes the consequences are similar."

At the unflattering suggestion that she might be guilty of boastful and brash behavior, Virginia sat up straight in her chair and donned an obstinate look. "I'm not bragging. I could do it. I could pick some man at random today and make him a household word."

Rita thought she deserved an Emmy herself for the outstanding performance she was giving. She'd win hands down in the category of best supporting actress. "If you say so...."

She assumed the demeanor of an indulgent mother.

Her patronizing tone only fueled Virginia's desire to prove herself. "I can see that you're only trying to humor me. Well, let's put my *bluff* to a test, shall we? And just to sweeten things up, how about a side wager? I'll bet you another lunch here at Le Bouves that I can do exactly what I claim. Loser picks up the tab, of course."

Rita pretended to mull over the proposition. "I don't know," she hedged. "My salary ees much smaller than yours. I would have to dip into my mad money should I loose."

"Lose—one *o*," Virginia remarked out of habit.

"Whatever." Rita's gold bracelets slipped down her arm and clinked together in a heap at her elbow as she propped her chin on the flat of her palm and cast a critical eye around the room. "Who picks our guinea peeg?"

"Pig," Virginia enunciated. "I'll let you choose the candidate for our experiment, but the choice is subject to my approval. That's fair."

Rita was already searching out the possibilities. "Okay, ees a bet," she agreed. "I chooz him."

Virginia had not been prepared for her to act so swiftly or emphatically. "For crying out loud, Rita. We're not picking out steaks at a meat market. We need to exert a little selectivity." She looked in the general direction Rita was pointing in.

"I know my beefcake," Rita insisted. "And he ees prime stuff."

"Who are you talking about?" Virginia could not figure out who she meant. There were three men in the general vicinity she was pointing to. At one table an older gentleman was seated in the company of either his daughter or a very young consort. At another were two business types, twentyish and well dressed but hardly hunk-of-the-month material.

"The one in the jeans. His buns ees nice, no?"

The only man in the place wearing jeans was also wearing an apron and was clearing dishes. "The busboy!" Virginia could not fathom her even suggesting such a preposterous idea. "Out of the question." She discounted the crazy notion straightaway.

"You want a man who looks good in a pair of jeans, no?"

"Well, yes, but—"

"But what?" Rita pressed.

"There's more to it than raw physique. The man has to be better than average looking and possess a certain style. A busboy hardly conforms to the criteria." Virginia couldn't believe she was even debating the absurd proposition.

"How do you know he eesn't handsome and charming? His backside ees better than average. Maybe his front side make your heart skip a beat, too." She signaled for the waiter.

Second-guessing what her impetuous secretary had in mind, Virginia whispered, "Don't you dare, Rita."

Rita paid no attention. She and the waiter exchanged words as she pointed out the busboy.

Virginia was mortified. "I can't believe you just did that!" she fumed under her breath. "You don't seriously expect me to go through with this?"

"You don have to marry him. Just look him over ees all." Rita could not see the harm in it.

"I don't believe it! He's coming over." Virginia shrank in her chair and shielded her face with a hand. "What am I supposed to say? How do I explain?"

Rita was preoccupied with sizing up her choice. "He ees very good-looking. I theenk maybe I should keep him for myself."

"You wanted to see me, ma'am?"

The lazy drawl caught Virginia by surprise. She glanced up and met the eyes of the man who addressed her. Rita had been accurate in her appraisal. The busboy was good-looking—extremely so.

"Uh, well, yes," she managed to sputter.

J.D. was impressed by the woman's fair looks. Not since he'd been a teenager and had experienced the hot and hard palpitations of his first major crush had he reacted so strongly to the mere sight of a female. A memory flashed before his eyes. Ashley Beaumont. Lovely, sensitive, untouchable Ashley. He hadn't thought of her in ages. It was the uncertain smile of the woman seated at the table that triggered the fond recollection. She somewhat resembled the girl who had stormed his senses at the tender and impressionable age of sixteen. She was a grown-up version of Ashley Beaumont, or what he imagined she must look like today. He blinked. The hazy image of a Southern belle faded. He clearly saw the attractive New Yorker before him and it was plain that her resemblance to a memory was only superficial.

There was an awkward pause as they both tried to collect their wits. Accustomed to thinking on her feet, Virginia fumbled in her bag for a business card. "I know this will probably sound crazy—" she couldn't believe that her hand was actually shaking as she rummaged through the handbag's contents for the small leather case "—but there is, uh, a position I'm trying to fill...." Her fingers finally located the damn card case. "The thought occurred to me that you could possibly be right for it." She extricated a card from the leather case and handed it to him.

J.D. glanced at the fancy script, then cast her a bemused look. "You're offering me a job?" he said incredulously.

Virginia slanted Rita a murderous look before answering. "Not exactly. I'm conducting interviews for the position. There is no guarantee that you'll be hired, but there is a chance. The only certain thing I can tell you at this point is that the job entails a great deal more money than you're earning here."

J.D. smiled down at her and, for a split second, the warmth he generated penetrated her frosty veneer. "I don't know anything about the advertising business, ma'am," he told her honestly.

"The position is for a male model. The agency I'm connected with is handling an account that wants to introduce a line of menswear into the American market. The idea is to have one man, one face, represent the line."

"I'm not opposed to work, so long as there's nothing shady about it," he stipulated.

"I assure you there is not. The agency and the account I speak of are both quite reputable. You don't have to decide anything right this moment. Think about it, and if you're interested in interviewing, come by our offices tomorrow." God! What was she saying? Rita's impetuousness was rubbing off on her.

Rita was thoroughly enjoying the mischief she'd instigated. She'd never seen her boss so off-center. Her composure had slipped just a bit—not much—but enough to make Rita wonder if it was only the unorthodox circumstances rattling her.

J.D. tucked the card into the pocket of his bibbed apron. "I'll surely consider it. Thank you, ma'am. Would you like me to clear those plates out of the way?" Regardless of her kind offer or what tomorrow might bring, he was still a busboy today. He was grateful for the job he had at the moment and wanted to render good service for the minimum wage he was paid.

Rita gestured for him to take away the cake and plates, but Virginia instantly countermanded the silent directive.

"No, please, it's not necessary. Later will be fine."

He acquiesced to her wishes with another dazzling smile and then withdrew.

Rita could hardly contain herself. "So, you like him, no?"

Virginia looked thoughtful as she watched him return to his duties. "There is something special about him."

Feeling Rita's eyes on her, she quickly regained her composure and drained the last remnants of her champagne. "Of course, the Southern accent is a major drawback. If by some remote chance he ended up becoming the Don Sebastian man, he'd have to remain mute. We couldn't have him speak a word."

"You would consider using him?" Rita had not expected Virginia to embrace the busboy option so readily.

"Possibly," she said, glancing again to her wristwatch. "We'll see what comes from the interview. He's pretty crude material."

"Ahh, but it was you who said you could take any reasonably attractive male and turn him into a sssssizzling sensation." A "Gotcha!" smirk spread over Rita's face.

"You may be gloating prematurely. I never claimed to be a miracle worker."

"I have faith in you."

"That isn't what you said a while ago." Virginia grinned. "Or were you just manipulating me into committing myself to a bad bet?"

"Me? How can you theenk such a thing?" Rita looked the picture of innocence.

"Based on past performance, it's a valid thought," Virginia said dryly. "Well, since we've blown out the candles, are you ready to head back to the office?"

"The party's over?" Rita whined.

"Afraid so. Our little bet means I have a thousand and one more things to think about. I'll leave you to pay your respects to the Trumps while I take care of having the doorman hail us a cab," she kidded her friend, getting up from the table and going in search of the maître d' to thank him and the staff for the excellent service.

Meanwhile, J.D. was tending to his menial tasks. As he spread a clean tablecloth on a corner table, his eyes traveled to the mystery woman in the chic black suit. He reached into the apron pocket, withdrew her card and pondered it for a moment.

Virginia Vandivere-Rice, Creative Director
Hanks, Udell & Partners.

He mulled over her fancy name and title. Why would an important lady such as she take any special notice of a lowly busboy? And what exactly did a male model have to do to earn his way? She had piqued his curiosity, but something about their brief exchange made him feel uneasy. Lucky breaks and easy money didn't happen to folks like him. Still... He glanced her way again as he returned the business card to his pocket. It would be foolish not to at least investigate what this male modeling position she spoke of was all about. Besides, it would be a good excuse to see her again. It wasn't the job offer that intrigued him; it was the woman named Virginia.

CHAPTER FOUR

THE MORNING WAS DREARY. Gray skies and drizzling rain only magnified the depressed condition of the poor Brooklyn neighborhood where J.D. temporarily resided. Another busboy at Le Bouves had put him on to the cheap lodgings after learning of his stranded situation.

"It ain't the best area of town but it's better than the Bowery flophouses," he'd told him. "The old widow that owns the place is kind of a kook but she treats her boarders okay. For an extra fin she'll let ya use the washer and dryer and borrow an iron. Tag along with me after work and I'll introduce ya," he'd offered.

And so it had happened that J.D. had settled in a rundown brownstone in one of the more drab sections of Brooklyn Heights, sandwiched between the East River and the navy yard. In its heyday, the cobbled street, the building and the landlady had been quite fashionable. But no longer. The neighborhood had deteriorated. The cobbled street was now rutted and littered, the brownstone had gone to pot, and Mrs. Tuddy, the landlady, well, she preferred to think of things the way they once were. Time had stopped for her. While technology and her neighbors had advanced through the fifties, sixties, seventies and eighties, Mrs. Tuddy had chosen to remain behind. She was stuck in the year 1940 and could not assimilate the changes that had occurred during the ensuing decades. At first J.D. had thought her crazy as a loon, but then he'd realized she was merely semicrackers and as happy as a lark cocooned in her eccentricity. She was content to live amid relics and cling to memories of what had been a sweeter period of her life.

As he stood looking out the third-story window down onto the wet street below, his mind, unlike Mrs. Tuddy's, was traveling ahead. He was thinking of the upcoming interview with the lady in black. He wanted to make a good impression, not so much because he thought he stood a chance of getting the job—that was unlikely. No, it was her, the puzzling customer from Le Bouves, he wanted to impress.

Ever since the brief encounter with her in the restaurant, she'd played on his mind. Perhaps it was just the unusual circumstances of their meeting. It couldn't be commonplace for busboys to be extended the opportunity she'd alluded to. There must have been a mixup of some sort. Maybe she had him confused with someone else, he reasoned. Or maybe the whole damn thing was a setup—a kind of inside joke that only the natives could appreciate. The one thing he'd discovered already about New Yorkers was that they were different from any other folk he'd ever known. He'd yet to figure them out. From the limited contact he'd had with them so far, the most he could conclude was that they ran hot and cold. He hadn't met a New Yorker yet who was tepid—quite the contrary of his fellow Mississippians, who were consistently lukewarm. But what of her? Was she hot or cold? More important, was she for real?

He glanced at the card in his hand. It was plumb flimsy from being fingered so much. It sure looked legitimate. Instinct told him that the attractive blonde was also the genuine article. Anyone could tell that she was an in-charge lady, accustomed to big deals for big money made in big boardrooms. The fact only added to his bewilderment. He hadn't a clue as to why such a woman would express an interest in him.

His eyes lifted and he stared into the distance. Since the Heights section occupied a bluff that rose sharply from the river's edge, the view, if nothing else, was grand. From his window he could see Lower Manhattan, the Brooklyn Bridge, Governors Island, the Statue of Liberty and the shipping factories and wharfs along the East River, all of which looked like a watercolor canvas when seen through a gray mist.

He raked a hand through his rumpled hair. He'd been awake for an hour, merely marking time until he thought Mrs. Tuddy would be up and stirring in the kitchen. He needed to borrow her iron and board to press his one and only shirt. He'd washed it out the night before in the bathroom basin and it was lying on a towel over the radiator in his room to dry. Since he hadn't the money to use the washer and dryer, he had no choice but to wear two-day dirty jeans to the interview. The best he could manage was a quick press and a fresh crease, providing Mrs. Tuddy agreed to lend him an iron.

Lucky for him that his new friend from work had let him borrow a pair of old warm-up pants to sleep in. Upon hearing about the unfortunate mishap of having his belongings ripped off, Mrs. Tuddy had been obliging, too. She'd given him a welcome package that contained a new toothbrush, a tube of toothpaste, a pack of disposable razors, a small can of shaving cream, deodorant, a plastic comb and a half-empty bottle of cologne. The cologne, she'd explained, was compliments of her dead husband. The brand name and the scent was pre-World War Two, but it served the purpose and didn't smell half-bad. J.D. was touched by her thoughtfulness and grateful as hell for the toothbrush and deodorant. Years of his mama emphasizing to him and his brothers that being poor was no disgrace and being unkempt or unmannerly was downright inexcusable had made him meticulous about personal hygiene.

He listened for a sign that Mrs. Tuddy was milling about down below. Nothing yet. He sighed and braced his forehead against the window.

He had a dull headache from the restless night he'd spent tossing and turning in a futile attempt to find some small section of mattress that wasn't lumpy. What was more, he was terribly hungry, and a little homesick. Being hungry wasn't a new experience, though. Many was the time that he and his brothers had been sustained by only a square of cornbread crumbled in a glass of milk before bed. Soul food was what his mama called the mixture. It was bland stuff but it had staved off the hunger pangs until morning when he and his brothers would try to beat one another to the table in order to get an extra portion of syrup bread. They'd sop up the molasses goo with thick slices, shoveling the sweet dough into their mouths as fast as they could. The gluttonous free-for-all always irritated their mother, who prided herself on rearing her children according to an exacting code of Southern gentility and honor.

J.D. smiled to himself, remembering his mother's proud ways. At the age of nine, he'd believed her to be as wise as King Solomon and her revelations more pointed and fearsome than those he learned in Bible study class. He had committed the unforgivable offense of having accepted a sack of apples from a neighbor for whom he sometimes did odd chores. His mother perceived this as an act of charity since he'd done nothing to earn the sack of apples on the particular occasion. Gratuitous gifts were unacceptable. It was all right to be neighborly and send a home-baked pie in exchange for a favor done, but one didn't give more than one was given, or give without a valid reason, such as a sickness or death in a family.

"We Mahues fend for ourselves, J.D.," she'd scolded him. "We may not have much but we've our self-respect. People in this county know us as being hardworking, honorable folk. A good reputation is nothing to trifle with and certainly not anything to be traded away for a sack of apples. It would be ungracious and would cause hard feelings to return the gift after taking it, but never do such a thing again, you hear? Things that come to you without sweat or sacrifice have no value, J.D. You'd do well to remember what I say."

Recalling the incident and his mother's words conjured up a slough of memories. He thought about home so hard he could almost smell the pungent pines and visualize the flatlands, black with rich silt. A sultry breeze was blowing. The clouds above were as fluffy and white as the cotton fields below. He could hear the laughter of children playing down by the levee; feel the lazy glide of the Tallahatchie's muddy waters through the sleepy Delta. He hadn't expected to miss it. How many evenings had he sat on the front porch daydreaming about the riches and excitement that surely existed beyond the magenta horizon?

J.D.'s head snapped up at the sound of someone coughing. Mrs. Tuddy had finally arisen. A chain-smoker, she hacked away from morning until night. The smell of coffee brewing was for real, not some homesick hallucination.

He grabbed his shirt and headed downstairs to ask about the iron. He thought again of his mother and how she would not approve. Maybe he ought to see if there was something he could do in return for borrowing it. Take out the garbage or fix the leaky faucet in the hall bath? The memory of trading away his self-respect for a sack of apples, half of which had been rotten, clung to him. Perhaps the cliché was true about taking the boy out of the country but not the country out of the boy. A person's upbringing shaped his character. That sense of self-respect his mother had instilled in him stuck the same as Delta mud. He wondered if he'd ever be able to completely shed it.

IT WAS NEARING NOON when Rita came bursting into Virginia's office. "He ees here," she informed her boss in a breathless voice.

Lost in the latest account analysis, Virginia hadn't the vaguest notion to whom Rita was referring. The only thing obvious to her was that Rita was flustered. "Who's here?"

"Your new sensation." The big old hoops at Rita's ears bounced as she pranced over to Virginia's desk. "Ayyyy! He ees hot stuff. Just looking at him makes me warm all over." She waved a hand in front of her face, fanning away a nonexistent flush.

"Get ahold of yourself, Rita. It's probably just another hot flash." Virginia didn't even try to humor her. She'd been dreading the prospect of the busboy's interview all morning. Secretly she'd hoped he wouldn't show up.

Rita's high spirits were not dampened in the least. "I will tell him you are ready to see him. Don be so stiff. You don want to scare him off. Theenk of the partnership that ees slipping through your fingers with each passing day." Rita knew exactly what buttons to push. With a smug lift of her head, she pivoted and proceeded toward the door.

"I'm not going to be pressured into hiring him. I'm only conducting the interview because it would be insensitive not to. After all, he came here in good faith. It's the least I can do."

"The least." Rita mocked her punctilious tone before slipping from the room.

Virginia smoothed her hair, straightened her jacket and squared herself in her chair. Why she bothered to adjust her appearance was beyond her. Nerves, she concluded. But why should she be uptight over an inconsequential interview with a busboy, for heaven's sake?

Rita rapped on the door, then eased it open, allowing the latest candidate for the modeling job access to the image maker.

Virginia stood up and extended a hand across her desk. "Hello. I'm pleased you could make it." She knew she sounded exactly as Rita had worried she might—stiff.

"Afternoon, ma'am." His voice was warm and silky, his clasp firm and calloused.

"Do sit down." She gestured to one of the teal-colored barrel chairs in front of her desk. Damn! Now she sounded like Margaret Thatcher. She reclaimed her own chair and smiled weakly.

"I suppose we should begin at the beginning," she mumbled while fixing her attention on scooting her chair closer to the desk. What a stupid thing to say! Where else would one begin? "I'm afraid I'm at a disadvantage. Usually I'm acquainted with the background of the person I'm interviewing, but in this instance I don't even know your name."

"Joe Dillon," he supplied, pronouncing both names as though they were one. Joedillon was the way she heard it.

"Well, Mr. Joedillon, as I mentioned—"

"Mahue," he interjected.

"Excuse me?" She raised her gaze to eye level and felt even more off balance when she engaged the kinetic brown orbs that stared back at her.

"Joe Dillon Mahue is my full name." Now it was Joedillon—pause—Mahue.

"Joedillon Mahue," she repeated, trying not to sound amused, which would be worse than stiff. "Just for clarity's sake, is Joedillon one name or two?"

He smiled easily. "Two. It's sort of a family tradition. All of us boys were named after my daddy. Then Mama tagged on a second name that was our own. My two older brothers are Joe Bob and Joe Ray. Then there's me, Joe Dillon. I think Mama figured it was a surefire way of making certain somebody came running whenever she called. She'd just holler Joe and one of us was bound to answer."

Virginia caught herself before her mouth fell open. "Very ingenious of her," she managed to say. What in the hell had Rita gotten her into?

"Yeah, well, I think she also had a deeper purpose in mind when naming us." He was going on, Virginia thought, as though he were merely trading small talk rather than applying for one of the most sought-after positions in all of New York.

"Really," she said, as if she cared.

"I believe she wanted us to know that all three of we boys were equal but special in her eyes."

Her stomach knotted and her breath caught in her throat. His speculation had hit her hard—as if someone had landed a blow to her midsection. Equal but special. What a wonderful legacy to have inherited. She actually envied Mr. Mahue his silly name. *Joedillon.*

Realizing she was saying nothing and more than likely was sitting there with a stupid look on her face, she recovered herself sufficiently to render a polite response. "Your mother must be a very wise and sensitive woman. You're fortunate."

"Yes, ma'am. She is and I am," was all he replied.

"Where exactly do you call home, Mr. Mahue?" She continued with the interview, making a conscious effort to have her grilling seem casual—just off-the-cuff chitchat.

"I'm from a small town in the Delta that nobody's much heard of. Cottonmouth, Mississippi." He relaxed a bit within his chair, leaning back and arranging his legs so that an ankle rested on an opposing knee. She noted that his jeans were faded from wear but neatly creased. His shirt was crisply starched and the whiteness of it contrasted starkly with his sun-bronzed skin. He wore boots, not of the Italian or English variety. No, his were honest-to-goodness cowboy boots.

"You're right. I've never heard of it. What distinguishes Cottonmouth from the better-known areas of Mississippi like Vicksburg or Biloxi?"

"The name pretty well says it all. Cottonmouth is made up of some of the finest cotton land in the whole of the South, and there's about a jillion water moccasin." He grinned widely at her reflexive recoil. She was terrified of snakes. The thought of having to contend with the repulsive creatures on a daily basis sent chills up her spine. How awful. She certainly did not envy Mr. Mahue his native habitat. Unable to help herself, she glanced pointedly at his boots. Snakeskin. Jeez!

"They're imitation," he said in answer to her unvoiced assumption.

She laughed nervously. Somewhere the interview had gotten off-track. She was uncomfortable. Minor details seemed magnified, such as the way Mr. Mahue's eyes followed her every move and the way her hair kept spilling forward across her face whenever she ducked her head to avoid meeting his gaze directly. She tucked the drape of blond hair behind an ear and steered the conversation back to specifics.

"May I ask how old you are, Mr. Mahue?"

"Call me J.D. Everybody does. I turned twenty-four last month." He shifted his weight and cast a glance about the room. The furnishings were expensive. The only concession to femininity was the color scheme—teal blue and peach. Mostly the walls were covered in huge posters framed in glass and brass. He supposed they represented ads she'd devised and was especially proud of. There was one for a popular diet drink, another for a fancy perfume and many more for such diverse items such as high-top sneakers, a lap-top computer, gourmet jelly, piña-colada-scented sunscreen and one of those express air-delivery services....

"Schooling?" she asked, recapturing his attention.

"High school is all. Where I come from, not many get the chance to go on to college."

"A college education is not a requisite for the position I mentioned." Sensing he was a little embarrassed, she tried to put him at ease. "Perhaps it's time for me to tell you a little something of the project we're in the midst of putting together. But first, can I offer you a cup of coffee or a soft drink?"

He wished it was solid nourishment rather than liquid refreshments she was offering. "Coffee sounds good. Thank you, ma'am."

She appreciated his good manners but wished he'd quit ma'aming her every two seconds. It made her feel like some spinster schoolmarm. She pressed the intercom button and asked Rita to bring them coffee. As a rule, she didn't make such personal requests of her secretary. Too many of her male peers treated the female staff members in a manner that demeaned their abilities and dignity. Nowhere was their idea of women's work detailed in any job description. She tried to set an example by not expecting any nurturing services.

But Rita delivered the coffee gleefully. She wanted to steal a peek and judge for herself how things were going. She beamed at Joe Dillon as she passed by and then set the two cups of coffee on the edge of the desk.

"Thank you, Rita." Virginia slanted a meaningful look toward the door.

"Mmm. Ees nice and *hot*." She rolled her eyes in a fake swoon, then bounced out again.

Virginia passed him one of the foam cups. "Sugar or cream?"

"Black's fine." He tasted the coffee in measured sips.

An awkward pause followed. Virginia swiveled in her chair, also sampling the coffee in slow, thoughtful sips. Then she turned back to face him. "Can I be perfectly candid, J.D.?" she said at last.

"Sure," he answered with a shrug.

"I approached you about the modeling position on an impulse. As I said, a college degree is not necessary but a certain degree of, shall we say, worldliness is essential. The designer we're representing is an important account for Hanks and Udell. It's absolutely imperative that we pull off this ad campaign. In order to do that we need a very special person who will be in keeping with the Argentine designer's image. Think of the position like that of an ambassador. As far as the public is concerned the model will be a representative of the designer himself. He *is* the Don Sebastian man."

"And you don't think a hayseed from Cottonmouth, Mississippi, fills the bill," he concluded. His tone carried no indication of insult or injury.

"I only meant to imply that your Southernness presents complications," she quickly added. "I'm trying to be up-front with you about certain difficulties that would undoubtedly arise were I to choose you. For instance, your Mississippi drawl is a major drawback. We plan to focus on the designer's Argentine essence. The ad strategy will be based on a South American theme. We visualized the Don Sebastian man as a caballero sort. You can see the problem we'd encounter at the onset. I mean, we couldn't have you speak in the commercials. Your accent would be out of character."

"Yes, ma'am," he readily agreed. "I can see how that'd be contrary to your aims."

"Then there's the added problem of your lack of experience. Even the most seasoned models would have trouble with the grand-scale exposure this assignment will entail. It is highly likely that the Don Sebastian man will become a celebrity of sorts. To be perfectly blunt, the image you'd be donning would have definite sexual overtones. In a matter of weeks, you'd be thrust into the national spotlight. It's not an entirely pleasant experience. People think of you as a commodity rather than a person. The pressure is tremendous. Your private life diminishes as your public persona grows. You would be subjected to long hours, endless shoots, extensive traveling, a grueling cycle of interviews and personal appearances. You wouldn't be Joe Dillon Mahue from Cottonmouth, Mississippi, any longer. Well, only on occasion, and those occasions would be few. You'd be the hot caballero, the designer's ambassador—the Don Sebastian man."

"You don't paint a pretty picture, Miss Rice." He polished off the coffee, leaned forward and set the empty cup on her desk.

His addressing her as Miss Rice caught her by surprise. What had happened to ma'am? Suddenly he was being much more formal. She didn't want to make a bad situation worse by telling him she preferred not to be addressed by her married name.

"Virginia. Most everybody calls me Virginia," she said.

He nodded. "I don't mean any disrespect, but after listening to the difficulties you've talked about, I have just one question."

"Which is?" She sat up in her chair, assuming a very businesslike posture.

"Why are we having this conversation?"

Why indeed? she thought. She said nothing for a moment while she studied him. Rita was right. She did know her beefcake. He was grade-A male. Damn handsome. Hot—really hot. What the hell! Why not be straight with the guy?

"Because, as I'm sure you must have heard many times before in your life, you are an incredibly good-looking man. What's more, you wear a pair of jeans well. And that is what we are selling the American public on. Jeans made to be worn by men but admired by women. 'Exclusively for men, especially for women,' is a theme we're toying with. I think you have the face and physique that turn women on. And that's the bottom line, J.D. If they're sold on you, they're sold on Don Sebastian. He makes a splash in the U.S. and we make a lot of money. By the way, a top model is paid well for his time. The going rate is a thousand dollars an hour." She awaited his reaction.

A low whistle escaped his lips.

"Of course, before we can even consider pursuing the matter further we must find out whether or not you photograph well. Our discussion today is just preliminary. I'd like to send you to our photographer and have some stills made. If we can get it done in the next day or two, I'll look them over this weekend and see what I think. But I must be honest and tell you that the proofs would have to be exceptional to override my reservations."

"I understand, but I have to be honest with you, too," he replied, looking somewhat overwhelmed.

"Please say whatever you wish. It's important that we both be candid." She wanted to add that it would also be refreshing not to be fed a line of bull for a change. Such was the norm in her business.

"It's not that I'm not flattered by your generous offer, but I'm not sure I'm the right person for the job."

"Why not?" She was taken aback.

"Well, ma'am—" he actually blushed "—for one thing, I think you've greatly overestimated the effect I might have on women. They don't take much notice of me. Where I come from, good looks don't matter as much as character, which is the second reason I'm a little leery of becoming involved in your project."

"I'm afraid I don't follow you," she said with just a hint of impatience.

"I'm talking about earning my wages. To be paid so much money just to don a pair of jeans and have my picture snapped doesn't seem right. All the pressure and long hours you spoke of don't bother me. I'm accustomed to both. It's the amount of money that I find unsettling. Back in Cottonmouth, it's what we call easy money. It's generally believed that whenever somebody succumbs to easy money, they've compromised their principles."

This was a first for Virginia. Was he actually sitting there and telling her that he was considering passing on the opportunity of a lifetime because the sum of money involved was prohibitively large? He had to be kidding!

"I assure you, J.D., that here in New York the sum in question is not out of line. It is not, as you say, easy money. Modeling is hard work. You'll earn every dime of the salary I quoted. It's all on the up-and-up."

He seemed satisfied. "Yes, ma'am. Then I guess there can't be any harm in going ahead with the pictures you wanted. I'll have to arrange it so that I don't miss any time from work. I can't shirk my duties at the café," he explained.

She thought his loyalty a bit misplaced but nevertheless was impressed by it. "Of course." She stood when he did. "If you'll give my secretary an idea of your schedule and a number where you can be reached, she'll work out the necessary details and then give you a call."

"I thank you, ma'am." He extended his hand to her.

"I'll be in touch," she promised, smiling when offering her own.

Once more, as in the restaurant, it was her smile that affected him. Once more, he felt a stirring deep within himself. Rumblings of distant desire. Involuntarily, his fingers tightened around hers.

His lingering touch had a definite effect on her, too. Mr. Mahue was either an extremely modest or a most naive man if he truly believed women did not take special note of him. She quickly extricated her hand in the pretext of once again securing the strands of strawberry-blond hair that had escaped from behind her ear.

He cast her an easy smile and then strode out of her office.

She sank back into her chair and stared at the spot where he had stood. He might just be the one. He was certainly different from all the others. A definite possibility.

The buzz of the intercom broke in on her musings. Rita informed her that the head partners wanted to see her upstairs.

She knew what it was they wanted to discuss: the Don Sebastian presentation. She couldn't help but grin at the thought of telling them that the success or failure of the agency's most prized account might very well rest with a busboy from a place called Cottonmouth, Mississippi. She could only imagine the look on their faces.

She savored the mental picture for a moment before going upstairs to tell them what they expected to hear. The meeting would be stuffy and standard. Mr. Hanks would ask about the status of the campaign. Mr. Udell would remind her of the exact date, time and importance of the upcoming presentation. She would reassure them that only a few final touches were required. The presentation would be sensational, she'd say. It was the best, most innovative concept she'd come up with to date. Nothing would go wrong.

God! She hoped that was true.

CHAPTER FIVE

THE WEEKEND DESCENDED before Virginia realized it, and she dreaded the very thought of the next couple of days. Visiting her mother was always an ordeal and if another person was present in the Connecticut country house, her stay was even less bearable. The presence of an outsider only gave her mother more of an excuse to go on and on about Billy, reliving every small facet of his amazing life and every tragic detail of his premature death. Virginia had heard the "Ode to Billy" so many times she could recite it from memory.

Fortunately, she arrived late Friday night and her mother had only energy enough to scold her between yawns. "It's dangerous for a woman to be traveling these dark roads alone. You never know what can happen. Something could go wrong with your car. Aunt Caddie's been here since noon. At least she has the good sense not to venture out in the dead of night. She's in the bedroom across from yours. Try to be quiet when you go up. And don't forget to turn off the lights. Night, dear."

No hug. Outward demonstrations of affection had never been Inez Vandivere's custom. Just a mild scolding, a big yawn and a scant, "Night, dear." Golly, gee, it was great to be home!

She slept late the next morning, probably more as a way to avoid the unavoidable than anything else. She'd known her mother would want to do the ritualistic trip to the small cemetery a few miles away where Billy was buried. She'd replace the withered flowers at the base of her son's grave marker with fresh ones, offer a silent prayer in his behalf and then wander the manicured grounds, talking of others long departed and pointing out the new headstones. It was all so depressing. Virginia could not see the purpose in it. She had arranged for perpetual caretaking. Yet her mother persisted in making the trip to the cemetery each and every Saturday afternoon. In the rain, in the cold, in the heat, she came with fresh flowers.

After the cemetery trek, Virginia went for a walk in the woods behind the house as a means of escaping yet another of her mother's tedious midafternoon tea-and-conversation ceremonies. These, too, were opportunities to discuss Billy the Adorable Kid, William the Conqueror—her child of such potential who'd been snatched away in the very prime of his life. Over and over again, she chronicled his days from the crib to the grave and not always accurately. Preserving his memory had become a personal crusade. Even the house was beginning to take on the appearance of a shrine.

Virginia followed a worn footpath that wound through the wooded thicket. Walking in the arena of her youth triggered long-suppressed memories and feelings. It invariably happened whenever she returned home. Though she was coming less and less often, she found herself dreading her dutiful sojourns more and more. She hated the way they made her feel. Insignificant. Jealous. Guilty as hell.

Following in Billy's footsteps had been hard enough when he was alive. She'd loved her older brother. How could anyone not have? He was a charmer. His sense of adventure and sharp wit made him irresistible to others. He was one of those people who could get away with doing or saying the most outrageous things. If anyone else had dared to try such stunts, they'd have been labeled reckless or crazy or both. But for Billy, such behavior was excused.

He got away with things because he was the best at everything—the best looking, the best student, the best athlete, the best salesman, the best con artist around. When one was the best at everything, people tended to overlook a few minor shortcomings. All of his life, that was the way it went. Nobody held him accountable. Most everyone was blinded by his devil-may-care charisma, especially his mother.

Three years younger, Virginia had grown up in his dynamic shadow, struggling for her own identity and yearning for a glimmer of the sunny praise he received. Her one and only distinction was to be Billy Vandivere's kid sister. The A's she made didn't matter, for he'd set the previous records. The athletic awards she won didn't matter, for he'd won all kinds of titles and had received a full scholarship for his efforts. College was a little better since they'd attended different universities. Her move to New York and subsequent success in the advertising business didn't matter, for Billy had already established himself as the chief executive officer of a California conglomerate and was making twice her salary. The one thing she'd managed to do first had ended in failure. Her divorce was not only a source of disappointment to their mother but a major embarrassment. If Billy had married, Virginia was certain he would have wed well and never have disgraced the family by incurring an unseemly divorce. As fate would have it, death had claimed Billy before a woman could.

Virginia rehashed the memories as she strolled the woods.

In a strange fashion, she had adored her older brother. She still did. But she'd also been jealous and resentful of him. God help her, she still was. Billy had treated his achievements cavalierly and sometimes he'd treated the people who loved him in much the same manner. He was a self-absorbed person and seldom noticed how his inflated ego undermined the confidence of others. He hadn't intentionally meant any harm. His narcissism was an unconscious trait, not a cultivated one.

Virginia's gaze traveled to a small clearing off the beaten path that had once served as a secret meeting place when they were kids. A few reminders still remained: a camping spot marked by a circle of charred stones, a rusty old wagon, and an arrow stuck in a nearby tree trunk.

Her eyes stung at the sight. How many times had she tagged after Billy to this clearing? She could almost hear herself whining, "Please can I play, too, Billy? I'll be whatever you want."

"Go home, Gin. Geeze! Can't I do anything without you being underfoot? I'm meeting the guys and we don't want any goofy girls around. So beat it, pest," came a ghostly voice from the past.

"If you don't let me play, I'm going to tell Mom about you sneaking out at night." The long-ago threat echoed in her ears.

She smiled to herself as she recalled how well the suggestion of tattling used to work. He'd usually relent and allow her to come along. Of course, she'd always be assigned some lowly role in the gamut of childhood games they played. Billy, on the other hand, was always designated as the leader in whatever adventure he and other kids conjured up, which was no more than right, since he was the inventive one among them.

As if it were yesterday, Virginia could still visualize him playing out youthful fantasies. One time, he'd be the roguish highwayman Robin Hood; she'd merely be part of his merry band of men. The next time, he'd be the noble chief Cochise; she'd be just another painted face in his tribe of whooping Indians. Even in play, he was the dominant force and she nothing more than a goofy girl with little imagination and even less value. It was as though the birth order had typecast them. Billy, the firstborn, was first at everything, and Ginny, the follower, had to be satisfied with second place. That was the way it was—the way it seemed it would forever be. For even in death, he still overshadowed her.

With a blink, the recollections of Billy disappeared, but the negative feelings her reminiscing had caused lingered. When would she overcome those feelings? When would she not feel insignificant, jealous and, worst of all, guilty as hell?

The wind picked up. Virginia lifted her face into the gust of fresh air and breathed deeply. She should be getting back to the house. Then again, why hurry? She was sure her mother was unaware of how long she'd been gone. She had probably dug out the family album by now and was boring Aunt Caddie to tears with page after page of pasted snapshots—Billy's life in review, from the crib to the grave.

SUPPER HAD BEEN TYPICALLY INEZ—bland. Her mother had a real talent for blandness and she was also a confirmed advocate of the nutritional value of anything brown—brown eggs, brown bread, brown rice, etcetera. The evening meal reflected her taste for bland, brown things. The roast beef was overcooked, under-seasoned, dry and very brown. The rice dish was tasteless and the wheat rolls were the same texture and color as cardboard. Even the yellow custard dessert was baked so it was brown on top and it, too, lacked any hint of spice. Virginia was amused by Aunt Caddie's tactful decline of a second helping.

"No, really, Inez. I couldn't get down another bite," she said between gulps of tea.

Aunt Caddie was related to her mother by marriage. She had the Vandivere red hair and a good humor. Since her father had passed away shortly after her birth, Virginia's concept of him was colored by her impressions of her aunt. She was a pleasant person, much more animated and jovial than her mother. Virginia found it odd that the two of them had struck up such a strong bond. Aunt Caddie had been the one to stay in touch, coming often for short stays and lifting everyone's spirits by virtue of her unfailing cheeriness. She took a special interest in her brother's children and seemed to be genuinely fond of her sister-in-law.

"So, Ginny—" she took stock of her niece from across the table "—we haven't had much chance to talk. How goes the ad business these days?"

"Fine," she answered, caught off guard by the sudden switch in conversation. Previously, Aunt Caddie had been speaking with her mother of an upcoming family reunion and whether or not they ought to consider attending.

"Every time I see those clever commercials you do on TV, I tell whoever I'm with that my niece is the genius behind the catchy slogans. I know it's not polite to brag but I'm so proud of you. Aren't you, Inez?" It was one of those rhetorical questions that was meant for emphasis yet required some form of an affirming response.

"Of course I am, Caddie. Virginia has done well for herself." Her mother began to clear the dishes. She displayed no great desire to pursue the matter.

Aunt Caddie smiled and went on. "So what are you working on at present? I'd like a preview of what new fangled item I will shortly be unable to live without," she teased.

Her mother carried a stack of dishes to the sink and made a big production out of scraping and rinsing them off. Her indifference made Virginia wonder once again why she subjected herself to these strained visits. "We're representing a new designer by the name of Don Sebastian. Well, actually, I guess I should correct myself and say that we're hoping to represent him. Whether or not we land the account will all depend on a presentation I'll be giving soon."

"I envy you. The work you do is so glamorous and exciting. It certainly beats trying to instill an appreciation of British literature in students who are much more fascinated with British rock groups." She sipped from her teacup and sighed. "Oh, well. It's a little late for me to be thinking of changing vocations. You, on the other hand, have such a bright future ahead of you. I have the utmost confidence that this Sebastian fellow will sign on once he realizes how inventive you are," her aunt predicted. "And then I think you should ask for a big fat raise. I doubt those ad agency people are paying you anything near what you're worth."

"I make a good salary." Virginia couldn't help but grin. Aunt Caddie hadn't the vaguest notion what she earned but the dear still felt she deserved more. "I do, however, have a strong incentive to seal the deal. Landing the account could mean a partnership for me." She said the last a little louder and more succinctly than necessary for her mother's benefit.

"How wonderful! Did you hear that, Inez? Ginny might become a partner in the agency," Caddie repeated just in case her sister-in-law might not have been paying attention.

Inez Vandivere dried her hands on a towel and turned around from the sink to face her daughter. "Why haven't you mentioned this before?" was her only comment.

Virginia wanted to be brutally honest and say, "When should I have told you? Between eulogies?" Instead, she simply answered, "The opportunity hadn't come up until now."

"I suppose you're planning to accept a partnership if it's offered?" There was a trace of disapproval in her tone.

Virginia was dumbfounded by her mother's reaction to the news. What the hell was wrong with accepting a coveted partnership in one of the most prestigious Madison Avenue ad agencies? "I most definitely am," she stated.

"Well, it's your business, of course," her mother said in that irritating fashion that implied she was about to make it hers. "But I wonder if it's a wise move on your part. Far be it from me to tell you how to run your life—" which was exactly what she had in mind "—but I should think you'd be more interested in pursuing a partnership of a different sort." That ambiguous statement made, she turned back to the sink and began scouring pots.

Aunt Caddie had been privy to similar skirmishes between mother and daughter. Behind her sister-in-law's back she shook her head bemusedly and shrugged her shoulders.

Virginia wasn't about to let the intimation slide. "Let me guess, Mother. I suspect the point you're trying to get across in your usual subtle way is that I should be directing my energies toward more worthy goals, such as snaring another husband rather than furthering my career." She could hardly contain her anger.

"Maybe now isn't a good time to go into it." Knowing how touchy the two were about the subject of Ginny's divorced status, Aunt Caddie tried to mediate.

Virginia ignored her attempt to smooth things over. "That's it, isn't it? The only title that counts in your books is an M.R.S." Her voice rose along with her temper.

"I never said that." Her mother kept scrubbing the pot.

"You did and you do, every chance you get." Virginia's blue eyes flashed as she stood up from her chair.

"You're blowing this way out of proportion, Virginia. I merely offered an opinion. If you prefer to devote yourself to a career at the cost of ever having a personal life, it's your choice. I would only remind you that you made that mistake once." Inez spoke in a very precise, unemotional manner as she carefully dried the pots and pans and stored them in their proper place in a lower cabinet. She was not prone toward disorder of any sort, conduct included.

Virginia had known all along that her mother held her responsible for the divorce, but this was the first time she'd directly placed the blame on her daughter.

Noting the wounded look on her niece's face, Aunt Caddie could contain herself no longer. "I think you're being unfair and old-fashioned, Inez. It's not like when we were young women. Ginny is part of a liberated generation. A majority of women today balance a career and a family, and they do it very admirably, I might add."

Inez took exception to Caddie's view and her butting in. "Ginny found it difficult to strike an even balance and I don't think her dilemma is uncommon. Women are working harder, juggling this and that, and the only thing I can see that they're succeeding at is making chaos of their lives. They're tired and frustrated and not any more fulfilled today than they ever were. Where is the liberation in that?" Inez pursed her lips.

Making a supreme effort to control herself, Virginia refrained from slamming the chair into the table. She gripped the back of it so tightly her knuckles grew white as she eased it into place. "Thank you for the assist, Aunt Caddie, but Mother seems convinced that ambition is a trait reserved only for males. Ambitious women make sorry wives. Isn't that true, Mother?''

Inez stood ramrod straight and tight-lipped. She thought her daughter's moody outburst uncalled-for and was shocked by her disrespectful behavior. She hadn't the vaguest idea what had come over her lately but she had no intentions of further airing their differences in front of Aunt Caddie.

Virginia threw up her hands. ''Why am I even bothering to debate the issue?'' She addressed the question to Aunt Caddie. ''It wouldn't matter if I told her that my job or the long hours I put in were not the reason for the divorce. She believes that to be the case and it would take an act of Congress to change her mind. I think you were right when you said now isn't a good time to discuss it.''

Inez was relieved. At least they agreed on that much.

Aunt Caddie was caught in the standoff. It seemed neither mother nor daughter was willing to budge from their respectively bullish positions. ''My, my,'' she sputtered. ''We're taking all this talk of modern women and traditional values much too seriously. Why don't we play a game of Scrabble instead?''

Virginia almost groaned aloud. Scrabble! Just what they needed—more word games. What fun!

''I'm afraid not tonight, Aunt Caddie.'' She tried to sound convincingly apologetic. ''I have a great deal to do before the presentation next week. As a matter of fact, I also neglected to mention that I'll be leaving very early in the morning.'' She, too, could be precise and unemotional. ''So I think I'll just turn in.''

She tried to muster a smile for Aunt Caddie's sake but failed miserably. Circling the table, she came to kiss her on the cheek. "It's always good to see you. Let me know in advance the next time you have a holiday from school and I'll get us theater tickets. I've a friend who's a distant cousin of the director of *Les Misérables*. I'm not promising but I'll see what can be arranged. You could join us, if you like, Mother." Virginia purposely included her mother only as an afterthought. She was much too mad to be kind.

Her mother donned a stony expression as she stood her post near the kitchen sink. A peevish "Mmm" was her reply.

"I think it would be wonderful!" Aunt Caddie bubbled. "Oh, and thank you for the chocolates, Ginny. You spoil me."

Virginia patted her aunt's bony shoulder and then glanced over to her mother. "I'm sure I'll be gone long before you're up. It's going to be pretty hectic next week, but I'll call when I get a chance."

"You shouldn't make the trip on an empty stomach. You were prone to car sickness as a child." Inez knew the gracious thing to do would be to wish her daughter good-luck on her upcoming endeavor, but she, too, was much too upset to be kind.

Virginia's chin lifted. "I'm a big girl now, Mother. I don't get carsick anymore."

They both were aware of the deeper, unspoken implication. *And I don't need your approval anymore.* Virginia intended to accept the partnership in spite of Inez's objections.

The weekend ended on much the same note as it had begun, with no hug, only another lecture on road safety. And a scant "Goodbye, dear."

It wasn't until Sunday evening that Virginia remembered the manila envelope in her attaché case.

The photography department had rushed it up to her office at five o'clock on Friday, just as she was leaving for the day. She'd been in a big hurry to get away before becoming sidetracked by yet another phone call and had slipped the envelope into her case without bothering to take a look at the contents.

Ensconced on the couch, the melodious voice of Whitney Houston playing on the stereo, she removed the envelope from her attaché case, pulled out the proofs and studied them one by one.

Her body perked from its slouch. She spread the proofs out on the cushions before her, crossed her legs Indian-fashion, reached for the glass of white wine on the coffee table and took long, thoughtful sips as she drank in the various poses of Joe Dillon Mahue.

That he was photogenic was obvious. He was one of those rare individuals who looked sensational from any angle. But there was something more. Something not so obvious but, oh, so necessary in the image business. Some called it chemistry, others referred to it as charisma. She preferred to think of it as magic, because in order for it to work it had to be seen yet unseen. It had to be a natural phenomena, not a trick of the lens. The busboy from Cottonmouth, Mississippi, possessed the necessary magic. He was a natural. She gulped down the last of the white wine and fell back against the overstuffed cushions. "Who'd have believed it?" she said aloud, laughing. "Well, Mr. Mahue, you're about to be discovered. Welcome to the crazy, upside-down world called New York."

CHAPTER SIX

IMMEDIATELY MONDAY MORNING Virginia had Rita get in touch with Mr. Mahue to have him come in and make a fifteen-second demo for the presentation. To say that she was upset to hear from Rita that Mr. Mahue had a conflict of interest and could not come in at the time she'd suggested would have been an understatement.

"He says he ees sorry but he's got dishes to bus. He wants to come after regular working hours," Rita informed her.

"You've got to be kidding me!" Virginia hit the roof. A whole crew would have to work around Joe Dillon's schedule and be paid time and a half. She was so infuriated by Mahue's skewed priorities, she didn't even show up for the shoot when it did finally happen; she was afraid she'd blow up at him. She had, however, laid out in detail the fifteen-second spot: set, mood, lighting, music—the works. Rita went in her place and filled her in later.

"Ees fabulous. So, so sexy. Wait till you see. Wait till everybody sees! America is gone to love him," she predicted.

"Whether or not a star is born is incidental," Virginia exploded. "How did the jeans look, Rita? Did they follow my instructions and do the tight shot on the back pocket? The close-up on Sebastian's logo?"

"The shoot was perfect. On those buns anything would look good. Can I pick 'em or what?" Rita bragged.

"I want to see for myself. Call production and tell them to put a rush on it. I want the tape on my desk A.S.A.P. It damn well better be good or everybody's working overtime until we get it right. I don't care how many times we have to reshoot." She flopped exhaustedly in her chair, webbed her fingers through her hair and cradled her forehead in her palms. *Oh, God! Please let it work,* she prayed silently.

It was late the next evening before she finally got to screen the demo. Everyone had gone home for the day. She sat alone in her dimly lit office, watching the tape again and again. She pressed the remote control, stopped it, studied it and rewound it until she finally concluded that her prayer had indeed been answered. Just as Rita had said, the fifteen-second spot was fabulous. It was sexy as hell. America was going to go crazy over Mahue and consequently they were going to go crazy over Don Sebastian designs.

Everything worked beautifully: the rugged pampas setting against a backdrop of a fiery sunset and lush green rolling hills; the Spanish guitar and castanets in the background; the profile shot of the sinfully sensuous Joe Dillon. The turquoise handkerchief tied at his throat was a great touch. A hint of gaucho macho. Then there was the phantom female hand that slid along his cheekbone, and the resonant male voice with the throaty Spanish accent announcing, "Designs by Don Sebastian," as the camera slowly panned down his body to the logo on his butt. At that point the camera moved out to take in Mahue's lower anatomy and give full scope to the jeans. The foot of the leg facing the camera was effectively raised and resting on a fence rail, accentuating the fine lines and tapered fit of the pants. Suddenly a shapely female leg appeared and hoisted itself in a flounce of red ruffles and white lace, the fandango skirt hiked to reveal creamy bare skin nestling against the inside of his thigh. The camera zoomed in on the suggestive pose. The throaty Spanish voice said, "Made for men, with women in mind," as slick, red-polished nails and slender fingers glided along the blue denim material to come to rest provocatively at the base of his butt.

She rewound, reran and reviewed the tape so much that hours passed without her realizing it. When at last she shut off the video recorder, she felt the most confident, the most excited and the most fatigued she'd ever been in her life.

Before heading home, she dashed off a note to Rita and placed it on her desk.

You were right. He's hot stuff. We have a winner. Get in touch with our Mr. Mahue and make sure he's on hand for the meeting Friday. Sebastian's rep may insist on a face-to-face before okaying the deal. Tell him no excuses acceptable. P.S. Yes, yes, yes, Virginia. There is a Santa Claus!

BY FRIDAY, Virginia was a bundle of nerves. The presentation was set for two. Only fifteen minutes remained on the countdown clock and Mahue had yet to put in an appearance.

"Where the hell is he?" Virginia jerked on her jacket. "I swear if he doesn't show up, I'll hunt him down and—"

"Ayyy! He will be here," Rita assured her while glancing nervously toward the open door. "Take deep breaths and don borrow trouble."

"Do you know if Sebastian's rep has arrived yet?" Virginia opened a closet door and inspected herself in the full-length mirror. "I should have worn the navy suit. It's more impressive." She turned sideways and placed her hands on her stomach. "God! Why did I eat lunch? I look like a damn blowfish. What did you tell me? Is Sebastian's rep here in the building, yes or no?"

Rita rolled her eyes. "She ees here."

"She? The rep is a woman?" Virginia faced the mirror again, flicking back her hair and examining her reflection more closely. "I think I'm breaking out in hives. Oh, swell, that'll be just perfect. My face will match this hideous cranberry suit. How long has she been here?"

Rita was accustomed to Virginia's ranting and raving. She always worked herself up before a presentation and switched from one topic to another like a race car switching gears.

"A few minutes ees all."

Virginia slammed shut the closet door and checked her watch. "I should be upstairs already. Dammit! I needed to talk to Mahue and prep him before—"

"Sorry I'm late. It was hard to get away. Friday lunch rush" came the breathless explanation from the doorway. "I ran the last six blocks," he panted.

Two pairs of eyes fastened on J.D.

"A cab might've been simpler and quicker, Mr. Mahue," Virginia retorted.

"Yes, ma'am, but I hadn't money for the fare," was his honest comeback as he tucked his loosened shirt back into the waistband of his jeans.

No jacket or tie. He was dressed as before in a white shirt, faded jeans and those god-awful boots. What did he think? That this was some casual picnic or down-home barbecue she'd invited him to? For crying out loud!

"We haven't much time," Virginia said curtly. "Come with me and we'll talk on the way up." She marched out the door and headed down the hall toward the elevator.

J.D. shrugged at Rita before hurrying to catch up with the cranberry whirlwind that had blown past him.

Virginia kept her gaze uplifted to the panel of lights above the chrome elevator doors as she rattled off instructions. "It's not necessary for you to sit in on the presentation. There's a lounge area off the conference room where you can wait."

She punched the call button again. Each passing second was accentuated by an antsy tap, tap, tap of her foot. "It's very possible that Mr. Sebastian's representative will want to speak with you personally before making up her mind. Don't be nervous. I'll be on hand to run interference should the need arise."

J.D. was as calm as could be. The only tension he felt was being emitted from her.

The elevator's arrival was announced by a dinging sound and the chrome doors opened wide. They stepped inside. Virginia pressed the button for the top floor and in a second the elevator began its ascent.

"You look nice." J.D.'s compliment took her off guard.

"The color's all wrong. Something darker would've been more impressive. But thanks anyway." She smiled stiffly.

"You'd be impressive in any color." He shot her a sideways look.

Her mind elsewhere, she was only half listening to him. "I hope you're right, Mr. Mahue, for I'm about to give what will probably be the most important presentation of my career." The admission slipped out before she could check herself.

"If you find yourself getting tongue-tied, just picture everybody in the room wearing nothing but their underwear and socks. It's a trick I used as a kid whenever I had to recite in front of the class. Try it," he told her just as the elevator arrived at their designated stop.

She grinned broadly at the mere thought of picturing stodgy Udell in his skivvies. Though the visualization technique he suggested was hardly new, his mention of it produced the intended result. Her pre-pitch jitters ebbed a bit.

"See, it works." He held the door as she exited from the elevator.

"Does anything ever rattle you, Joe Dillon?" she asked, stopping in the center of the hallway and waiting for him to join her.

His eyes slowly perused her person, from the spritzed bangs at her forehead to the gold tip of her alligator shoes. "Not very often, and when it happens, it's generally because the circumstance or person means something real special to me."

The languishing manner in which he regarded her succeeded where words had failed. Even in her hyper state, Virginia recognized the unmistakable overtones of infatuation. Only an insensitive fool could have missed it. She knew she should discourage him, set the record straight here and now give him the standard lecture about professional boundaries. But instead she found herself just standing there like a dummy, as though she had nothing better to do than bask in the warmth of his smoldering brown eyes. Worse yet, Mr. Hanks chose that inopportune moment to emerge from the executive men's room a few feet away. With a none-too-discreet clearing of his throat, he let her know they were anxious to get under way in the main conference room.

"I'll be right there, sir," she told him, grabbing J.D.'s elbow and hustling him down to the lounge at the opposite end of the hallway. "It shouldn't take more than an hour. Just sit tight and I'll get back to you." She spun around and started back in the other direction. Luckily the corridor was deserted so no one was witness to her panicky mutterings.

"I don't need this distraction. Concentrate, Ginny," she coached herself between sucking in deep breaths and buttoning up her jacket. "Think jeans. Think multimillion-dollar deal. Think partnership." Halfway to the conference room it dawned on her that she'd forgotten to apprise Joe Dillon of one itty-bitty detail. She swore beneath her breath, pivoted and trotted back to the lounge. "Oh, by the way, I decided it would be easier all the way around if we shortened your name to Dillon Mahue. It sounds better, don't you think?"

Before he could voice an opinion, she ducked back out of the lounge and hotfooted it down the hall to present her discovery, Dillon Mahue, to the woman who had veto power over both of their destinies. The pressure was on.

CLAUDIA SHAPELL WAS a tough cookie who didn't waste time or mince words. No sooner had the formality of introductions been observed than she made her position eminently clear.

"I'd like you to know that I'm not just an associate of Mr. Sebastian's. He and I are equal partners. He creates the fashions and I handle the business end of our endeavor. I have carte blanche on all financial matters. It will be my decision, and mine alone, whether to choose to have your firm promote us in the States. I wanted you to understand from the onset that although I keep a low public profile, behind the scenes it is quite another story. It's me you must sell on your campaign, not Sebastian. That said, please proceed with the presentation."

Claudia Shapell was not going to be a pushover. Her soft features, honey-colored hair and silky voice were deceiving. It was her calculating green eyes that gave her away. Beneath the attractive exterior was a woman who preferred the fragrance of power to that of imported *parfum*. And on her the scent was becoming. Virginia wasn't upset by the woman's assertiveness. Quite the contrary. What really bothered her was that she herself hadn't had the foresight to wear something as imposing as Claudia Shapell's black leather outfit. The pressure mounted.

Play by the lady's rules. Be as direct and assertive as she is, Virginia told herself. *Remain standing throughout the presentation. Make her look up to you. Capitalize on any small advantage.*

She smiled confidently and took her place at the head of the conference table. If she accomplished nothing else, by the end of the presentation Ms Shapell would at least know they were two women of like spirit—sisters united by a mutual desire to succeed in a man's world. She would see Mr. Hanks's and Mr. Udell's input for exactly what it was—merely the lending of their esteemed reputations and important connections. So far, their only major contributions had been pulling out Ms Shapell's chair and blowing a lot of hot air and cigar smoke around the room. Oh, yes, Ms Shapell would soon know who'd shouldered the brunt of the creative commitment to Don Sebastian's designs. Virginia squared her padded shoulders and proceeded to lay out the theme and ad strategy that Hanks, Udell & Partners planned to implement.

It went quickly. The entire time Virginia pitched the concept, Claudia Shapell did not venture an opinion, did not ask a question, did not change expression, did not so much as move a muscle or bat an eye. Subsequently, Virginia couldn't get a reading on her. Did the woman like it? Hate it? Was she blowing it? Bombing up here? The whole time she was speaking, a line from a deodorant commercial kept swimming in her head. *Never let them see you sweat!*

She noticed the sweat prints her fingertips left on the plastic cartridge as she slipped the tape into the VCR at the finale of the presentation. The kiss of death. She was sweating. In a second or two, beads of perspiration would trickle down her forehead and those sharp green eyes would see right through her phony bravura.

She dimmed the lights, turned on the TV and punched the play button on the video recorder. She had no backup plan, no alternate tape to show. She'd been so certain that the sole-focus, one-line-teaser route was the way to go. Now, suddenly, she wasn't sure at all.

Virginia forgot herself and sank into a chair, forfeiting the small psychological advantage she'd held. What the hell! What did it matter? she thought.

"Don Sebastian Designs..." She didn't bother to watch the fifteen-second spot. She was too preoccupied with trying to second-guess what the heads' reaction would be when they lost the account.

"Made for men, with women in mind..."

Claudia Shapell leaned forward in her chair, placed an elbow on the table and thoughtfully traced her bottom lip with a forefinger. "I would like to view it again," was all she said.

Hallelujah! At last, a flicker of interest. Virginia sprang into action, rewinding and replaying the tape for Shapell's review. As the other woman studied the tape, Virginia studied her. Oh, yeah, it was there on her face. She liked what she saw. Virginia just wasn't sure what it was about the fifteen-second spot that appealed to her. Did she appreciate the carefully developed creativity? Or was she more impressed by Mahue's innate sensuality? At this point, Virginia didn't care, so long as it grabbed her.

At the end of the second screening, Ms Shapell sat back in her chair. "I like it. It's provocative but tastefully done. I wasn't at all sure about the single model focus, but now that I've seen the young man in question, I think it may be effective. I'm taken with the image he projects. Yes, I think he serves our purposes nicely."

Udell and Hanks looked visibly relieved.

"It's a sound concept, Ms Shapell. I'm positive it will produce the kind of response you had in mind. Don Sebastian's jeans will be a hot item in the U.S."

A faint smile spread across Claudia Shapell's glossed lips. "You can quit selling me, Ms Vandivere. I'm all but convinced to sign with your agency. Before I do, however, I'd like to meet with the young man you've selected to be our image bearer."

"Yes, of course. I anticipated that you might like to do that. He's in a lounge down the hall. I'll send for him." Her hand stretched toward the intercom.

"Oh, I'm afraid I can't at the moment. I'm flying out to Argentina tomorrow and my day is tightly scheduled. Perhaps he could meet with me this evening and we could chat over dinner. It'd be more personal."

"Whatever is convenient." She readily committed J.D. Nothing short of a sudden death—his own, if he didn't agree to it—would stand in the way of his making the dinner engagement.

"I'm familiar with most of the faces on the modeling circuit. His is a new one. Am I right in assuming that he's a recent discovery?"

"I thought it smarter to go with someone who will only be associated with your line," Virginia explained.

Her sidestepping of his lack of experience amused Claudia Shapell. "Then he has no previous modeling experience," she astutely deduced.

"No, but I think he's a natural. I highly recommend that we go with him. He has that certain something that no amount of experience can produce. In two words—male mystique.''

"I agree, but before I commit our line and a sizable portion of our capital to your ad strategy, I would like to assure myself that this young man is a good investment. I'd like to know that we share similar views and a common goal. I'm sure you can understand my hesitation. After all, we would be placing enormous faith in a relative unknown.''

Virginia could not argue with her logic. "I understand perfectly.''

"Good, then I'll have my secretary make the arrangements and call to confirm with you the time and place of tonight's meeting.'' Udell and Hanks were both on their feet to assist her as she stood from her chair. They were invisible to her. She focused her attention on Virginia. "You're very good at what you do, Ms Vandivere. An association between us in the future looks promising.'' She nodded approvingly. "In any event, I'll be in touch by Tuesday at the latest.''

"Thank you. We at Hanks and Udell are extremely excited about this campaign. We look forward to serving you.'' Thank goodness she remembered to mention the agency. Hanks and Udell disliked their employees taking individual credit. Teamwork was the phrase for the day—every day. Virginia donned a very businesslike posture, standing tall in her cranberry suit but a little to the side as the lady in black leather made a sweeping exit from the conference room. Hanks and Udell almost collided at the double doors when their prized client suddenly stopped short.

"Oh," she said as an afterthought, turning back toward Virginia, "what's the young man's name?''

She almost forgot herself and said Joe Dillon. "Dillon Mahue," she answered correctly.

"Mmm. Dillon Mahue." She tested the sound of it, then half smiled as if intrigued by a private thought. "The reservation will be in my name. Tell the gentleman to be on time. I dislike being kept waiting."

Virginia felt numb after her departure. To be so near to closing the deal and then to have Shapell insist on a private audience with Joe Dillon . . . "Damn, damn, damn!" she fumed, banging her fist on the table. She sank into one of the cushion swivel chairs, dropped her head back and stared resignedly up at the paneled ceiling.

The Sebastian deal was beginning to take on all the characteristics of a situation comedy. A bad one at that. Virginia didn't know if she wanted to laugh or cry. All the long hours of brainstorming and worry, and then to have everything hinge on the outcome of a cozy little dinner party. Really, it would have been almost laughable if it wasn't so grossly unfair. Virginia closed her eyes and rubbed her temples. Flashes of a memorable Tracy-Hepburn flick went through her head—chilling visions of *Guess Who's Coming to Dinner*. "Oh, God," she groaned, opening her eyes and hauling herself upright in the chair. She felt sick at her stomach.

Joe Dillon wasn't cut out for the kind of sophisticated mind game that would be played out tonight. The silver setting alone—two forks and three spoons— would undoubtedly throw him. He'd be uncomfortable and probably clumsy. There wasn't time to coach him. He'd have to wing it.

She tried to pull herself together. Maybe they'd get lucky and Ms Shapell would find his Southern mannerisms utterly charming. After all, Joe Dillon did display a certain degree of good breeding. And if he just didn't mention the fact that he bused dishes at Le Bouves on the side, maybe, just maybe . . .

Virginia knew she was kidding herself, but what choice did she have except to go through with the farce? She exhaled as she got up from the chair. Leaving her high hopes behind, she went to seek out Joe Dillon in the lounge.

She found him reading a magazine and relaxed as ever.

"How'd it go?" he asked.

"Fine," she lied.

"You didn't need me, huh?" He put aside the magazine and stretched lazily.

How to tell him about the major complication and make it appear minor? That was the trick. She tried to act nonchalant. "Well . . ." she hedged, unbuttoning her jacket and sitting down on the couch beside him. "Your meeting with Ms Shapell had to be rearranged. She's a busy woman."

"So when are we supposed to get together?" He wasn't thrown by the news.

"Tonight," she informed him. "Ms Shapell would like for the two of you to meet for dinner and talk then."

J.D.'s expression sobered instantly. "I'm afraid I can't do that," he stated flatly.

"This isn't an invitation you can afford to decline, Joe Dillon. You have to go," she insisted.

His jaw set stubbornly. "I can't afford to accept, either," he replied, as if that explained things and nothing more needed to be said.

"Why not? What's the problem?" Her frayed nerves were beginning to unravel altogether. She had to work hard at keeping her tone moderately civil.

"I'm broke. Flat busted. I didn't have money for cab fare and I sure don't have money to take a lady to dinner." He looked off into space, obviously embarrassed by the admission.

Virginia treaded carefully. She could see that his Southern pride was badly wounded by having been forced to make such a personal disclosure. "I'd forgotten about the cab. I should have realized the reason for your reluctance. I'm sorry. I didn't mean to embarrass you."

"It's all right." He dismissed the matter of his lack of funds with a shrug but still kept his eyes averted.

"You're not expected to pick up the tab for the dinner," she ventured. "Since it was Ms Shapell's suggestion, she'll be paying. So there shouldn't be a problem with your going."

"Yes, ma'am, there is." He was polite but determined. She could see a small muscle at the base of his jaw beginning to tick.

"What now?" She didn't have his self-control. Her impatience with him showed.

"Back where I come from, going to dinner with a woman is considered more social than business. I'm not sure I like the arrangement," he told her bluntly.

"Oh, for Pete's sake," she said scoffingly. "That may be true in Cottonmouth but it's not the case in New York. Business is transacted in a social setting all the time. It doesn't mean anything. You share cocktails and a meal while hashing out a few details. We're not talking a date-date. It's strictly business. It's inconsequential that the participants are male and female. You are merely two professional associates who happen to be meeting in public rather than in private for the sake of expediency. That's it. Nothing complicated or compromising. It's no big deal.'' It was partly the lecture she'd intended to give him on professional boundaries and partly a crash course on local customs.

"If you say so," he relented, though he sounded unconvinced.

"Trust me on this, okay?" She thought that would be the end of it.

"I still can't do it," he said matter-of-factly.

She wanted to choke him with her bare hands. At her wit's end, she didn't know what else to do but just tell it like it was and put herself at his mercy. "Look, Joe Dillon—" she turned to face him squarely "—I understand pride. I have enormous pride, too, but this account means so much to me that I'm willing to swallow my pride and beg you, if that's what it takes. The Sebastian campaign isn't just another run-of-the-mill deal. It means a lot to me personally. If I land the account, I'll be offered a partnership in the agency."

She couldn't believe she was actually telling her secret aspirations to an almost total stranger. It was the act of a desperate woman. She raked a hand through the tuft of bangs in a frustrated gesture. "Believe me, if I could make it happen without asking this favor of you, I would. To be perfectly honest, I think it's grossly unfair that something I've worked years to attain should end up being gauged on the basis of a casual dinner affair. But the simple fact is, Ms Shapell won't sign without evaluating you first. If you decline to attend tonight, I can kiss any hope of a partnership goodbye. I want it, Joe Dillon. It would mean the realization of all my efforts. It's what I've dreamed about. I want it so badly I'd do most anything to make it possible, including pleading with you to change your mind and go. What will it take to get you to agree? Please, just tell me and I'll try to comply."

J.D. sat dumbfounded. Suddenly she seemed so vulnerable, so different from the woman who'd been calling all the shots. "I don't want to mess things up for you. I'd do it in spite of my misgivings but I don't have anything decent to wear. My bag was stolen the day I hit town and these clothes are all I've got. I hardly think they're fitting."

"Is that all!" She laughed in relief. "We can solve that problem easily enough. We'll buy you an outfit for tonight and—"

"I couldn't let you do that, ma'am. Taking gifts I haven't earned goes against my grain. It wouldn't be right."

That damnable stubborn pride of his resurfaced. She had to come up with a way around it. She rephrased the suggestion. "But you have earned the money for the demo tape we shot. I believe I owe you for two hours' work. That would be more than enough money to buy a suitable ensemble for this evening. I'll just cut a check and—"

"No bank is going to cash a check for me. I'm new in town. It isn't likely they'd take my word for it that the check was good."

She wasn't about to give up. Too much was at stake. "Okay, I see your point. Let's do this, then. I'll advance you the cash until Monday morning when we can go to my bank and I'll vouch for you. That way you'll have no problem opening an account. You pay me back and deposit the remainder of the money. In the interim you can buy the clothes you need, make the dinner date with Ms Shapell and still manage to keep that gentlemanly honor of yours intact. Please, Joe Dillon,'' she urged him, reaching out and touching his arm. ''Help me here. I'm running out of options.''

He shook his head and grinned. ''I suppose that'd be all right.''

''At last.'' Her entire body went limp.

''But I have a condition of my own,'' he stipulated.

''Anything,'' she blurted.

''Another dinner date. You be my guest and it's purely social, not strictly business.'' He seconded the demand with a lingering look.

She was stunned—stymied. Having dinner with him would complicate things terribly. It was important to maintain a professional distance with co-workers. It would be awkward, not to mention potentially disadvantageous to both the ad campaign and her career. Under any other circumstances she'd be flattered by his obvious attraction, but considering the potential consequences, it just wasn't worth the risk. Then again, if she refused him, he might refuse her. She needed his cooperation or else she could scrap one major account and chalk up a partnership. Dammit! What should she do? Stick by her standards or serve her ambition? Why did life so often come down to an either-or proposition?

He studied her as she wrestled with a decision. He shouldn't have been so bold as to ask her out, but the opportunity had presented itself and he'd acted impulsively. He sensed she was searching for a tactful way to decline. He had to have been crazy to think she'd want to keep company with the likes of him. The lady was out of his league entirely. "If the idea doesn't appeal to you, we can forget it." He gave her an out.

"Uh, no, that's not it. I was merely thinking that there must be scores of women in New York who'd make better dinner companions than I would," was her spur-of-the-moment ad-lib.

He saw through the polite ploy. "Look, Virginia. I didn't just fall off a turnip truck. I can pretty well figure out when I'm getting the runaround. It's okay. I understand. Somebodies like you don't mingle with nobodies like me. It's a given I learned a long time ago. I just forgot it for a moment, is all." Amazingly, he didn't sound offended, merely a little disappointed.

He'd drawn the wrong conclusion entirely. "You misunderstand me, Joe Dillon. I assure you I only meant to imply that you might be more comfortable with someone more your own age and in a less intimidating position. There's a certain strain that develops between people when one signs the checks that another depends on." There, she'd said it in a roundabout fashion.

"The age difference doesn't matter to me. And I don't mind the strain in the least," he said simply and sincerely.

She had to admire his determination. Once he set his mind to something, Joe Dillon Mahue was not easily dissuaded. "All right," she agreed at last. "I accept your condition then."

Now it was his turn to be stunned—stymied. He sat back, taking a moment to absorb her affirmative answer.

The situation was already awkward, she thought. Someone had to make a move. She stood up from the couch and smoothed nonexistent wrinkles from her skirt. "We should hurry. There's a lot to do and only a few hours left to do everything. Ms Shapell dislikes being kept waiting. Her words, not mine," Virginia was quick to clarify. "Since I can't break away to accompany you, I thought I'd ask Rita if she'd go along to show you the best shops and buys. Do you mind?"

"I'd be grateful for the help but I wouldn't want to put Rita out any." In an easy move, he was on his feet and ready to fulfill his end of the bargain.

"Are you kidding! She loves an excuse to shop. Just don't let her talk you into anything outrageous. She can get carried away at times," she warned him, turning her back and walking off.

His gaze dropped to just below her peplum jacket. He became semihypnotized by the sensuous sway of her hips and silky swish of her skirt. It would seem that Rita wasn't the only one who could get carried away at times. What he was thinking at that very moment was also outrageous. He wanted his boss. He wanted her every bit as much as she professed to want that partnership. It never occurred to him to wonder if their two desires were mutually exclusive.

CHAPTER SEVEN

DUE TO SOME CURIOUS TWIST of fate, J.D. somehow managed to make a favorable impression upon Ms Shapell. She signed with the agency the following Tuesday. Though Virginia had phoned Joe Dillon over the weekend to press him for details about the dinner date, she hadn't been able to get much information out of him. About the most he'd say on the subject was that he thought things had gone *okay* between him and Ms Shapell. Virginia couldn't figure out whether he was being overly modest or deliberately evasive. Either way, his reluctance to divulge specifics really irritated her. The only thing he was inclined to discuss at length was their upcoming misadventure. It had been a ridiculous conversation. He kept talking about a ride in the park while she underwent a mild nervous breakdown. She'd spent three long, paranoid-filled days wondering whether the deadline date would be forever regarded as Black Tuesday or Fat Tuesday. Even when Udell had informed her of Shapell's decision and offered her a congratulatory pat on the back, she had still been skeptical of the good news.

"But has she actually signed?" she'd asked, worried.

"Relax, Virginia. The contract is being sent over to her as we speak. The Sebastian account is ours. Or more precisely, it's yours," Udell had amended with

a broad grin. "Ms Shapell insisted on two stipula-
tions. One was that you be personally responsible for
every aspect of the campaign. And the second was that
Mr. Mahue exclusively represent Don Sebastian Designs. Money is no object. We've been instructed to
offer him whatever amount it takes to ensure that his
face is not associated with any other line. Obviously
she's quite taken with him."

"Obviously," she'd answered numbly.

"Mr. Hanks and I are very pleased, Virginia," he'd
told her between puffs on his Cuban cigar. "The Sebastian account means a great deal of added revenue,
not to mention immeasurable PR for the firm. It goes
without saying that we are impressed by your performance and have every intention of recognizing your
efforts in a highly visible way in the not-too-distant
future." Puff, puff. Hint, hint.

She had hardly been able to contain herself. She had
had an overpowering impulse to run a victory lap
around Udell's desk, her arms uplifted, shouting,
"Yes! Yes! Yes!" like some gold medalist in the
Olympics. Of course, she had not executed such a
theatrical stunt. It would have been poor form.
"Thank you. I can assure you that I'll handle the account with kid gloves."

"I'm confident you will," he'd said, extending his
hand to the first and only female in the history of the
firm to be deemed potentially worthy of a partnership.

Finally, she'd thought to herself, *the recognition
I've always wanted.* There would be no more tagging
after the big boys. No more being just another painted
face in a tribe of Indians. She was going to assume a
more important role. Soon she would rise to the

mighty ranks of the male chiefs. At thirty-two, Virginia Vandivere had succeeded in stepping out from the shadows and was at last being allowed to shine. Nothing—absolutely nothing—stood in her way now. It was only a matter of time—days or, at the most, a month or two—before her lifelong ambition would be realized.

Virginia had been so engrossed in her thoughts she'd stood there transfixed, clasping Mr. Udell's hand so long and so tightly that he'd grown uncomfortable.

"Er, uh, well," he'd stammered when extricating his hand from her grip.

"Oh, excuse me," she'd apologized. "I guess I'm a little excited about the news. I should tell my crew. They worked very hard on the campaign. I think a small celebration is in order." She'd quickly composed herself and was once more wholly the professional woman.

"Yes, and be sure to include Mr. Mahue. I suspect he deserves a lot of the credit for bringing Ms Shapell around."

"Yes, of course. I'll convey our gratitude," she'd said offhandedly, as yet unaware what a profound part the gentleman from Cottonmouth would eventually play in her life....

J.D. HAD DECLINED HER INVITATION to come join the impromptu celebration. He had, however, taken advantage of her good mood and used the opportunity her phone call had presented to finalize the arrangements for their dinner date. Since he'd already planned the entire evening and had even taken the liberty of making reservations, she could hardly postpone complying with his condition. Reluctantly she agreed to accompany him to dinner at the Russian Tea Room the following Saturday evening.

J.D. could think of little else the remainder of the week. At dusk on Saturday he sat on the edge of the bed in his cubbyhole, half-dressed and suddenly only half-sure he should have arranged the evening at all.

He looked over at the new coat, shirt and tie hanging on the outside of the closet door. The clothes he'd recently purchased were certainly fine enough for the occasion. For once he wouldn't feel shabby or ashamed. He glanced to his wallet on the dresser. For the first time in a long while, he had money enough to spend. With Rita's help he'd planned a pleasant outing. But still he had doubts about being a suitable escort. After all, what did he know about big evenings on the town? Stimulating conversation? Sophisticated moves?

"You shouldn't have done it," he muttered to himself as he tugged on his socks. "And this time you can't blame Mason for the jam you're in." He slipped his feet into the wine-colored loafers, then stood and wiggled his toes. The shoes were stiff and cramped his feet. He preferred his broken-in boots, but wearing them was out of the question.

He sank back down on the lumpy mattress and stared at the shiny loafers. What difference did all the new finery make? Underneath he was still the same person. Fancy clothes and flashy money didn't change a man. Facts were facts. He was a common fella looking to impress an uncommon woman. It had been foolish to think he could. Hell, he hadn't even known where to take her tonight! The entire evening had been Rita's suggestion. He probably shouldn't have told her about the condition he'd forced on Virginia, but he'd wanted their date to be special and had needed a knowledgeable New Yorker's advice.

J.D. expelled a deep sigh before hoisting himself from the bed. The insecurities he was battling made him feel like an oafish kid. He'd forgotten what it felt like to be wildly excited about the prospect of being with a woman while dreading it at the same time. It had been a long time since it had happened to him. In fact, he hadn't experienced those smitten symptoms since Ashley Beaumont.

Crossing to the closet door, he took down his starched dress shirt and began putting it on. As he fastened the buttons, his mind traveled back to the Delta and a sweet hazy summer long ago.

Ashley wasn't from the Delta. She hailed from somewhere outside of Vicksburg and was merely visiting her mother's relations. Prior to her arrival, all anybody talked of was the fact that her daddy was from one of the finest of Mississippi families and how peculiar it was for him to have married a woman who was Delta born and bred. According to gossip, the Beaumonts were filthy rich and lived a life-style becoming of royalty.

Indeed, he thought he had glimpsed a princess when he'd set eyes on the Beaumont heiress for the first time. He was mesmerized by the sight of the enchanting creature ensconced in a circle of chatting and giggling local girls. To the unworldly sixteen-year-old, she seemed a rare flower in a garden of weeds; she appeared so fresh and elegant in contrast to the sweltering heat and plain surroundings. And when she looked his way and actually smiled at him, his heart melted into a pool of quivering muscle.

Thereafter, wherever he went and whatever he did, he was only half-aware of what he was doing. The other half of him belonged to her—to Ashley. He was constantly searching for her, hoping, praying he might run into her again. Occasionally he would, and the mere sight of her would make him tingle all over. At night he would lie awake in his bed in the upstairs loft; the airless quarters would be filled with his brothers' snores, and his head with thoughts of the lovely Ashley. For hours he'd stare up at the ceiling and fantasize about her. They'd meet unexpectedly at the shady stream back in the piney woods where he sometimes went to fish and study on things. At first they'd be shy, but gradually they'd warm up to each other. He imagined her smelling as sweet as magnolias, and her laughter would be plumb musical. She'd be amused by his Delta stories and tell him he was the most fascinating person she'd ever met....

In his vivid imaginings, she'd wind up scooting closer to him as they exchanged confidences and deep, lingering looks. The outcome of the secret tryst never varied. She'd inch closer and closer to him until her delicious body was pressed so tightly up against his that he could feel every hard and fast beat of her heart. Then, she'd slip her fingers through his hair and lift her soft pink lips to his own in an invitation to be soundly kissed. He'd forge her to him and almost make her swoon with a kiss that lasted forever. That was the best part of the fantasy—how without much practice he was just naturally a sensational kisser.

Usually it was then, just as the pair of them were stretching out on the cool grass and she was murmuring feverishly, "I want you so—I swear I'll want you forever! I don't care if you're poor and I'm rich . . . it didn't matter to my daddy. Make love to me, J.D.—right here, right now. Let's not waste another precious minute...." Usually it was then that his fantasy would be disturbed. Generally it was his older brother, Joe Ray, with whom he shared a bed, giving him a hard poke in the ribs with an elbow and telling him to quit his squirming or else nobody was gonna get any rest. If he hadn't known better, he'd have believed that Joe Ray persisted in ruining his fantasy on purpose. But his brother couldn't know what he was thinking. Nobody knew of his secret feeling for Ashley—not even her, because it wasn't anything more than a stupid fantasy, just wishful thinking.

J.D. smiled wistfully as he reached for his tie, put it on and mindlessly looped it into a knot. He continued to dwell on the past as he finished preparing for his dream date in the present....

That hazy summer had turned out to be the best and worst time of his life, for to his amazement a major portion of his fantasy came true. The attraction between him and Ashley was not as instantaneous as he'd imagined. And he certainly was not nearly as accomplished a lover as he'd been in his fantasy. But strangely enough, they did meet up at the shady stream one afternoon. They did exchange words, but mostly they were awkward with each other. However, the next day she returned as he'd hoped she would. She came most every day thereafter, except Sunday, when she had to observe a day of worship. For the next few weeks they met on the sly at the shady stream and talked about themselves at length. To this day, he wasn't sure whether or not Ashley really smelled sweeter than magnolias. But she did wear good-smelling perfume and her laughter was most definitely musical. She was smart, too. Well-read. Soft mannered. And her eyes were the bluest of blue. Every time she looked at him it darn near took his breath away.

Looking back, he realized that he must have been crazy to think things could have ever worked out between them. But in those days he wasn't thinking really clearly. As the summer came to an end and the day of her departure from the Delta neared, they both closed their eyes to what even a blind person could see. Instead, they experimented with kissing and everything became a blur when their youthful passion exploded. In those last days they were making love every afternoon by the stream. And though she was amused by his stories and hungry for his lovemaking, she never once uttered the feverish words of his fantasy. She never said she didn't care about the differences between them. She never told him it didn't matter that he was poor and she was rich. She never brought up the example of her daddy.

And he'd never noticed until later—until after she was gone from the Delta, until after he'd written her letter after letter. She only bothered to reply once.

Dear J.D.,
It was wonderful hearing from you. I sometimes miss the Delta. I will always remember it fondly and you, too, of course.

I leave for Boston at the end of the week. Daddy is sending me to an exclusive girls' school. At first I was against the idea but now I'm looking forward to the change. I'm bored with Vicksburg, anyway.

I probably won't have much free time to write. Please understand. This past summer was special but we both knew it couldn't last forever. I'll cherish the memory of it, as I hope you will. Goodbye and God bless.

Ashley

He'd kept the letter several years after receiving it. He'd read it so many times that the words were engraved on his brain. *I sometimes miss the Delta.* She'd never mentioned missing him. *I will always remember it fondly and you, too, of course.* She'd included him only as an afterthought. Between the lines was a clear message. *The fact is, I couldn't consider a boy from the Delta a serious suitor. You were a summer romance. It was fun but it's over.* Please understand, she'd asked.

It had taken him a while to understand. It had taken even longer to get over her. Eventually the hurt of her rejection had worn off, but the reason for it stuck with him. He came away from that summer having learned two things—how to make love to a woman and how badly it could turn out if you chose the wrong woman to pleasure.

J.D. blinked and the hazy summer memory evaporated. He found himself looking at his own reflection in the tarnished dresser mirror. His oxford shirt was buttoned and tucked in. The silk Fumagalli tie was knotted and straight. He didn't look at all like the poor, oafish boy of his youth.

Having forgotten his apprehension about the coming evening, he wondered why he'd recalled that long-ago summer and Ashley. Then he remembered the moment he'd first met Virginia and how he'd been struck by her vague resemblance to his former lover. A grown-up version of Ashley was what he'd initially thought. In all honesty, they didn't look that much alike. Mostly it was the blue, blue eyes and the shy smile that made him think of Ashley.

Then it dawned on him—the obvious connection between the two women. He'd said it himself, without fully realizing the significance of the observation. *Somebodies like you don't mingle with nobodies like me. It's a given I learned a long time ago,* he'd told her.

But she'd argued the point, citing their age difference and working arrangement as the problem, not his plain roots or meager finances. Was he just being overly sensitive? Was the somebody-nobody connection merely a product of his overactive imagination? After all, he'd been engaging in plenty of fantasy lately. Perhaps he was simply confusing one fantasy with another.

No, he decided. The cold, hard reality of it was that he was indulging in wishful thinking about Virginia. It was rare for a man to have one fantasy fulfilled. What were the chances of it happening a second time? *About a zillion to one,* he figured.

But that didn't mean they couldn't have a nice evening. J.D. shrugged off his concerns, tucked his wallet into the back pocket of his pleated slacks and collected his sport coat from the hanger on the closet door. The reservation was for eight. He had an hour yet but he wanted to arrive early at the restaurant. It had bothered him that Virginia had insisted on coming separately. Back in Cottonmouth, a gentleman picked up a lady at her doorstep and delivered her home again. He guessed they did things differently in New York. Though he was trying to adapt, he wondered if he'd ever truly become accustomed to Yankee ways.

CHAPTER EIGHT

THE LAST THING VIRGINIA NEEDED or wanted was Rita hovering about while she was trying to get ready for her dinner date with Mahue. It was rare for Rita to pay an impromptu visit to her Upper West Side apartment and never, ever, did she come by on a Saturday night. In fair or foul weather, in sickness or in health, Rita went dancing in Spanish Harlem on Saturday nights. Even when her second husband refused to go anymore, Rita left to cha-cha the night away, which was how she came to meet husband number three. Her unprecedented appearance at Virginia's place on Spanish Harlem night made Virginia *muy* suspicious.

"Aren't you late for the Latin cotillion?" She cast her a sideway look, then jiggled into her slip.

"No. Things don get hopping until later." Rita seemed in no particular hurry as she plopped herself down on the vanity stool and examined the vast array of nail polish bottles, one by one.

Virginia smothered a groan. Rita wasn't budging. "See something you like?" she asked, her perturbation evident.

"No," Rita said honestly. "All you have ees these pale colors. I need something to match my outfit. Ees new. What you theenk? Ees me, no?"

Virginia gave up. It was obvious that Rita was stalling when she knew damn well that Virginia wanted her to go. The flashy getup she was wearing made Virginia's eyes hurt just to look at it. She resembled an over ripe, neon tangerine with ruffles. Everything considered, Virginia decided it was best to be diplomatic. "Definitely you, Rita," she agreed, following up with a more frank assertion. "I'm positive you have no less than a dozen shades of orange nail polish at home. You came by to snoop, not to borrow. I don't know how you found out, but you know, don't you?"

"Know what?" Rita played dumb.

Virginia was not in the mood to engage in game playing. "That I'm going to dinner with Mr. Mahue, that's what." She didn't wait for a reply or even glance in Rita's direction. Turning on her stockinged heels, she hid herself inside the closet, thankful to have the excuse of deliberating over thirty or so wardrobe selections. "It's not what you think. It's not a date-date. He cornered me into agreeing to have dinner with him."

Rita had lost all interest in the nail polish. She sauntered over to the closet door to watch Virginia go through the process of elimination. The faster and more furiously she explained the situation, the faster and more furiously the hangers zipped across the clothes bar. "If I hadn't accepted his condition, he wouldn't have kept the appointment with Shapell." It took her only a split second to look over and then reject each outfit in turn. Nothing looked right. Everything was either too businesslike or too casual. She didn't buy clothes for date-dates because she didn't go on date-dates. She was becoming more frustrated by the hanger.

"I intend to set Mr. Mahue straight tonight. I'm going to make it perfectly clear to him that there can be no more of these conditional dinners. Damn! I don't know what to wear. Maybe the black suit . . ."

"Ees no good. You'll look like you are going to a funeral," Rita put in.

"Well, then, it's fitting, because that's exactly how I feel." Virginia yanked the black suit from its hanger, snatched up a pair of black high heels from the shoe rack on the closet floor, then breezed past Rita and dumped the whole kit and caboodle on the bed.

Rita let her blow off steam. She knew Virginia well enough to realize that her sulky indifference was a cover-up. She was behaving temperamentally because she was anxious. It had been a very long time since her friend had dealt with a man on any level but a professional one. Rita was thoroughly convinced that Virginia was afraid to let herself become intimately involved again. Her ex-husband's infidelity had caused her to question her womanly appeal. Being the best ad woman in the business was her boss's way of compensating for feeling inadequate after working hours.

"I theenk you are making a fuss over nothing. The man ees not asking you to have sex with him, only dinner. You make mountains out of anthills."

"Molehills," Virginia corrected her. "And I am not exaggerating the predicament I'm in. Fraternizing with contract labor is not smart. It can give rise to all sorts of sticky complications." She grabbed up a hairbrush from the vanity and began whipping it through her hair. "My only interest in Mr. Mahue is seeing to it that he fulfills his obligations to Hanks and Udell. I get paid to make him irresistible to other women, not to play footsie with him under the table. I can't believe I let myself be coerced into accepting his invitation. Technically I'm his boss and—"

"But only temporarily," Rita pointed out.

Virginia took no notice of her words, continuing her tirade. "It's bad practice to socialize with staff. It undermines one's credibility."

"Ayyy! You're hopeless." Rita shook her head and deposited herself on the bed with a bounce. "Obligations, complications. Your life ees full of them. You make my head ache with all your talk of it."

Virginia decided she was wasting her breath. Besides, Rita wasn't the one she needed to convince. Joe Dillon was the person to whom she should deliver the speech on professional ethics. And she intended to do just that at dinner. "So take two aspirin and go dancing," she said testily. "Mr. Mahue's my worry. I'll handle him."

"Okay, fine. Go ahead and ruin a nice evening. I don suppose it matters to you that he has gone to a lot of trouble to make tonight special for you." Virginia could feel Rita's dark eyes boring through her as she got up and fished the shoes out from beneath the suit. "Business ees business. What ees a man's feelings, so long as he learns just who ees *número uno*?"

"Not fair, Rita." Virginia balanced on one foot as she slipped on a shoe.

"Ees you who ees unfair. You don have to be boss twenty-four hours a day. You could at least wait until after dinner to cut his pride to pieces." Having spoken her mind, Rita wiggled off the bed and shook her hips so that the tangerine tiers fell into place.

"You're being overly dramatic. I seriously doubt he'll be as devastated as you'd have me believe." Virginia hobbled about in a clumsy attempt to slide her foot into the other shoe.

Rita slanted a look back over her shoulder as she headed out to cha-cha land. "You may know proper English but Mundo knows men. Your *caballero* has a strong will and passionate feelings. If it was me, I'd wish to make love, not business, with him."

"Good night, Rita," was Virginia's brusque reply.

Taking the hint, Rita waltzed out of the bedroom. "I theenk maybe you will have regrets come Monday." Her smug hum floated back through the doorway.

"I assure you I'll have none," Virginia declared. "Tonight Mr. Mahue and I will reach an understanding and by Monday the touchy situation between us will have been resolved."

There only resounded a slam of the front door.

Virginia decided that perhaps she should heed her own advice and take two aspirin herself. She had one hell of a headache from anticipating the evening ahead. Rita's visit had put her way behind. She was already twenty minutes late and it'd take at least another twenty minutes to put herself together.

In her hurry to dress, she forgot about the aspirin. Throughout the cab ride over to the restaurant, she periodically closed her eyes and rubbed her throbbing temples. Without some form of relief, the headache would soon escalate into a major migraine. Rummaging through her purse produced only a package of breath mints. By the time the cab stopped outside of the Russian Tea Room, she'd prescribed a strong drink for herself. *Yes,* she thought, *that should do it.* It'd ease her frazzled nerves and alleviate her headache all at once. She already had her drink order in mind before the maître d' said, "Oh, yes, Mahue—party of two. Your table is upstairs. Follow me, please."

"STOLY OVER ICE," she told the waiter.

Joe Dillon had never heard of such a drink. "Make it two," he said, thinking it easier to duplicate her order than to select or pronounce anything from the wine list. No sooner had the waiter departed than he grinned broadly and asked, "What exactly are we drinking?"

"Stolichnaya. It's a Russian vodka," she enlightened him.

"What's it mixed with?"

"Ice," she said with a trace of amusement,

"That's it? Just ice?"

She nodded.

"I've never tried it. Russian vodka isn't a commonplace drink back in Cottonmouth." He settled back against the banquette's plush upholstery and cast an awed look about the upstairs dining room. He'd never seen anything like it. The decorating scheme was kind of Christmasy—ruby-red upholstery, forest-green walls and giant chandeliers in the shape of big gold balls with tinsellike stuff dripping down. A store of paintings hung all over the room. Russian art, he guessed. Probably hundreds of years old. The room fairly glittered with polished brass trim work, and there were big brass urns next to each pink linen-draped table. While he'd waited for Virginia to arrive, he'd asked the waiter about the huge urns. The gent had explained that they were called samovars and that they were once used to brew tea in Mother Russia. J.D. figured the tea must be awfully powerful tasting being brewed in something so grand. He was disappointed to learn that they were only used in a decorative capacity. But that was his only complaint with the fancy place. It was a sight to behold.

Virginia noticed his preoccupation with the decor. "Do you like the artwork?"

"Yes, ma'am. I like it fine," he said simply, dismissing the artwork and settling his gaze on her. "You look pretty as a picture, too."

"Thank you," she answered stiffly, relieved when the waiter interrupted with their drinks. Thinking Joe Dillon might need extra time to study the menu, she advised the waiter that they'd like to browse the selections at their leisure.

When she once again returned her attention to Joe Dillon he was holding up his glass in readiness of a toast. She wanted to skip the gesture and just quaff down the vodka, but it would have been rude. Mechanically she raised her glass and clinked it against his. "To a productive and profitable business venture," she said, carefully avoiding making eye contact as she sipped the chilled vodka. She took a small amount of satisfaction in having been slick enough to beat him to the toast.

Joe Dillon studied her over the edge of his glass as he sampled the vodka. Her face was strained and her body tense beneath the very basic, and obviously very expensive, black suit. It was evident to him that she was twice as uncomfortable as he was. But why? he wondered. He set aside the vodka with a grimace. "Strong stuff," he remarked.

"It takes a bit of getting accustomed to." She sipped again, looking off at nothing in particular and twiddling with the pearl necklace at her throat.

J.D. decided making small talk wasn't breaking the ice. He wanted to put her at ease. Being basically a direct person, he opted to address her jitters straight on. "You seem uptight, Virginia. Is it me?"

She was taken so off guard by his intuitiveness that she actually looked up and met his questioning gaze. The vulnerability she encountered in the brown orbs that stared back at her made it impossible for her to be completely truthful. "I have a headache, that's all," she explained.

"Is it me?" he repeated, refusing to relinquish her eyes or the issue.

What should she say? *Yes, dammit! It's you. First you make me feel awkward and then you make me feel guilty for feeling that way.* "No, uh, well, not exactly," she hedged. She took another swig of vodka.

"So I'm only partly to blame for your headache," he deduced, grinning lazily.

She found herself smiling back at him in spite of herself. "It's getting better. The vodka is helping."

"Then let's get you another," he suggested, signaling for the waiter before she could stop him. "Two more of the same," he told the fellow.

Virginia could feel her face getting hot. The waiter probably thought her a lush. Damn! The evening was going to become a circus if she didn't get a grip on herself. She needed to take charge of the situation and guide the conversation around to what needed to be said. Instead, she was stalling—behaving like some shrinking violet because she hadn't the nerve to dissertate on the rules of their relationship just yet. She needed time to work up to it. Switch gears. *Get him off track,* a small voice inside her head whispered.

"I like your new clothes. Very New York," she commented, making a big production out of swirling the ice in her glass with a swizzle stick.

J.D. didn't want to push her. It wouldn't be polite. "Rita helped me pick them out. It wasn't her first choice but I couldn't go along with what she'd originally had in mind."

"I can only imagine," Virginia replied, relaxing a smidgen.

"No, I don't think you can. A man could get arrested wearing an outfit such as the one she wanted me to try on. The color alone was indecent."

She laughed at the thought of what Rita must have tried to thrust on him. Thank goodness the man had an innate sense of style. He did look nice. Extraordinarily so.

As he related the details of the shopping adventure with Rita, she found herself becoming less inhibited and more taken with him as a person. He wasn't just a commodity or a complication; he was witty and warm and easy to be with. Or maybe it was just the Russian vodka doing its bit. She wasn't certain, but she was definitely mellowing out.

By the time the waiter checked back to see if they were ready to place their dinner order, she was actually beginning to enjoy herself. It occurred to her that Joe Dillon might be concerned about appearing ignorant of Russian cuisine. She thought she would spare him the embarrassing ordeal, but as she was about to order for them both, he opted to do the honors. Her amazement couldn't have been more apparent as he proceeded to order her favorite dishes: borscht—beet soup; shashlik—pieces of lamb roasted on spits; pirojok—small meat pies; and blini—rolled pancakes filled with cottage cheese and covered with sour cream.

"Are you psychic or what? How did you know my favorite dishes?" she asked as soon as they were alone.

"I did my homework," he said with a wink, at which she visibly stiffened. Judging from her reaction, he got the distinct impression that she disliked the idea of his researching her. He felt obliged to explain. "I wasn't prying, Virginia. I wanted to take you someplace you liked. I was afraid the menu wouldn't be in English and I didn't want to risk getting tongue-tied or ordering everything backward. So I asked Rita and she told me what you liked to eat and where to get it."

She was a little flattered that he'd gone to the trouble. "Are you always so accommodating?"

"I like to please a lady, if that's what you mean."

What a delightfully uncomplicated complication he was. No bull, just unsettling forthrightness. Men with lines she knew how to deal with. The gentleman from Cottonmouth was another matter. She didn't know quite how to react to him.

As they shared dinner and conversation, her headache lessened considerably. She was still unsure which had alleviated the awful pressure: him or the vodka she'd consumed. Before she realized it, she was talking about herself, telling him private things she rarely discussed with anyone. He listened attentively, as though he truly cared what she had to say. He had a talent for timing—asking a pertinent question when it was appropriate or making a profound comment at the perfect moment. Somehow, without her really being aware of it, he'd gotten her to reveal the darker side of herself. She hadn't intended to talk about anything so personal as her divorce, but to her utter astonishment she heard herself mentioning her former husband.

"What went wrong?" he asked.

She considered giving him some glib answer, but she hated ruining the candid rapport between them. It was refreshing to be able to be totally oneself with someone. For some inexplicable reason she felt she could trust him. In a matter of a few hours, the emotional distance she'd been so determined to maintain had evaporated. It was crazy. Her intentions had gotten all muddled—turned around. *The vodka. It had to be the vodka,* she reasoned. *No more for you, Virginia.* She silently swore off the stuff, shoving the half-finished drink away before answering.

"I wasn't enough for him. In all honesty, I don't know whose fault it was—mine or his. We both were trying to establish ourselves in separate careers. Maybe we got too wrapped up in making it at the expense of each other." She hadn't told anyone what she'd just told him, not even Rita. Deep down she sometimes wondered if she'd played a part in her ex's discontentment. It had all been so clear when she'd found out about his many indiscretions. He was the infidel; she the wronged wife. With the passing of time, however, she'd questioned the legitimacy of what she'd thought had transpired in the past. Had it actually happened as she remembered it? Or was that only her personal version of a painful experience? Which came first? The chicken or the egg? His indiscretions or her withdrawal from him? Her eyes grew opaque as she stared off into space.

J.D. ventured an opinion. "It seems to me that there are bound to be times in a marriage when a husband

and wife's attention is divided. But if a person is sure about his or her own feelings, they don't feel threatened by a lull. If a man needs attention so badly as to take it anywhere he can get it, the discontent comes from within, not from without."

It was as if he'd read her mind. "How did you know what I was thinking?" she asked incredulously.

"I guessed. Women have a tendency to blame themselves. Probably because we men have convinced 'em that it's their place in life to be all things to us at once—wife, mother, lover and friend—and if they fall short in any given area, they've done us an injustice. Most of us are spoiled little boys who expect the impossible but don't much want to put ourselves out any in order to have our every whim fulfilled. We're kinda blind to our own shortcomings. It's easier to point out the woman's failings. If we lay the blame at her feet, we don't have to look to ourselves or do any changing. It's worked pretty good for centuries. So why mess up a good thing?"

He'd piqued her curiosity. "You're very astute when it comes to women. Are you speaking from a theoretical or personal point of view?" She smiled amusedly while leaning forward and cradling her chin in a palm.

"I don't claim to be an authority on women," he said quickly. "Far from it, in fact. I'm just philosophizing. We do a lot of that back in Cottonmouth. Mostly 'cause there isn't a whole heck of a lot else to do 'cept to occasionally exchange ideas or swap stories."

"You mean there haven't been a host of women in your past? I would've thought differently." She hadn't meant to speak her thoughts aloud. The remark simply slipped out before she could check herself.

He didn't seem at all nonplussed by the question. "I'm no ladies' man, Virginia. Once there was a special woman. It was a long time ago and nothing came of it."

"Who was to blame for things not working out?" she asked, testing him.

"Why me, of course," he said with a wink.

"Something makes me think not," was her pensive comeback.

"Would you like another drink?" he asked.

"No, thank you." She forced all thoughts of him away, straightening and withdrawing into her plastic persona.

Joe Dillon was baffled by the sudden change in her. One minute she was friendly and receptive, the next moment she was cool and aloof. She changed moods like a chameleon changed colors. Mostly, she was intense, but tonight she'd loosened up just a bit. Enough so he realized that underneath all the guarded intensity lurked a sensitive and desirable woman.

"We need to talk, Joe Dillon."

He knew by her tone that whatever she had on her mind, it most certainly wasn't of the same nature as what was on his. "I thought that was what we were doing."

His smile was disarming. Why'd he have to be so damn good-looking? So young, so warm, sexy and Southern? Rita's words mocked her. *If it was me, I'd wish to make love, not business, with him.* Virginia fidgeted in her chair. "Well, yes, but there are other, more serious matters we need to discuss—a few things we need to get straight."

"Okay," he said, wiping his mouth with his napkin and glancing around for the waiter. "We can do some serious talking during our ride in the park."

Vaguely she remembered his mentioning it on the phone. "I don't think a ride through the park is conducive to conducting business."

"Wasn't it you who told me that in New York people conduct business in a social setting all the time?"

He had her there. *Good going, Virginia,* she thought to herself. "Yes, but I didn't mean—"

"It'll be less noisy in the buggy. The fresh air will help your headache," he insisted, catching the waiter's eye and telling him in sign language he was ready to settle the tab.

She searched for a tactful way to decline. "It's late. I doubt you could even find an available carriage or driver on such short notice, and even if you could, it's dangerous to travel into Central Park at night. There are muggers everywhere."

He merely grinned, then pulled out his wallet and began counting out the cash for the check. "I rented a buggy and driver until midnight. I'll expect he'll take us wherever we want to go. I also think I can fend off any muggers we meet on the ride. We backwoods types learn how to fight early on." He was only half teasing.

It dawned on her that he must have spent a good deal of his earnings from the demo on the evening. She couldn't fathom why he would make such a sacrifice. "Don't you think it's a bit extravagant hiring a carriage for an entire evening?"

He placed the money to cover the tab and tip on the silver tray and eased out of the booth. "Yeah, a bit," he admitted, offering her a hand up. "But I happen to think you're worth it."

How could she refuse him? She exhaled a sound-less sigh and gave him her hand. "You've some smooth moves for a backwoods type, Joe Dillon," she remarked as they descended the stairs.

"When you get to know me better, you'll realize my intentions are always genuine."

She said nothing more as he took her arm. The gentleman from Cottonmouth had a hold on her, and not just in the physical sense.

THE JAUNT THROUGH CENTRAL PARK in the moon-light was a delightful change of pace for Virginia. The soothing sway of the gas-lit carriage and the clop, clop, clop of the horses' hooves as they plodded along had an opiatelike effect on her. Soon she became totally unaware of the driver in the top hat and waistcoat perched on the seat above them.

Her senses were too filled with the cool caress of evening air, the spring smell of rhododendrons, aza-leas and wisteria, and the sounds of tranquillity—twittering birds, gurgling brooks and splashing water fountains. But most of all, she was absorbing the di-vine silence within the inner-city sanctuary. As the carriage rolled along past the famous Tavern on the Green, with its flagstone terrace and gaily colored umbrellas, it occurred to her that she'd been so wrapped up in the serene atmosphere that she'd for-gotten to engage in conversation. Feeling terribly re-miss, she decided the least she could do was act as Joe Dillon's tour guide. She began to point out land-marks and areas of special interest as they made their way past the plaza, the zoo, the Mall, Belvedere Cas-

tle and the concert ground. As they rode by the bal-
ustrade with its broad steps leading to Bethesda
Fountain near the lake, she relayed bits and pieces of
the park's history.

Joe Dillon leaned this way and that, full of wonder
and questions. It was a reawakening for Virginia to
view it all again through his appreciative eyes. She felt
as if she were seeing the Ramble, Belvedere Lake, the
Great Lawn and Shakespeare Garden, with its old oak
from Stratford-upon-Avon and English flowers from
the poet's work, for the very first time.

She pointed out the central promenade, the stately
buildings that housed the Metropolitan Museum of
Art and the American Museum of Natural History,
and the obelisk's two hundred tons of granite known
as Cleopatra's Needle. Though he could not see them
very well, she told him of the bronzed busts of Burns
and Scott and Beethoven and tried to describe the
sculptures of Alice in Wonderland and Hans Chris-
tian Andersen as best she could.

He was astounded by the number of recreational
sites—playgrounds and boat houses, tennis courts and
baseball diamonds. "Wow! It's something, huh?" he
uttered disbelievingly. "Your parks are bigger than the
whole of Cottonmouth."

She laughed at his misconception. "Central Park is
unique, even for New York. Most parks don't compare in size or scope," she explained as the sight-seeing
tour came to an end and the carriage rolled through
the gates, back to the big-city furor beyond the park's
stone walls.

"I have to admit, the ride was fun," she told him,
regretting it was over so soon.

"I was hoping you'd say it was the pleasant company you enjoyed." There was a trace of wistfulness in his mild tone.

"It goes without saying," she assured him.

"It shouldn't," he countered. He'd wanted a sincere response, not an automatic one. "People ought to say what's on their mind or in their heart." Unexpectedly he grazed his fingertips along her cheek in the pretext of brushing the baby-fine wisps of hair back from her face. "The wind blew your hair out of place," he said softly.

Suddenly realizing she was holding her breath, she exhaled and reached up to secure her hair behind her ear. Whenever she felt uncertain, she reacted by becoming very opinionated about the source of her discomfiture. "It's sometimes impossible and very often unwise to express your true thoughts and feelings, Joe Dillon," she stated primly.

To which he replied, "It's always possible and usually preferable to leaving things to be assumed."

Which was precisely the point she'd intended to discuss all evening—wrongful assumptions. He'd finally given her the opening and she was letting the opportunity slip away while he wrestled with the unthinkable prospect of his kissing her in the moonlight. Was she nuts?! "It's funny you should mention assumptions," she blurted. "In a way, it pertains to what I had wanted to discuss."

"You're referring to the serious talk we've yet to have," he surmised.

"Yes," she insisted, just as the driver reigned in the horses and the carriage lurched to a stop.

"Okay," he agreed, tapping the driver on the shoulder and thanking him for his services. "We can do our talking on the way home. How far do you live from here?" He jumped out of the carriage and held out his arms.

"I can—" his hands clamped around her small waist and in a smooth, effortless lift, he deposited her on the ground "—manage," she uttered stupidly.

"Can we walk it?" he asked.

"Well, yes, I guess so. But it'd be quicker to catch a taxi."

"I'm in no hurry. It's a nice night for a stroll."

Some stroll, she thought. Her apartment was a twenty-block hike from where they were and *he* wasn't wearing high heels.

"Which way?" he asked.

Glumly she pointed in the direction they needed to proceed in. The driver tipped his hat to her as they passed. She was sure he was thinking what easy targets they were for muggers. Nobody with any sense strolled the New York streets at midnight.

Joe Dillon noticed she was lagging a little behind him. "You're not still worried about muggers, are you?"

"No, uh, of course not," she lied, falling into step beside him.

He took her arm as they walked along the boulevard. "So, what was it you wanted to discuss?" he prompted her.

She hesitated, unsure of how to broach the subject. "It concerns our future relationship, Joe Dillon," she began, stepping down a curb and then up another.

"Uh-huh," he said blandly, pointing to a grate in the sidewalk in a silent gesture for her to watch her step.

He walked briskly. She had to take two steps to his one to keep pace. Gingerly she tiptoed across the grate. "I don't want you to take what I'm about to say personally, but I have to be blunt," she said apologetically.

"Uh-huh," he replied again.

"There are certain ground rules we must adhere to, Joe Dillon. It's important for us to respect each other professionally." Up and down the curbs again. Another damn grate in the sidewalk.

She ventured a glance in his direction. He didn't look particularly upset. So far, so good. She was, however, getting a little winded. His idea of a stroll was more like rigorous exercise.

"I respect you a lot," he answered.

"I appreciate it," she puffed. "But I don't think I'm getting my point across to you. Us seeing each other socially complicates our working arrangement. We could become too familiar and it would doubtlessly affect our professional objectivity. You see what I mean?"

"Not really," he drawled.

She almost missed the next grate. "Maybe I'm not phrasing this right," she tried once more. "It's hard enough for a man to work for a woman. The male and female egos get in the way. In order for you to become what I hope you will, I have to call the shots. There can be no distractions or dissension. I have to be solely focused on you as an image I'm trying to promote, not as a man I'm trying to please. If we were, uh, personally involved it would eventually filter over into our business dealings. A disagreement outside of work could affect both of our performances on the job. Or vice versa. So you see, it's best to avoid mixing the two. Believe me, it seldom works.''

Three blocks down. Only seventeen to go. Damn! Was she getting through to him? He wasn't responding.

Joe Dillon was having difficulty understanding the rationale. He couldn't figure out why it was okay for him to socialize with a lady in authority in one instance but not in another. Miss Shapell had gotten personal. A little too personal for his taste. Throughout the business dinner her knee had kept rubbing against his under the table. At first he'd thought it was an accident, but every time he moved his legs, she'd shift hers. By the end of the evening, his knees were plumb chafed from all the bumping and brushing going on under the table.

''Socializing in the sense of furthering a business connection is one thing. It's accepted practice—good business. It's when personal intentions enter into a professional relationship that it becomes bad business,'' Virginia babbled on, double-stepping to keep up with him. More engrossed in making her point then watching where she was going, she missed a grate. Her heel went down into the latticed metalwork and she almost tumbled headlong onto the pavement. J.D.'s quick reflexes and firm grip were all that saved her from an embarrassing spill.

Humiliated beyond words, she balanced precariously on one foot and tried to wiggle free her heel. ''Oh, swell. It's stuck,'' she grumbled.

''Hold still and let me see if I can work it loose.'' He bent down to assist her.

She braced a hand on his shoulder, continuing to try to pry the wedged heel from the grate.

"Slip your foot out," he suggested.

She did so, slightly miffed she had not thought of the simple solution herself.

"It's jammed pretty good. I'm afraid I'm going to break off the heel if I tug much harder," he told her.

"Do it anyway. We can't stand here all night." She was growing more flustered by the minute. If they had taken a taxi as she'd suggested, she wouldn't be in the asinine predicament. The designer shoes had cost a fortune.

J.D. gave a yank. He shot her a sheepish look when he held up the left shoe minus a heel. "Sorry. It'd take a team of mules to tow free your heel. It's gonna be hard walking the rest of the way."

She sighed and glanced around in the hopes of spying a taxi. One was never around when you needed it. "There's not a taxi in sight and I've no intentions of hobbling home," she told him flatly.

"You could take off your other shoe," he pointed out.

The mischievous glint in his eyes only added to her exasperation. "Get serious. Barefoot in the park is not my idea of fun," she fumed. "You're the resourceful backwoods type. What do you propose we do now?

She gasped when he hoisted her off the pavement up into his arms. "What on earth do you think you're doing?"

"Carrying you home," he calmly replied.

"It's a gallant gesture but impractical, Joe Dillon. My apartment is still a long way from here," she protested.

"I used to tote bales of cotton. I expect I can pack you a few blocks." He shifted her weight a bit.

"We can hail a taxi. There's bound to be one come along in a minute."

"If one passes, I'll flag it. But in the meantime you don't want to be a sitting duck for the muggers, do you?"

As much as she hated admitting it, there was a certain logic to his reasoning.

"You want to help me a bit here by putting your arms around my neck? It'd make it easier going."

She did as he requested, not sure it was all that much of an assist.

He didn't seem at all taxed by his burden as he walked along the avenue. Nor did he pay much attention to traffic signals at the crosswalks. He dodged the cars and ignored the honks and shouts of the testy New York drivers.

"Whaddya color-blind, pal!" Honk. Honk. "Hey, bub, you gotta death wish or what?" Screech, screech. "This ain't lovers' lane, Romeo!" were but a few of the bellows directed at them.

It wasn't the heckling that made Virginia cringe. It was their conspicuous traveling arrangements. Passersby were gawking at them. What if someone she knew saw them? Someone from the agency or, God forbid, a client! She'd be the laughing stock of Madison Avenue. Yet, even in her mortified state, she was keenly aware of the sinewy play of the muscles in his neck and shoulders, disturbingly cognizant of his cologne. Her reputation could be in the sewer at any moment and she was more sensitive to brawn and musk than to her dilemma.

"You were saying?" he cued her as they proceeded down one curb and up another, steadily heading toward her Upper West Side abode.

The whole damn scene was ludicrous—him acting the part of the chivalrous gentleman aiding a damsel in distress while she expounded on the necessity of remaining personally detached and sermonized about professional ethics. "I was trying to impress upon you the importance of keeping our relationship on a strictly business level." She squirmed uncomfortably within his embrace.

He grinned, boosted her up a bit in his arms and continued walking. "Yeah, well, where I come from people aren't so formal. Just because you work for a person doesn't mean you can't be sociable with 'em. I can respect you as a boss and like you as a person at the same time."

She couldn't decide if he was incredibly dense or merely unbelievably stubborn. She said nothing more and let him carry both the conversation and her for the remaining blocks. As they came within range of her apartment building, a taxi finally appeared. "Wouldn't you know it. We're almost at my door and now a taxi shows up," she said grumpily.

"Which building is yours?" he asked.

"The one with the blue canopy up ahead," she directed him.

She had expected him to set her down at the revolving glass door, but instead he carried her on into the building and then proceeded to the opened elevator. Only once they were inside did he gently set her down.

"Thank you," she murmured disconcertedly, squaring the suit jacket on her slim shoulders and smoothing her skirt. "You really don't have to go up with me."

"We backwoods types have old-fashioned ideas about seeing a lady to her front door. What floor?"

"Eighth," she said, relenting as she slipped off her one good shoe and stood in her stockinged feet. She chanced a circumspect look over at him as the elevator doors shut. He appeared pensive. She wondered what he was thinking. No doubt he would be glad for the evening to end. She'd hardly been a fun date.

The strained silence in the close quarters of the elevator was becoming obtrusive. She tapped her stockinged toes and concentrated on the clank of the elevator cables. Nothing was resolved between them. If anything, the situation was more awkward than it had been. At the moment she couldn't even make casual conversation, let alone some profound statement about keeping their association platonic. She felt rattled and more than a little claustrophobic.

It seemed forever until the elevator finally arrived at the eighth floor. The doors had only partially opened when she made good an escape and pattered down the carpeted hall to her apartment door.

J.D. followed her lead. She could feel his warm breath fanning the back of her neck as she fumbled in her purse for her keys. "I, uh, had a nice time, Joe Dillon," she jabbered inanely. Once she'd located her keys, she turned and offered him a stiff smile. "I'm sorry if I put a damper on the evening by telling you I can't accept any more invitations from you. I hope you understand."

He gave her a bemused look. "Yes, ma'am. I think I do. But I'd like to make sure I haven't misinterpreted your meaning," he said.

"Of course," she responded graciously.

He moved closer. She retreated a step. He leaned forward, bracing his hands against opposite sides of the door and trapping her between his arms. Her back flattened against the apartment door. He spoke low and slow.

"If I have it right—" one hand cupped the back of her neck and the other tipped up her chin and lifted her wide eyes to his "—something as personal as this between us would be out of the question." His lips brushed ever so lightly but suggestively over hers.

She shuddered and closed her eyes. Her mutinous body was betraying her, reacting to stimulus, not reason. "Yes," was her breathless answer. "It's totally out of the question."

He pressed his body nearer to hers—so near that she could distinguish each button on his shirt, his belt buckle and the rocklike definition of the muscles in his thighs. Gliding his hands through her hair, he drew her mouth to his in a deep, lingering kiss. "And no way can that happen," he commented as he released her lips.

She melted against him, sighing. "Precisely. It can't happen." *Ginny, Ginny, Ginny,* a voice inside her head said scoldingly. *What are you doing? Have you taken leave of your senses?* Yet her body functioned of its own will, yielding to, cleaving to, craving the man from Cottonmouth.

His arms enfolded her and he nestled a cheek in her silky hair. "I just needed to be clear on what you wanted," he whispered throatily. "My wants are simpler," he stated, taking her by the shoulders and moving away from her. "But judging from what you've said, I guess I won't be able to satisfy them. So I'll abide by your rules and say good-night." He cast her a wistful smile, then turned and walked away.

She stood there paralyzed, watching his tall, lithe figure move toward the elevator. Her heart thundered in her chest. She knew it would be the craziest, most reckless thing she'd ever done in her life if she was to call after him. Yet she wanted to. Oh, God! How she wanted to. Her throat constricted. Her lips refused to form the words. *Let him go,* her saner self cautioned.

He pressed the elevator call button.

She forced herself to look away and mechanically insert the key into the lock.

"Oh, what the hell!" was her only advance warning of the amorous ambush in store for her. She barely had time to look over her shoulder when, with the grace and accuracy of a falcon, he swooped down on her and plucked her off her feet once more.

"We can't, Joe Dillon. It'd be a big mistake." She sounded unconvincing even to herself.

He gave the door a push with his foot and marched into the darkened apartment with her cradled in his arms. "If you only had one opportunity and a few short hours in which to sell yourself, what would you do?" he asked her.

"It's not the same," she argued.

"The heck it isn't, darlin'," he replied, moving on blind instinct toward the bedroom.

CHAPTER NINE

WHAT FOLLOWED WAS UNREAL to Virginia—like a dream sequence in which she was both a participant and a spectator. It was as though she had divorced herself from the responsibility of their lovemaking; her body reacted, but her mind remained detached from the actual act.

Everything was exaggerated—time, motion, sensation. It was all so strange, so incredibly sensuous.

She didn't allow Joe Dillon to turn on a light.

"You're wrong if you think the darkness will hide your feelings, Virginia," he told her.

And oh, how right he was.

When he eased her feet to the floor and had her stand with her back to him while he reached around and slowly unfastened the top few buttons of her jacket, all of her propriety disintegrated into lust. A thousand small shock impulses traveled through her body as he slipped the jacket midway down her arms and grazed his lips from shoulder to shoulder and down her back in an excruciatingly slow and divinely erotic fashion. She was no longer a woman of substance, only a spineless mass of tingling, raw nerves.

He eased his hands down her arms, smoothly peeling off her jacket and sensitizing her to his touch all at once. She stood transfixed, saying nothing and surrendering everything with a deep, expressive sigh. Joe

Dillon knew what she refused to recognize—that she wanted an excuse to do what she knew she should not. She wanted permission to misbehave.

So he told her, "I'm the one who wants this most. If it backfires on us, it's my doing, not yours." Crisscrossing her arms with his, he pulled her against him, shifting the bulk of her weight to him. "You smell as good as I imagined, and feel even better," he whispered in her ear. "If it's only going to be once, I want to make it a memory that'll last a lifetime."

Indeed she knew she would always remember the way he lifted the hair from her nape and bowed her head forward, relieving her of the strand of pearls around her neck and stringing beads of kisses in its place. Also etched in her subconscious forever was the mental picture of how he methodically and expertly undressed her. Crazy, insignificant things registered with her: the shafts of street light spilling through the opened slats of the miniblinds; the play of shadows and light on his exquisite physique as he stripped out of his clothes; the naked desire in his admiring eyes as they drank in her womanliness from head to toe; and the realization that even work-roughened hands could be gentle and incredibly knowing when exploring and pleasuring her body.

She felt thoroughly comfortable with him—uninhibited and, oh, so hungry. Not even her ex had stirred such a fire in her. She wanted to rush things—test the extent of his passion without fully realizing the expertise of his foreplay.

But not Joe Dillon. He had taken his time getting her into bed, and when he finally did make his move, he wasn't going to just lay her back and have his way.

"Sit with me a spell," he requested, patting a spot in the middle of the bed. She did so a little hesitantly.

"People don't take the time to savor each other," he said. "It's an important part of what happens between a man and a woman. When you care for someone, it's just as necessary to tell 'em in words as it is in action." He took her hand and drew it to his lips. One by one he kissed each fingertip and in between fingers. He told her how lovely and bright, sweet and sexy he thought her to be. "I don't say these things lightly. It's been a long time between women, Virginia," he murmured against the soft inner flesh of her wrist. "I'm no Don Juan but I'll do my best to satisfy you. I want to give you pleasure and never bring you grief."

She was touched by his honesty and mesmerized by his sensitivity. "Just looking at you gives me pleasure," she heard herself admit. Suddenly it was she doing the exploring. Tentatively at first, then more boldly, she conducted a hands-on survey of his masculine terrain. Her slender fingers traced the angled contour of his cheek, then charted the slope of his broad shoulders. She ran her palms over his wide chest, taut stomach and hard thighs. Touching him became an addiction. She couldn't stop herself. "What have you done to me, Joe Dillon?" she asked bewilderedly, coming up onto her knees and webbing her fingers through his hair. "In a matter of moments you've managed to turn my world upside down. Black is white, wrong is right. I know better than to be doing this with you, and yet I can't deny I want you. I'm out of control and I hate it," she confessed in a ragged voice.

She was stunned by the forcefulness with which he forged her to him—amazed by the ease with which he rotated their linked bodies so that she was stretched out on the mattress beneath him and he was braced above her. "The world isn't always a black-and-white, wrong or right proposition, darlin'. Some things can't be controlled. Bottled-up emotions have a way of exploding on a person after so long a time. Just when you least expect it, someone comes along and shakes up the feeling deep inside, and the lid pops off, spewing what you've been containing every which way at once." He kissed her trembling lips and the hollow of her throat while simultaneously smoothing a hand along her hip and outer thigh.

"I never meant to add to the pressure," he assured her, gliding his lips between the divide of her breasts, over her midriff, then inching his way back to nuzzle a cheek in the soft swell of her bosom.

Her back arched, and purring sounds escaped from her as his tongue made delicious swirls around each apricot nipple in turn.

"I've no grand designs in mind," he whispered against her feverish flesh as she writhed in delirious anticipation.

She was only half listening to him. Her immediate need overrode everything else. Wantonly, she wound her arms around his waist and drew her hands up his muscled back. "About those feelings deep inside, Joe Dillon," she said, gasping and lifting her head off the mattress to claim his mouth hungrily. "They're getting stronger by the second. Either love me or leave me, but for God's sake do one or the other before I really do explode...."

He made love to her then—slow, steamy, thorough, unforgettable sex—many times over and in a variety of ways. She was shocked to discover how enduring and creative a lover the gentleman from Cottonmouth could be. Somewhere in the back of her mind she wondered where in the world a backwoods type like him had learned so much about pleasing and satisfying a woman. And when everything was over and done, he filled a porcelain basin with hot water scented with fragrant oil and bathed her with warm hand towels. She felt terribly self-conscious and tried to resist his soothing ministrations, but he told her to hush and enjoy the pampering. It was the most wonderfully relaxing, singularly sensuous experience of her life.

And when the luxurious bath was complete, he joined her in bed, drawing her into his arms and against the curve of his reassuring body. Every so often, he smoothed back her hair and kissed her temple. She felt cherished and kittenish within his steadfast embrace. She'd never been more content, more exhausted or more confused in her entire life. The same repetitive questions kept beating in her brain. Why did he have to be so damn good-looking? So young, warm, sexy and Southern? It would've made things infinitely easier if he'd been a total washout as a lover.

Half-asleep, she was unaware that she'd spoken her secret thoughts aloud. The last thing she remembered was the comforting sound of his laugh as his arms encircled her tighter and his body heat permeated her being. It felt odd, but nice, not to go to sleep alone.

It was nearly noon the next day when she awakened. Joe Dillon was no longer in her bed or her apartment, but he was definitely still in her system.

At first she believed the flashback of the night before to be nothing more than a vivid dream, but then gradually the foggy state she'd been functioning in lifted. In the bright light of day she could not hide from the realization of what had actually transpired between them. The telltale traces of his presence confronted her as soon as she glanced over to the empty side of the bed. The covers were flung back, and she could see where his head had lain by the indentation of the never-used pillow. His musky scent still clung to the sheets, and his tie was cavalierly draped over the bedpost.

When the full implication of what she had done hit her, she lurched upright in the bed. Her stomach did a flip-flop as she recalled specific details of her appalling behavior. It was then that she spied the porcelain basin left on the bathroom sink. The memory of his toweling her down sent her sprawling back on the bed with a sickened groan. "Oh, God!"

She pulled the covers over her head, unable to face the glare of daylight or the consequences of her runaway hormones just yet. Another muffled "Oh, nooo!" pretty well summed up Virginia's reaction. She had an overriding impulse to deny anything had ever happened. He represented a weakness in her character she could ill afford to admit. By the time she finally collected herself enough to crawl out of bed, she'd already decided to seize the convenient out he'd given her. After all, the whole sordid mess was really more his fault than hers. He'd said so himself. She had tried to impress upon him the reality of their situation—tried to tell him it would be a mistake to cross over the line. As far as she was concerned, there was only one way to handle the indelicate matter of their interlude: pretend it had never occurred. She planned to treat the episode as a momentary lapse in good form and judgment—an unfortunate slip of the old hormones that she never intended to repeat or refer to again. What was more, she was determined to see to it that Joe Dillon did the same.

She raked back her wild hair from her eyes and pulled on a terry cover-up. Unwittingly her gaze traveled to the tie looped over the end bedpost. The sight of it only served to magnify her embarrassment and guilt. It suddenly took on the appearance of a hangman's noose dangling from a gallows. She quickly snatched it and strode to the dressing table, stuffing the offensive object inside her purse.

I theenk maybe you will have regrets come Monday. Rita's warning rang in her ears.

I assure you I'll have none. Her own smug words came back to haunt her.

She sank onto the vanity stool and stared in disbelief at her disheveled figure in the mirror. "Just look at yourself," she said aloud. "How will you ever pull it off? He'll see through you. Everyone will. Dammit! You knew better," she scolded herself. "What are you? Self-destructive?"

Even as she looked at the visible effects of the previous night, it was still inconceivable to her that she had actually compromised a mega-important campaign and a coveted partnership for a few fleeting hours of fantastic sex.

She slumped forward, chin in hand, and expelled a disheartened sigh. "And that isn't the worst of it," she said reflectively. "You did it again. Different man, same mistake. Wasn't it you who swore you'd never again go out with a man who was better looking than yourself? And what do you do? Not only do you go out with him but you compound the colossally stupid blunder by tumbling into bed with him. And this one's almost ten years your junior. Way to go, Ginny. Dumb move. Really dumb!"

Disgustedly she turned away from the silly creature in the mirror. She didn't want to confront her again until the twit had pulled herself together. That would mean a hot shower, several cups of coffee and a couple hours of reflecting on her options. At least!

CHAPTER TEN

WHEN RITA LOOKED UP and took stock of her boss Monday morning she knew immediately something was terribly amiss.

"You don look so good," was her blunt appraisal. "The flu bug bite you, too? Half the office ees out sick."

Virginia took the messages Rita held out to her, delaying a response until after she'd glanced through them. "I wish. Put everything on hold and come into my office."

Her brusque manner tripped Rita's alarm system. In spite of the forewarning, her body started at the slam of the office door. She wasted no time complying with the summons, only pausing long enough to pour them both a cup of coffee before slipping into the inner office and nudging shut the door with a practiced bump of her hip. "I thought you could use it," she ventured, passing Virginia a cup, then planting herself in one of the chairs in front of the desk. "Whas up?"

Virginia took a sip of the coffee, then unclasped her purse and plucked Joe Dillon's tie from inside. "This," she stated flatly, holding out the tie for Rita's inspection.

Rita's eyes followed the swaying object dangling from her boss's fingertips. "A man's necktie?" Unable to deduce the significance, she merely shrugged.

"It's Joe Dillon's," Virginia explained, dropping the tie to the desk and herself into her chair. "I wasn't going to take you into my confidence, but I have to talk to someone. I have a burning need to unburden myself and there isn't anyone I can trust but you, Rita. I'm in a terrible fix," she confessed.

"You slept with him," Rita astutely guessed.

Virginia nodded. "Unbelievable, huh?"

"Ees surprising but not shocking," was Rita's tactful reply.

"It's appalling behavior," she insisted between swallows of coffee. "I can't believe I did it. I don't know what came over me. One minute I was making it clear to him that nothing of a personal nature could go on between the two of us, and the next minute we were rolling around on the sheets." She chugged down the last of the coffee in nonstop gulps, then crushed the foam into crackling bits with a clenched fist. "I keep going over it in my mind. Asking myself again and again how I could have been so rash, so utterly stupid, so...so..."

"Horny?" Rita filled in the appropriate blank.

"Thanks a bunch." Virginia pitched the pulverized cup into the trash can.

"Don mention it." Rita flinched at Virginia's sudden bolt from the chair. It took acrobatlike agility to stop her own coffee from spilling over the rim of the cup and onto the expensive upholstery.

"I guess I can forget about any hopes of receiving the Adwoman of the Year award. If word of this leaks out, the only recognition I'll get from my peers is a roasting for biggest screwup of the century. It'd be exactly what I deserve, too."

Rita decided to let Virginia wallow in self-recriminations for a bit. It was only another anxiety attack. Her fretting and pacing were good therapy. She'd eventually wind down.

"I jeopardized the Sebastian campaign. I risked a partnership. I compromised my principles."

Rita's head swiveled from right to left as Virginia strutted back and forth, back and forth. "What's more, I broke a solemn oath I made myself to never ever become involved with a man who was better looking than me. It's shades of Rob Rice all over again. History repeating itself. Handsome men are nothing but trouble. Men! Huh!" Virginia threw up her hands, then let them drop to her sides. "Joe Dillon's barely beyond the age of consent. My God! Give or take a few years either way and I could be a child molester or his mother!"

Rita stifled a laugh. Virginia was really stretching it in order to feed her guilt. A man in his mid-twenties was no *niño*. "You are being too hard on yourself. He ees legal and probably more seasoned than you. My hunch ees, he was pretty good, no?"

Virginia shot her a lethal look. "Give me a break, will you, Rita? Whether I give him an X, R or P.G. rating is hardly the issue here. Somehow I have to get across to Joe Dillon that my interest in him is purely professional and make him understand that what happened between us was a matter of stupidity, not chemistry."

Rita shook her head. "How can you say that? Chemistry ees what made the sparks fly between you two. You cannot just dismiss it with a snip of your fingers."

"It's a snap of the fingers, and yes I can," Virginia stubbornly contended.

"He will know differently."

"Please, Rita. I need a little moral support, not an argument. I also need you to run interference for a bit, just until I can figure out a way to smooth things over. You can buy me some time by giving him the runaround. The 'She's not in but she'll get back to you' routine. Be my go-between for a while. You can begin by slipping this into a plain manila envelope and seeing to it that it's delivered to him." She treated the tie as if it were contaminated waste material, holding it between a thumb and forefinger and at arm's length, then dropping it like a bomb into Rita's lap.

Rita was uncomfortable with the request. "Ees not right, Ginny. You don treat a man who has made love to you with so little respect. You should talk with him yourself. Explain in person. I theenk it is your own reaction you are afraid of, not his."

Rita's astute deduction came too close to the truth. Virginia instantly went on the defensive. "That's nonsense," she said in a scoffing tone, taking her seat behind the desk once more.

"You can't avoid him forever," Rita pointed out. "Besides, if he means nothing to you, it should not be difficult to tell him so."

"I'm not talking forever, Rita, just a few measly days." Her head was starting to pound and her exasperation beginning to mount. "And would you stop implying that I'm harboring some sort of romantic feelings for the man? We had dinner together, which somehow led to us having sex together, which now has made for a very uncomfortable situation. That's it. Nothing more," she stated succinctly.

"What you describe ees casual sex, but you don act so casual about it. I know what I say because I have had more experience with men than you. I am not easy but I am human. A few of my dance partners ended up bed partners. One I even married. The others, they were no big flames, only one-night flickers. When we meet, we smile, sometimes we dance, but we are not hot for each other anymore. It ees not uncomfortable for us. Sex with a man ees only uncomfortable when it ees more than a passing moment or...how you say?" She searched for the right phrase. "A passing fancy."

"Must you always analyze everything to death?" The criticism erupted from Virginia before she could check herself. "I don't need a shrink or a surrogate mother at the moment." Again, Rita's body jumped when Virginia slammed her palms against the desktop. "All I want or require is an efficient secretary who can do what she's told." The instant the cutting rebuke passed her lips, Virginia regretted saying it.

Rita's dark eyes flashed. Both hurt and anger registered on her face as she stood up, set the half-finished cup of coffee aside and placed a hand on a jutted hip. "When have I not done what you ask? And sinz when do you bully the people who work for you?"

Virginia felt perfectly wretched at having taken nasty and unfair advantage of a loyal friend. "I'm so sorry, Rita. You're a whiz of a secretary. I couldn't get along without you. It's me that's the problem. Pay no attention to me today, okay?" She pleaded for her forgiveness with a contrite look.

"Sure." Rita wasn't one to hold a grudge. "I have a question, but I don want you to bite my head off again."

Virginia assured her with a nod.

"If things was different and you were not the boss and there was no campaign or partnership to worry about, would you give him a second chance?"

She thought over the question for a moment. "I honestly don't know. We're different people, Rita. The only thing we seem to share in common is great sex."

"There ees bread and there ees butter, but together they are good," Rita reminded her.

"Yes, well, there is a campaign to consider and there is the fact that I am his boss for the present, so I doubt we'll ever know whether or not we might have been good together." Virginia looked away, pretending to be impatient to get to the daily business at hand.

Rita took the tie and the hint and started to take her leave. "Oh, I almost forget," she said, stopping in her tracks and turning around to face Virginia with a sheepish look.

"You forgot," Virginia tutored her.

"I know. I know." Rita missed the point entirely. "Ms Shapell called a minute before you come in. I did not have a chance to write it down but I remember the message. She wants to talk to you. Something about a charity benefit and Mr. Mahue."

Virginia nearly made another faux pax by blaming Rita for what was really her fault. She'd been the one to sidetrack her secrétary. "It doesn't sound too terribly urgent, but go ahead and put in a return call to her." She waited until Rita was out of hearing range to vent her frustration. "Damn! Great first impression. The woman's going to think you're totally incompetent or else you value her account so little that you can't be bothered to return her call."

Her day had barely begun and already it was shaping up to be an exercise in crisis management. Throughout the years there had been a few isolated instances in which she'd wondered why she put herself through it all and if it was worth the aggravation—times when she contemplated switching careers and doing something far less demanding, like fading into bohemian oblivion and writing poetry, perhaps. Greenwich Village had been the favorite haunt of Paine, Poe, Whitman and Twain. She wouldn't have to go far. Inspiration could quite literally be waiting around the corner.

She entertained the crazy thought for all of five seconds before Rita buzzed her.

"Ms Shapell ees on line one."

Virginia punched the appropriate button and picked up the receiver. Though she halfway expected Claudia Shapell to present yet another wrinkle for her to iron out, she really hoped it wouldn't be the case.

What Claudia Shapell wanted to discuss turned out to be a ghastly contretemps for Virginia. The prized client was insistent upon Joe Dillon escorting her to a highly publicized high-society affair. It was one of those trendy black-tie bashes where dream dates with New York's most eligible bachelors were auctioned off and the proceeds donated to a worthy cause. This particular year the money was designated to go toward aiding the homeless.

Ms Shapell had it in mind for Joe Dillon to be included among the auctionees. She thought it would make for terrific—and free—PR. Virginia had had to talk fast to dissuade her, hammering home the exclusive angle of the campaign. Selling him to the highest bidder could subliminally undermine his marketability as a patented trademark of Sebastian Designs, she argued. Fortunately Ms Shapell saw the logic, but she remained firm on the idea of Joe Dillon acting as her escort for the evening. The advance exposure would give a boost to the launch of the line, she'd reasoned.

Virginia had no choice but to once again commit Joe Dillon. Worse yet, Ms Shapell insisted on her attending, as well, stating that it had been difficult to finagle the two extra guest tickets, but she wanted to show her appreciation for the superb job Virginia had done thus far. She was adamant about making it a foursome. Grudgingly Virginia agreed to the tedious arrangement. By the end of the conversation, she was thinking in terms of death by firing squad. It would be infinitely quicker and far less painful.

Unable to face Joe Dillon, she had Rita do her dirty work. Rita reported back to her that he was most displeased about being inducted into escort service and even more upset about the secondhand manner in which he was told. According to Rita, she'd had to talk like a Dutch uncle to get him to agree to the arrangement. The notion had struck Virginia as funny, considering Rita's Puerto Rican accent.

A lot less funny was the fact that she could find no male takers for the fourth ticket. None among the ranks of her peers or subordinates was available to accompany her on the night in question. Either they were otherwise committed or they were attending the function with someone else. A few, she suspected, had invented previous engagements because they felt uneasy about socializing with the boss.

The prospect of going stag did not bother her half as much as the ordeal of having to face Joe Dillon alone. So, as a last resort, she drafted Rita to go along, on the strict condition that she tone down everything—her clothes, her jewelry and, most especially her sex drive.

Rita cheerfully agreed. She would have agreed to wearing a paper sack over her head, so long as there were peepholes from which to ogle all the gorgeous hunks on auction. Her only regret was that she had but one life's savings to donate to the worthy cause. Of course, she wisely kept her intentions of bidding a secret for fear that Virginia would nix that, too....

THE FOURSOME ARRIVED in separate pairs and at separate times the evening of the charity auction. Wishing to make a fashionably late appearance, Claudia Shapell had served Joe Dillon cocktails at her place before setting out for the hotel.

Virginia and Rita milled about the lavish banquet room for a bit. Virginia was scanning the sea of faces, looking for Claudia Shapell; Rita was just generally gawking.

"Oh, look, Ginny." She pointed at a tall, dark gentleman two tables away. "Ees David Copperfield, the magician. Ayyy! He ees even better looking in person."

Virginia quickly knocked down her arm. "We're supposed to be rubbing elbows with the rich and famous, not fingering them like convicts in a lineup. You can't go around oohing and aahing all night. Be nonchalant, okay?"

The mayor walked past them at that exact moment, causing a small gasp to escape Rita's lips. "Ees him. Ees the mayor. He smiled at me. Did you see?"

"I saw. Will you quit standing there with your mouth hanging open and come on?" Virginia walked ahead, wondering why she had ever thought it would be in her best interest to bring Rita along.

Rita tagged after her, more intent on watching the beautiful people than on where she was going. Consequently, she collided into Virginia's back when she stopped short.

"Oh, God!" Virginia exclaimed, her blood running cold suddenly.

"Whas wrong?"

"It can't be. What in the hell is *he* doing here?"

"Who?" Rita craned her neck and rose on her tiptoes to get a glimpse of who it was that had immobilized Virginia. "Oh, God!" She echoed Virginia's sentiments as she spied the source of her apoplexy.

Standing only a few feet away from them was Virginia's ex-husband.

"Maybe if you turn around ver-ry slow-ly, he won't notice you," Rita suggested.

Too late. At precisely that instant he made eye contact. "Great! He's coming over. What do I do now?" Virginia whispered.

"Act nonchalant," Rita reminded her. "Then spit in his eye."

As if things weren't awkward enough, Virginia caught sight of Claudia Shapell and Joe Dillon also making their way toward them. She wished the floor would open up and swallow her.

"Well, well, if it isn't my favorite ex-wife," Rob greeted her, loudly enough so that anyone within a twenty-yard radius could overhear.

She braced herself and forced a smile.

"Last count, I was your *only* ex-wife," was her cool comeback as he bent to kiss her cheek.

"Some things never change. You're as lovely and bitchy as ever." Devilment flashed in his eyes as he exchanged his empty glass of complimentary champagne for a full one from the tray of a passing waiter. "It's good to see you, Ginny. How many years has it been since our split?"

"Not nearly enough," she shot back.

Rita rolled her eyes and snatched a glass of champagne for herself.

Rob's attention was quickly diverted to Claudia Shapell as she and Joe Dillon joined the circle. Being a connoisseur of big breasts and big bucks, Rob found her appealing right away. "I thought the evening might be dull, but—" he let his gaze travel over the other woman's strapless dress appreciatively "—it's taking on a whole new dimension. I'm Rob Rice," he smoothly introduced himself, claiming Claudia Shapell's hand and ignoring Joe Dillon's presence completely.

J.D.'s eyes locked with Virginia's as his date and her ex exchanged flirtatious pleasantries. He disliked the man at first sight, and not just because of his pushy manner, which would have been enough. His animosity went much deeper and was more of a personal nature. It had nothing to do with Claudia Shapell and everything to do with Virginia. It really galled J.D. that the man had been first with her. It was all he could think of.

"...and this is my escort for the evening, Dillon Mahue." Miss Shapell's slight press of his arm recalled him.

Rob Rice held out his hand.

Joe Dillon was more inclined to land a fist to his jaw, but his good Southern upbringing prevailed. He

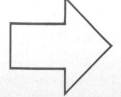

NO COST! NO OBLIGATION TO BUY! NO PURCHASE NECESSARY!

PLAY "LUCKY 7" AND GET AS MANY AS SIX FREE GIFTS...

HOW TO PLAY:

1. With a coin, carefully scratch off the silver box at the right. This makes you eligible to receive one or more free books, and possibly other gifts, depending on what is revealed beneath the scratch-off area.

2. You'll receive brand-new Harlequin Superromance® novels. When you return this card, we'll send you the books and gifts you qualify for *absolutely free!*

3. If we don't hear from you, every month we'll send you 4 additional novels to read and enjoy. You can return them and owe nothing but if you decide to keep them, you'll pay only $2.74* per book, a savings of 21¢ each off the cover price! There is *no* extra charge for postage and handling. There are no hidden extras.

4. When you join the Harlequin Reader Service®, you'll get our monthly newsletter, as well as additional free gifts from time to time just for being a member.

5. You must be completely satisfied. You may cancel at any time simply by sending us a note or a shipping statement marked "cancel" or returning any unopened shipment to us at our cost.

You'll love your elegant 20k gold electroplated chain! The necklace is finely crafted with 160 double-soldered links and is electroplate finished in genuine 20k gold. And it's yours free as added thanks for giving our Reader Service a try!

clasped the jackass's hand but he did not return his phony smile. He couldn't imagine how Virginia could have cared for somebody such as the likes of him.

"I see by the rosebud in your lapel that you're one of the prizes to be auctioned off tonight, Mr. Rice." Claudia returned the once-over.

He glanced to Virginia before answering. Her heart made a dull thump at the wicked glint she detected in his eyes. Even when they were married, Rob had always taken some sort of perverted enjoyment in making off-color remarks that would both infuriate and embarrass her. He was going to say something incredibly gauche just to watch her squirm.

"My ex-wife might differ with you about my being a prize. Or were you planning to make a bid for me, Ginny?" Right on cue, he delivered a wicked wink. "It might be worth it. It's a nice package up for grabs—a cozy weekend in Vermont at one of those wonderfully rustic old inns. Just the two of us. We could do a little skiing, talk about old times in front of a crackling fire, and later on I could give you one of my famous back rubs. As I recall, you were always game for a massage." Rob had intended to jab only his ex with the pointed barb. He was unaware that he'd struck a raw nerve with Joe Dillon, as well.

"Maybe the lady isn't interested in a cheap thrill." In the absence of a response from Virginia, J.D. took it upon himself to answer for her.

Rita wanted to kiss him for coming to the rescue.

Virginia was stunned speechless.

"Have I inadvertently stepped on your toes? I was addressing the suggestion to my former wife. Which lady are you referring to?" Rob's mouth was set in a leer.

"Any and all," J.D. answered, his tone deceptively mellow. Only Virginia saw the telltale tick of a muscle in his cheek.

The two men glared at one another. Each wished the other would present an excuse to step outside and square off.

Claudia Shapell was not disconcerted by their sparring in the least. In fact, she seemed highly amused by the whole thing. "I suspect that a weekend with Mr. Rice might be a very popular item on the block tonight. The question is, is he worth the high price he'll bring?" She arched a brow.

Virginia had to bite her tongue to keep from offering a knowledgeable opinion. Rob most definitely could drain a bank account and strain a woman's nerves. He loved center stage and playing the part of a rake.

"We can easily dismiss your doubts. All you have to do is crook your pinkie at the auctioneer and a weekend of back rubs and bliss can be yours."

"Excuse me. I feel a trip to the men's room coming on." A disgusted J.D. left Claudia Shapell to fend for herself. Since she'd all but invited the jerk's advances, he felt no strong obligation to safeguard her questionable virtue. In fact, as far as he was concerned, he thought the two of 'em deserved each other. Something about the way they were licking their chops reminded him of a pair of wily foxes that caused ten kinds of mayhem raiding everybody's chicken coops back in Cottonmouth. He and Mason had finally tracked 'em down, but only after the cunning critters had run them in circles. Right now, all he was interested in tracking down was a waiter. It was going to be a long, miserable night and he wanted a long, tall drink.

Virginia lost track of the conversation as she watched Joe Dillon's tuxedo-clad figure merge with and then be swallowed up by the swell of bodies.

She blinked at the poke of an elbow in her ribs. "Lez powder our noses," Rita suggested. It wasn't very inventive but it was the best Rita could do on the spur of the moment.

"Yes, uh, well..." She could hear herself babbling like an idiot. "You'll understand if I don't participate in the bidding when your turn rolls around, Rob. One woman's dream date is another woman's nightmare." Her chin lifted and her gaze hardened as it fixed on her former husband. "Of course, don't let me influence you, Ms Shapell. He does have his moments."

"Thank you for that qualified endorsement. Let's keep in touch. A nasty divorce is no reason not to be friends." He slanted her a challenging look, then grinned broadly. He intended to be obnoxious to the bitter end.

Virginia ignored him and gave Rita a subtle push in the direction of the ladies' room.

Rita kept glancing back as they made their way through the shoulder-to-shoulder crowd. "Can you believe it? Who was coming on to who? I theenk she ees a bitch and I don mean just her attitude."

"Who cares?" Virginia muttered, slowly making her way toward the cash bar instead of the ladies' room. "Let's have a drink and forget about the pair of them."

"Don you have any feelings? What about Joe Dillon? You can just leave him in that Shapell woman's clutches." Rita followed her to the bar.

"Shh! Don't mention names. Someone could over-hear you."

"I don care," Rita persisted.

Virginia wedged herself in at the bar and placed their order. "A margarita, no salt, and a gin and tonic with a twist, please."

"If you don do something, I will." Rita kept look-ing around in the hopes of spying Joe Dillon.

"He's a big boy. And has the thought ever oc-curred to you that he might not want us bird-dogging him all evening?" Virginia paid for the drinks and handed Rita the frothy margarita, praying to good-ness it would shut her up for a bit.

"He don want to be here. Ees your fault he's stuck with her. And ees your responsibility to look out for him." She only paused long enough to suck down a mouthful of roses of lime and tequila. "He ees a lamb in the woods and that she-wolf will gobble him up if you don protect him."

"All right, all right. I think you're blowing this way out of proportion, but if it'll ease your mind, we'll check up on him. Just for the record, it's a babe in the woods, not a lamb."

"Whatever." Rita instantly set off in search of Joe Dillon.

"Don't you dare do or say anything to insult her," Virginia said, following her. "She's an important client and we can't afford to alienate her. I find it hard to believe that she harbors any unscrupulous inten-tions toward Joe Dillon. He's not her type."

"He ees male, no? Than he ees her type." Rita weaved in and out of the throng of guests.

"She isn't going to seduce him, Rita. She's a shrewd businesswoman. She wouldn't risk her position and reputation for a roll in the hay,'' Virginia insisted, sloshing her drink when someone bumped into her from behind.

"Hmmph! In a heartbeat,'' was Rita's reply. "Didn't you?''

Virginia stumbled a step. She grabbed hold of the back of Rita's dress and restrained her. "How about I arrange a coast-to-coast hookup. Then you can broadcast my sex life to the nation,'' she seethed under her breath.

"There they are. She has him cornered by the piano.'' Rita wriggled from her boss's grasp and proceeded like a torpedo toward her target.

Virginia hurried to catch up to her. "Behave yourself. Not one word or gesture that could be construed as a moral judgment,'' she warned her.

Rita did not answer, which made the knots in Virginia's stomach coil even tighter.

"Oh, there you two are. We were wondering what had become of you.'' Claudia Shapell's smile was not as warm or welcoming as her tone.

"We stopped off at the bar.'' Virginia held up her drink as proof. "It looks as though they're about ready to begin the auction.''

"Yes. I see by the program that your ex-husband is scheduled to be auctioned next to last. He must be something special. Every year they save the best until the end. He's runner-up to David Copperfield. Not bad.'' She appraised Virginia's ex-husband the way an avid collector appraised rare goods.

Virginia was only half listening to her. It was Joe Dillon who was occupying most of her attention. He looked ill at ease and he had not engaged her eyes once since she'd returned. What's more, his cheek muscle was still twitching. Obviously he was in a sullen mood.

Feeling Claudia Shapell's gaze on her, she realized she had yet to respond. "Rob is a popular soap star. I suppose the organizers thought he'd hold a special appeal for the ladies."

"Oh, really! I didn't know. I seldom watch daytime television."

Was it her imagination or was Shapell pressing her cleavage up against Joe Dillon's arm in a suggestive fashion?"

Rita cleared her throat with a painfully obvious, "Aaah-hem!"

"Uh, it's not actually half-bad, for a melodrama," Virginia said inanely. Melodrama was an appropriate choice of words, since she had the sense of being smack-dab in the middle of one.

She saw Joe Dillon stiffen and inch away from Ms Shapell. He had yet to say a word or venture a glance in her direction. Was he angry with her? Of course he was, she reasoned. He couldn't be very pleased about the way the evening was progressing or the way she'd been avoiding him. He probably thought she couldn't give a damn about what had happened between them. He was wrong. She had thought about it more often than she cared to admit. Sometimes, when she closed her eyes, she could feel his touch on her skin, hear his slow, soft words, visualize their bodies entangled and moving in perfect rhythm. But then she'd snap to her senses and realize the dangerous head game she was playing. Denying him was the hardest thing she'd ever done, but necessary. She had to block it from her mind. To do otherwise would be to risk both of their futures.

It wasn't just herself she was thinking of. Joe Dillon had a chance to become something more than a sharecropper's son—to know a better life than what was in store for him back in Mississippi. Depending on how she conducted herself, she could either make him or break him. Only a fool would trade the solid opportunities that lay ahead for them both for great sex in the here and now. She had no choice but to pretend nothing intimate had gone on between them. It was the only way to guard against the inevitable consequences of behaving inappropriately again.

"Claudia, don't you look fabulous." A woman in a glittering red gown waved and made her way over to them. "How wonderful of you to come."

"You've outdone yourself, Marion. The auction looks to be a bigger success than last year." Claudia returned the compulsory hug from the woman, who was obviously an organizer of the charity event.

"Yes, yes. It's a wonderful turnout. But we were very fortunate to have such delicious bachelors to auction off. They've all been so giving of themselves," the woman pointed out. Then, her eyes zeroed in on Joe Dillon. "Oh me, oh my," she cooed. "It would seem that we missed a golden opportunity. Whoever have we here?" Her red-polished nails smoothed the black satin lapels of his jacket.

Virginia saw Joe Dillon wince. She knew he found the woman's forwardness both distasteful and degrading. She was treating him like so much male flesh and he wanted no part of it.

Virginia was about to intervene when Claudia saved her the trouble. "Sorry, Marion," she said silkily, plucking the woman's fingers from Joe Dillon's person. "Mr. Mahue is off limits. He only graciously consented to act as my escort for the evening. I'm afraid he's not for sale."

"Are you sure you wouldn't like to volunteer as one of our eligible bachelors, Mr. Mahue?" The woman spoke in a baby voice while batting her false eyelashes at him. "It's all in fun, and a quality piece like you could provide much-needed revenue for a very worthy cause."

Piece! As in a piece of meat or a pound of flesh. J.D. could not believe the woman's nerve. "No, ma'am," he said flatly. "The cause may be a fine one, but I don't fancy myself being sold off like some stud stallion expected to service a bunch of nags." He hadn't meant to be so rude and crude, but he'd had it with being paraded and pawed.

Rita covered her mouth with a napkin to keep from spewing her margarita all over herself.

Virginia managed to keep a straight face.

Claudia was taken off guard but quickly recovered. "Dillon didn't mean that the way it sounded, Marion." She rushed to make amends. "Being from the South, he's a little sensitive about auctions of any sort. These Confederates still carry the scars of slavery and loathe any reminders," she told her confidentially. "He's new to New York and not yet accustomed to how things are done. Please don't take offense." She figured Marion was a big enough airhead to buy it.

The woman donned a tolerant expression. "Are you two an item?" she asked, as if it had some bearing on whether or not she would choose to forgive him.

"Of sorts. He's under exclusive contract to Don Sebastian," she explained.

"How nice," was the caustic reply. "I thought perhaps he was your private property." She shot Joe Dillon a haughty look.

"Only in a business sense," Claudia assured the social butterfly.

"Mmm, I've heard that before." Seemingly satisfied with having inferred her skepticism, the woman marched off, wisely taking her red-glittered self out of range of Claudia's glinting green eyes.

"I would prefer it if you didn't express yourself quite so metaphorically, Dillon. When in Rome, do as the Romans do," she lectured him. "Oh, well, no harm done. The woman's unimportant," she decreed, looping her arm through Joe Dillon's and glancing around. "We should mingle. The whole idea behind this evening was to gain some advance exposure for you and the line."

As if to prove a point, Claudia slipped her bejeweled fingers up the pleats of his shirt to his black bow tie in the pretext of squaring it. "Much better," she said with a pat. What she really meant to declare was that he was indeed her private property and no one trespassed without her consent.

His chin snapped up and he looked directly into Virginia's eyes. She could plainly read his thoughts. He was in a murderous, not mingling, frame of mind. And it was her sudden demise he seriously contemplated.

She shrugged her shoulders in a helpless gesture and said, "I think Miss Mundo and I will be leaving shortly. It's been really nice but I have a great deal to accomplish tomorrow and—"

"I understand completely." Claudia waved aside her excuses with a flick of her wrist. "I won't keep Dillon out too late. I know you want him fresh for the camera. Good night.''

Joe Dillon said nothing—nothing at all. He didn't have to; his face mirrored his feelings. He was totally disgusted, thoroughly humiliated and angry beyond words.

Claudia Shapell was oblivious to his reluctance as she pulled him along into her social circle.

Rita shook her head disapprovingly and said to Virginia, ''You should be ashamed.'' Fed up herself, she headed toward the exit.

''What?'' Virginia feigned ignorance. Her gown swished as she threaded her way through the crowd of boisterous bidders. ''What do you expect me to do?'' she asked in a hushed voice. ''I'm his boss, not his guardian.''

''He ees green, Ginny. And you are taking as much advantage of him as she. She wants his body and you want his soul. He don stand a chance!'' Rita hissed back.

Virginia caught her by the arm at the doorway. ''You're really upset with me about this, aren't you?'' Rita had never before censured her so strongly.

''Ayyy!'' Rita threw up her hands in utter frustration. ''You demand too much, Ginny. You boss him, reject him, coerce him and shame him, and still you expect him to be your *caballero*. Anything for an account, anything to please a client, but nothing for the man who serves your interests.''

Virginia glanced around to make sure no one was listening to their conversation. ''Shapell isn't some demented sex maniac, for God's sake. Joe Dillon isn't being stalked like helpless quarry. And even if your invented suspicions had a smidgen of validity, Shapell wouldn't dare act on a primitive impulse. Too damn much is at stake. Besides, whether you believe it or not, I am keeping an eye on him. I wouldn't let him get trapped in a sticky situation.''

''Hmmph! If you ask me, ees *she* who has her eye on him and he already ees trapped in the spider woman's web. I don want to talk about it anymore.''

''Fine, neither do I,'' was Virginia's snippy reply.

The subject was dropped. They shared the taxi, but Rita contributed very little to the conversation during the ride home.

CHAPTER ELEVEN

VIRGINIA WAS JARRED AWAKE by a nonstop pounding on her front door. Groggy and disoriented, she hauled herself from the bed and stumbled through the darkened apartment. "Okay, okay," she muttered under her breath, bouncing off various pieces of furniture as she blindly made her way to the door. She had the presence of mind to keep the chain latch in place until she identified who it was. Propping her drooping head against the doorjamb, she opened the door a crack and peered at the blurry figure of the intruder through the slit.

"What time is it?" she asked dumbly.

"Way past my patience," Joe Dillon told her. "Open up unless you want your neighbors to get an earful."

"Okay, okay, but could you wait until I can find my robe?" She brushed her hair back from her eyes and yawned, unable to rouse herself from her stupor.

"No. I don't care if you're in your birthday suit. Let me in. Now." He rattled the chain.

Virginia eased the door open a bit more and slipped off the lock.

Joe Dillon charged inside like some raging bull. "Could you turn on a damn light?"

Concern overrode her modesty. She complied with a flick of a lamp switch.

In spite of his blazing anger, Joe Dillon was not sufficiently insulated to absorb the shock of her scantily clad figure. The cropped tank top and slit boxer shorts were too much to take; the white satin fabric, her bare hips and her long, shapely legs caused his blood to run even hotter. "Yeah, you had better get a robe," he contradicted himself.

Half puzzled, half conscious, she went into the bedroom and returned a moment later in a tattered and faded football jersey that came to her knees. "I can't find it," she mumbled, staggering to the couch and dropping onto the plump cushions with yet another big yawn. "Do you realize it's two-thirty in the morning, Joe Dillon? Can't whatever you have on your mind wait until—"

"Until when?" he exploded. "Until you feel like taking calls? No, ma'am. I won't be put off any longer. I had one lousy night because of you, so I figure it's no more than right that you have one lousy day because of me."

Her head rolled listlessly back against the pillows. "Okay, you have my attention," she lied. "What's wrong?" Her lids drifted closed.

Something inside of him snapped at the sight of her nodding off. He strode to the couch, clamped his big hands around her upper arms and hoisted her onto her feet. "I listened when you insisted on doing the talking. And you're damn sure going to show me the same courtesy." He gave her a hard shake.

"Stop it!" She tried to wrench free from his grip. "What in the hell do you think you're doing!"

He deposited her on the couch with a jolting bounce. "You've got it backward. It's me who ought to be posing that very question to you. So wake up, Ginny darlin', because I want a clear answer.''

She rubbed her smarting arms. "I'm awake. Wide awake. See!'' She glowered, giving him bug-eyed proof. "So, do you want to give me a hint as to what this is all about, or am I supposed to guess?''

Her pouty attitude made Joe Dillon want to shake her again but he restrained himself. "Take a stab at it,'' he spat.

"You're unhappy about having to act as Ms Shapell's escort.''

"Bingo! And unhappy would be putting it mildly.'' He jerked off his black tie and jacket and pitched both into a nearby chair. "I don't know who I'm more disgusted with—me or you. One of us is a poor judge of character. I hired on to do modeling. I'm not in the stud service business. If that's what's expected you can find yourself another flunky. I'm not your Johnny Reb callboy.''

"No one expects you to provide, uh...'' She tried to find a polite term for the sleazy deed.

"The hell they don't,'' he snapped back. "I know when a woman is on the make. In case you haven't noticed, your client is giving me all the right signals. The woman's on me like flies on sugar and I've no intention of becoming her candy man.''

Virginia's sluggish brain was beginning to grasp his meaning. "What exactly has she done to make you so certain she wants something to start between the two of you?'' She felt obligated to ask the question, but a sinking feeling in the pit of her stomach told her she wasn't going to like his answer.

J.D. leveled a steely look at her. "I've got *some* dignity left. I don't have to supply you with details. My word ought to be good enough."

Virginia expelled a sigh. "It's not that I don't believe you, Joe Dillon. I'm sure you feel that something wrong is going on. But it's possible that you've misinterpreted Ms Shapell's actions and are mistaken about her intentions. You're new to New York and green at the business. Everything moves at a faster pace here—including the people. The ad business is somewhat like show business. It's a lot of flash. The people involved are pushy and showy. There's always a lot of touching and kissing going on. What you might consider as being flirtatious, Ms Shapell might think of as merely being friendly."

He raked a hand through his hair. "You're right about one thing," he conceded. "I don't understand the Yankee mentality. Where I come from, when a woman gives a man inviting looks and rubs his leg under the table, she's generally got something intimate in mind. Do you honestly believe that New York women are so different?"

He'd asked for an honest opinion, but if she answered truthfully he could very well walk off the job and leave her high and dry. How far should she go to save an account and appease a client? She'd assured Rita that she was keeping an eye out for Joe Dillon. A neat trick when one was conveniently looking the other way. Who was she kidding? She'd seen the warning signals for herself—subtle indications of familiarity that went beyond what was appropriate or acceptable.

"I suppose not," she reluctantly admitted.

He looked baffled. "Are you saying that I've got a legitimate gripe?"

"I'm saying it's a possibility," was her dismal reply. "Come into the kitchen. I'll put on a pot of coffee and we'll talk about it further."

As he watched her jersey-draped figure walk into the kitchen, he thought about how she'd done it again—changed colors like a chameleon. He unfastened the top few buttons of his shirt and rubbed a hand across the back of his neck. His righteous madness was wearing off but not his frustration. He was caught between a rock and a hard place—between two women and cross-purposes. One wouldn't let him back into her bed and the other was pressuring him to crawl into hers. "A fine kettle of fish you've gotten yourself into," he grumbled to himself before joining Virginia in the kitchen.

She said nothing at first. He decided to follow her lead and do the same. Not until after the coffee was brewed and poured and they were seated across from each other at the table did she speak.

"I've been thinking over the problem." Her tone was flat. "Let's assume the worst and say you're right about Claudia Shapell."

"I'm not making it up," he put in.

She gazed thoughtfully into her cup of coffee. "Don't be so touchy, Joe Dillon."

"Put yourself in my place," he challenged her.

"I did," she told him matter-of-factly. "A woman doesn't work her way up through the ranks of a male-dominated field without encountering a certain amount of sexual innuendo. In some instances it goes beyond innuendo. Men make passes and women have limited options as to how to deal with the dilemma.

Ignore it, be good-natured and brush it off, register a private objection in the form of 'No dice, buster,' give in and put out or lodge a formal complaint.''

She paused for a reflective second and sampled the coffee. "You can't imagine how many women have been passed over for a promotion or were forced to quit high-paying positions because they refused to play pat-a-cake with the boss. Many found it simpler to move on rather than put up with the constant come-ons from their peers. The problem has existed for women for years. Only lately has it started affecting men in the workplace—it's only been within the past ten or so years that women have risen to positions of power. Strangely enough, a small percentage of those women have been guilty of the very same abuses as their male peers.''

"What's sauce for the gander is sauce for the goose,'' he said dryly.

"Right. Now we have reverse sexual harassment as well as reverse discrimination.'' She slanted him an assessing look over the edge of her cup. "If you're convinced that Claudia Shapell falls into that small percentage of women, you're faced with the options I mentioned. But consider your decision carefully, Joe Dillon. There is so much at stake. If you pull out on me at this critical point, we stand to lose a bundle. I've already set up location shoots in Argentina and bought television and radio time. The pasteups for magazine ads are in progress. We're talking thousands and thousands of dollars invested in you. There is also the small detail of a contract. Breaking one is nasty and costly business.''

He smiled ruefully and set aside the coffee mug. "I know I've got a thick Southern accent, but some-

times I think we talk different languages, Ginny darlin'."

She wondered when and why he'd gotten it in his
head to call her Ginny darlin'. But she decided now
was probably not a good time to go into it.

"You speak in dollars and cents and contracts. I'm
talking about a man's honor."

"I'm not discounting your feelings. I know you
have enormous pride. I don't blame you for resenting
being treated in such a demeaning manner."

"Or, as you ladies are prone to say, like a sex object." His voice was a little less hostile but not his eyes.

Virginia smiled weakly. "What I'm trying to tell you
is that I have to think of the broader picture—the ir-
reparable damage your sudden departure from the
campaign at this late stage would cause. Hanks and
Udell's entire strategy is centered upon you. No you,
no campaign. No campaign, no account. No account..." She caught herself at the last second.

"No account, no partnership," he finished for her.

She got up out of her chair, keeping her back to him
and taking her sweet time when refilling their coffee
mugs. "I'll be held accountable for the setback to Don
Sebastian. Whatever else she is, Claudia Shapell is a
cost-efficient, hard-nosed businesswoman. She'll be
satisfied with nothing less than my head on a silver
platter."

Joe Dillon detected the slight sag of her shoulders
beneath the man-size football jersey. "Surely the
agency wouldn't fire you over one account? Besides,
I'll be glad to tell 'em my version of things."

If the situation had not been so grim, Virginia
would have found it laughable. She sighed, then returned to the table and handed him the mug. "Sexual

harassment is a difficult thing to prove, Joe Dillon. Shapell would just deny it. Whose side do you think Hanks and Udell will take? The Don Sebastian account means big income to the agency. Make no mistake, I'll be dropped like a hot potato."

"Damn," was all he muttered.

"It's a tough, competitive business. Big accounts are what it's all about. People are expendable," she explained.

They lapsed into brooding silence.

"What did you do?" he finally asked.

"About what?" She was so preoccupied with thoughts of her dismissal, her attention had drifted.

"When men made passes," he said. "How'd you handle it?"

"I don't want to influence you." Suddenly she felt the full weight of her responsibilities. To which did she feel the stronger obligation? The Madison Avenue agency or the gentleman from Cottonmouth?

"I've got a mind of my own. You won't sway me," he assured her, lying through his teeth. He was already wavering. Originally he'd planned to tell her he was washing his hands of the whole sordid business. Now, suddenly, he couldn't help but remember the revealing discussion they'd shared in the lounge the day of the presentation—her telling him how the Sebastian account meant the realization of a lifelong ambition. He vividly recalled how she'd pleaded with him not to jinx her golden opportunity to become a partner. Looking at her across the table, he wasn't so sure anymore about his reasons for wanting out. What really was prompting him to dig in his heels like a mule? Was it purely his dignity he was trying to redeem? Or did he secretly want to get even with Vir-

ginia for treating him like some fatal infection? Ever
since they'd slept together, she'd behaved as if he were
a rat carrying the bubonic plague.

"All right," she gave in, reclaiming his wandering
attention. "I chose to overlook the come-ons. I tact-
fully ignored the innuendo and sidestepped situations
that were potential danger zones. It's a fine line to
walk and distracting as hell. I won't tell you that I
didn't resent it. Mostly because it was so damn unfair
to have to always be on guard. It was twice as tough
for me as it was for my male peers. They could keep
focused while I was forced to keep looking over my
shoulder and weigh every word I said. I even had to
select the clothes I wore accordingly. It was an unend-
ing tap dance. To some degree it still is," she admitted. "And shuffling and sidestepping work only so
long as the sexism is implied rather than acted on.
Nobody ever came right out and gave me an ultimatum."

J.D. sat mulling over everything she'd said. "Yeah,
well, I haven't been out-and-out propositioned just
yet. She's a wily animal but I suppose I can duck and
dodge her awhile longer," he deliberated out loud.

Virginia's face lighted up. "I know it's a lot of
pressure, and under any other circumstances I
wouldn't ask it of you, but this is so important to us
both, Joe Dillon. You have to believe me. I'm not just
thinking of the agency or myself. With the exposure
you'll receive from the campaign you'll be able to
write your own ticket in this town. Everyone will want
you. You'll be inundated with modeling offers."

He grinned wryly. "You're awful sure about me. I
may not be cover boy material."

"Oh, you are, Joe Dillon," she said certainly.

"Yeah, well, even so, I'm not real keen on the idea of being a pinup. What's more, I don't have a burning desire to linger in New York too long," he told her, equally as certainly.

"But that's crazy. Where else could you make as much money? And you will, you know," she emphasized. "I don't think you realize how much money is involved. In a few short months you'll have earned what it would take a lifetime to accumulate back in Mississippi. An opportunity such as this doesn't come along every day. You'd be a fool to throw it all away because of a temporary case of homesickness."

He shrugged, dropping his gaze and twiddling with the mug. He was heartsick, not homesick. "It isn't the Delta that I yearn for," he said simply.

"Then what?" She hadn't a clue as to what would satisfy him.

He raised his gaze to hers and looked deep into her puzzled eyes. "How long do you intend on avoiding the subject of us?"

"Us?" She pretended not to catch his meaning.

"I would've thought you might've gathered by now that I don't go to bed with a woman unless she means something special to me." He did not make it easy for her to skirt the issue.

"I never questioned your motives." She collected their mugs and escaped to the kitchen sink. "I think we've had to hash through enough for one night. Do you suppose we could save the conversation of *us* for later? It's four-thirty in the morning." She was practically begging now.

He got up out of his chair and came to where she stood.

She turned around and faced him, still holding the mugs in her tightly clenched fingers.

Wordlessly he took them from her and set them in the sink. His hands clamped around her small waist, and with a smooth lift he settled her fanny on the countertop.

"What I have to say won't take a minute." He reached up to right the football jersey, which had slipped off one shoulder. He drew a deep breath, let it out slowly, then said what was on his mind.

"I'm a plainspoken person. I don't know any other way to be. It might be smarter to keep my feelings to myself but I can't see how it would change anything." His eyes fixed on hers. Was it resignation or determination that she perceived within the dark orbs? "I'm in love with you, Ginny darlin'. I guess I was from the moment I set eyes on you in the restaurant."

She started to speak but he pressed his fingertips to her lips.

"I know what you're going to say and, believe me, I've argued the same points over and over again to myself. It's crazy. It only happens that way in the movies. People call it love when it's really something else. But those arguments don't hold water. Inside, I know, just like a person knows when he's hungry or sleepy, which direction to walk when he's lost, or when his time is growing near. I've been thinking a lot about the lines from Ecclesiastes my mother used to recite to us as kids. *To every thing there is a season, and a time to every purpose under the heaven*."

She was stunned by his declaration. Maybe none of what was happening was real. Perhaps she was dreaming. Or maybe her mind had finally snapped from all the strain. It was bound to happen sooner or later. She had been functioning under tremendous pressure of late. He wasn't in her kitchen, professing his love and quoting Ecclesiastes by dawn's early light. It was just a figment of her overtaxed mind. In a moment, she'd awaken to find herself alone, in her bed, a little confused but otherwise unaffected by these wild imaginings.

He took advantage of her dazed state, catching her at the front of the silky jersey and gently towing her closer until their lips were but a breath apart. "You can act like you don't care. You can tell me daily that I'm wasting my time. But I'm not giving up on you so long as there's that spark of hope whenever I kiss you," he solemnly vowed, claiming her mouth with a needy urgency that shook them both.

"This isn't happening. It isn't possible," she uttered bewilderedly when their lips finally parted.

"Anything's possible if we want it bad enough," was his husky reply. "Do you honestly believe if you say, oops, pardon me, I didn't mean for that to happen, it erases things? You're too savvy a woman to kid yourself that way."

What she was experiencing was not a persistent dream. It was a persistent Joe Dillon. "It's you who's kidding himself," she said huffily. "We're total opposites. Besides, I'm much older than you." She shoved him back with her palms and jumped down from the countertop.

"Look on the bright side. You wouldn't have to worry about me dropping dead and making you a young widow."

"You're making me crazy, Joe Dillon." She raked the sides of her hair up, giving a convincing performance of a woman about to pull her hair out. "I'm shipping you to Argentina on the first available plane. You and I need to put some distance between ourselves.''

He slipped his hands into the pockets of his tuxedo pants and slanted her a challenging look. ''You can send me packing but it'll only delay what's bound to have to be settled between us. I'm a stubborn cuss. Been that way ever since I was little. Whenever my heart was set on having something, I couldn't seem to take no for an answer. I guess I never outgrew the irritating habit.''

''I really am feeling the effects of sleep deprivation. My brain is numb and my body is screaming for a few hours' rest. Have a heart, Joe Dillon. Go home so I can go back to bed,'' she pleaded.

He could see she was exhausted. Without further protest, he walked into the living room, collected his jacket and tie from the chair and made his way toward the door.

''Are we squared away about how to deal with Ms Shapell for the present?'' she dared to ask him once he was out in the hall.

''I'll try it your way, but if the woman makes it clear that she expects sexual favors in return for the high wages I'm being paid, I'm through—no ifs ands or buts about it.''

''Mmm,'' she murmured drowsily, more interested in climbing back in her own bed than considering the farfetched possibility that Claudia Shapell might try to harass Joe Dillon into hers. ''Enjoy Argentina, Joe Dillon.'' She yawned widely.

''Yeah. Try to miss me a little, Ginny darlin'.''

She shut the door on him.

CHAPTER TWELVE

JOE DILLON LEARNED MORE than just the tricks of the trade during the location shoots in Argentina. Much to his chagrin, Claudia Shapell manufactured reasons to make impromptu consulting trips to South America during his three-week stay. Even when they were shooting in the remote rain forests and at Iguaçú Falls, she showed up to observe. She'd wave and watch from a distance, patiently waiting until the crew was dispersed for the day to move in on J.D.

He tried to get out of her dinner invitations and repeated offers to act as his tour guide. "Don't be silly. You're not imposing. I want to do it," she'd insist. "Hurry and change. San Carlos de Bariloche is only a few kilometers away. It's one of the more popular resorts in the Argentine Alps. I know a lovely little secluded spot where we can dine and watch the sun set over the Andes."

The woman knew her way around, in more ways than one. She came up with more colorful places to visit faster than he could think up excuses. Predictably they always wound up in some romantically picturesque setting, strolling arm in arm, with her confiding in him how lonely it was at the top and hinting in every conceivable way that she wouldn't be averse to his spending the night with her. On more than one occasion she presented him with a lavish gift, and each time, he politely refused. In every instance she'd assure him that the gift was not meant as a bribe, only as a bonus, and then she had the gift delivered to his hotel room the following day. With each delivery, he was reminded of the sack of apples he'd taken as a kid and all the trouble he'd gotten into for accepting the gift he hadn't earned.

He thought about his mother's long-ago warning: "A good reputation is nothing to trifle with and certainly not anything to be traded away for a sack of apples.... Things that come to you without sweat or sacrifice have no value, J.D. You'd do well to remember what I say."

He didn't want to risk insulting Claudia Shapell by returning the gifts. But each time he scrawled his John Henry across the bottom of the delivery ticket, he felt as though he were signing away a bit more of his self-respect. He'd add the latest "bonus" to the stack of unopened bribes and wonder how in the hell he was going to redeem his honor without offending his benefactress. Joe Dillon was tap-dancing as fast as he could but he really didn't know how much longer he could keep it up. During their side trip to San Carlos de Bariloche, Claudia Shapell had actually patted him on the butt. She'd been amused by his startled reaction. "Don't be a prude, Dillon," she'd said, laughing. "I'm paying for the privilege."

At each stopover, he purchased a postcard by which to send the latest news and his love to Virginia. Always they began with the endearment, "Ginny darlin'," and ended with, "All my love, J.D."

Virginia saved them all but never answered a single one. Oddly enough, her lack of response made no impression on Joe Dillon. He continued his long-distance wooing. Each succeeding postcard contained more loving lines than the one before. He crammed as much sentiment as possible into the small space allotted him. The last one she'd received was especially revealing.

Ginny darlin',
We did a shoot at Iguaçú Falls yesterday—a two-mile-wide wall of roaring water tumbling over a two hundred and thirty foot drop. It's a sight to behold. Took my breath away. I feel a connection with this land. Did you know that they grow cotton here? If there's such a place as God's country, this is it. Last night, I sat in my hotel room thinking about what a wonderful life we could build together here. There's fertile soil and breathing space for me, and plenty of promoting for you to do. I'm sure you're thinking I've stayed in the sun too long, but I've never been more clearheaded....

All my love, J.D.

Whenever she had an exceptionally stressful day, she'd find herself drawn to that particular postcard. She'd reread the scribbled thoughts and, for a fleeting moment, take solace in the adventurous notion of escaping the rat race and running off to Argentina. But then she'd quickly get control of herself, drop the postcard back into the small cedar box with all the others and slam shut the lid.

The ad campaign would be set into motion soon. The on-site crew had been expressing the footage from each shoot by air back to the production department before moving on to the next one. The countdown was under way at Hanks and Udell. There remained only a few short days and some last-minute touches before Don Sebastian Designs would be launched in the States.

She was always shaky when an ad campaign was about to be put to the test. Prelaunch jitters, she reasoned. Maybe a little worse than usual, but then she'd not had a partnership riding on the outcome before. The sleepless nights, the frequent lapses in concentration during the day had nothing to do with Joe Dillon. She promised herself a long vacation once the campaign was solidly installed. Anywhere but Argentina. . . .

"HERE EES THOSE BROCHURES from the travel agency you wanted." Rita dropped a dozen or so colorful pamphlets on her desk. One depicting the splendors of Argentina was strategically placed on top of the pile.

"I specifically said anywhere but Argentina," Virginia reminded her, picking it up and dropping it into the trash can.

"So sue the travel agency," Rita said with a dismissive shrug.

Virginia slanted her a frosty look.

"And here ees your mail for today." She set the stack on Virginia's desk. Joe Dillon's postcard was on the top of the heap.

"I suppose you read it?" Virginia picked up the postcard and aimed it accusingly at Rita.

"Ees not in an envelope. I cannot help it if my eyes trip over a word or two."

"You devour every syllable," Virginia accurately surmised. "So where is our Mr. Mahue at present?"

"What do you care?" was Rita's snippy answer.

"You've been temperamental for days. Why don't you just come out with it and tell me what's eating at you?" Virginia figured she would regret giving her secretary an opening, but it was becoming harder and harder to ignore her cranky humor.

"Well, sinz you ask..." With a swish of her dark mane, Rita settled in a chair.

"Is this going to be a long list of complaints?" Virginia said it in a kidding tone, hoping Rita wouldn't answer in the affirmative.

"Do you want to hear or no?"

Against her better judgment, Virginia gave Rita a go-ahead gesture.

Rita pursed her lips. She weighed what she was about to say carefully, for she risked not only a long-standing friendship but possibly her job, as well. Ginny wasn't the most collected person under the best of circumstances and lately her fuse had been shorter than ever. A ticking time bomb, in fact. She wouldn't take well what Rita felt obliged to say. "I'm worried about you, Ginny," she said in her most serious voice. "I theenk you are making a big mistake with your life and as a friend I can keep my mouth shut no more."

"I've a good idea where the conversation is leading and I'd just as soon not discuss it any further. So unless you have some work-oriented complaint to register..." Virginia shoved back her chair. The topic of Joe Dillon was a closed subject.

"Sit down," Rita said sharply. "I will only follow you if you try to walk out. For once, you are gone to face a problem straight on."

Semistunned by her imposing manner, Virginia sank back into her chair. "What is that crack supposed to mean?"

"It means you cannot continue to behave like a child when things get heavy in your life. You are a grown-up woman and ees time you started acting like one. Every time you have a personal crisis, you fall back on old habits. When trouble lays in your path, you make like a turtle and draw into a crusty shell. Ees what you did with your brother, your mother, your ex-husband, and now you do the same with Joe Dillon."

"I'm really not in the mood for a bunch of psychoanalytic crap, Rita," Virginia shot back. "There's no deep-seated denial pattern to how I deal with the people in my life."

"That's the point. You don deal with them. If someone you care for disappoints you, you shut yourself away from them because you don want to risk the pain that comes from opening up your heart to another. I theenk you are afraid to tell them how you feel. I theenk you believe if you admit to them that they have the power to hurt you, you only invite more heartache. How can they ever prove differently, if you don give them a chance?"

"Right," Virginia said scoffingly. "I'm at fault. Aren't you forgetting how many chances I gave my ex-husband? And how did he prove himself? He'd tell me one lie after another and sleep with one woman after another."

"Ees a mystery to me why you react as you do. For years you knew he was sleeping with other women. You were the turtle once more, hiding in your hard shell and not poking out your head so you would not have to see what was going on. You did the same with your brother. Instead of speaking up and telling him he was stealing all the attention, the turtle said nothing and crawled off to find sunshine of its own to bask in. And because you are afraid that your mother will say aloud what you have always thought to be the truth—that she loved your brother more...that he was her favorite child—you squeeze tighter into your own space where her rejection cannot penetrate."

Rita knew she was striking sensitive nerves. Virginia's face was the color and texture of granite. "There *ees* a pattern, Ginny. You've made it so. And if you do not recognize the fear, it will paralyze you. What good is it to be a big success if there ees no personal satisfaction in what you do? More money, more power ees not a substitute for happiness. What Joe Dillon offers ees more enriching than big bucks and a fancy title, but you let a chance at real fulfillment pass you by because you are afraid of history repeating itself."

"You've lost me," Virginia said numbly.

"You are like the mad doctor who created Frackenheim," Rita put forth.

"Frankenstein," Virginia corrected her, still in the dark as to where the analogy was leading.

"Whatever," Rita went on. "The mad doctor, he both loved and feared his creation. I theenk it ees how you feel about Joe Dillon. You have made him into a sensation, something women dream of. Soon, no matter where he goes, they will be throwing themselves at him. It ees like a rerun of a bad movie. You see Rob Rice, not Joe Dillon. You theenk he will be another heartbreaker, playing musical beds like your ex. And you are wrong to make such comparisons. They are two different men. Joe Dillon has a level head and a faithful nature. Neither will be turned by a pretty face or a willing body."

"I suppose I do make unconscious comparisons." She leaned back in her chair with an audible sigh. "I won't deny that I'm attracted to him. Any woman would be. My life was all neatly laid out before he came into it. Everything was proceeding just as I planned. I wasn't looking for a romance. My only ambition was to be considered one of the best in the ad business. Then, you had to spot Joe Dillon in the restaurant, and suddenly my life goes haywire."

"You call your life neat. I say it was boring before Joe Dillon. The only excitement you got was from competing in business." Sensing that Virginia's shell was cracking, Rita dared to say more. "You pushed yourself not because you wanted to prove that you were better than all the other kids on the ad block, but because of a childish need to outdo your brother. You got what the guest shrinks on afternoon talk shows call a fexation."

The proper term was "fixation." No matter how badly Rita butchered the word, she'd accurately labeled Virginia's hang-up.

"You could not even stop when he died. You still compete with a ghost." Rita hated being so cruelly blunt with her friend. She had the glazed look of someone in shock. Rita's first husband, Kid Chi-Chi Rivera, had worn the same punchy look after being KO'd in the fourth round of one welterweight title match.

"I didn't realize..." Virginia's voice was low and thick, like that of a person emerging from the twilight effects of anesthesia. "I mean, I knew besting Billy was part of why I drove myself so hard in the beginning..." She rose up slowly out of her chair and walked to the window. The view from the top of Madison Avenue was what she'd worked so hard to achieve, but as she looked down on the street that symbolized her goals, her vision of the future blurred. "I thought it was just my guilt over being secretly jealous of him that haunted me after his death. Somewhere, somehow, the sibling rivalry became an obsession with me."

She hugged her midsection to ward off the icy feeling welling in the pit of her stomach. "Dear God, Rita. You're right. I've been like a runaway train racing along on an endless, going-nowhere track. I wasn't going to stop until my mother was forced to admit that I was equal to him. I had to hear her say that she was as proud of her daughter as she was her son. She never did and I converted her silence into fuel. There was plenty to feed both my resentment and my ambition. By the time of Billy's accident, I'd built up so much steam I couldn't throw on the brakes." Her eyes brimmed with tears and she shuddered in spite of the tight grip she tried to keep on herself.

Rita came to where she stood at the window, handed her a tissue with one hand and patted her shoulder with the other.

"I know what you're thinking," Virginia said between sniffs and swipes at her tearstained cheeks. "I'm behaving like a child again—blaming my mother for what's really my fault and being a big crybaby."

Rita smoothed Virginia's hair and spoke lovingly. "Even grown-up women cry, Ginny. Ees a way to shed the bitterness. I don mean to upset you, but for too long I have stood by and done nothing while I watch you grow more intense and less satisfied each day." Gently taking her by the shoulders, Rita turned Virginia away from the window and forced her to engage her eyes. "As a *niña*, you decided a turtle was not a lovable creature. Then the turtle chooses a wild hare for a mate and his bed hopping only convinces her all the more that she ees not desirable or deserving. Ees not true, Ginny. Beneath that protective shell ees a lovely and lovable woman, but you must stick your neck out, take a chance, if you are to ever get over a childish fear.''

Rita smiled reassuringly. "Mundo knows men. Joe Dillon has a good and true heart. He loves you deeply but there ees a limit to his pride and patience. If you care for him, you had better tell him so. For once, the slow turtle had better act quickly or else live with regrets forever.''

With a wink and another pat, Rita left Virginia to think over her advice. She turned back to the window, standing motionless and staring reflectively out at the Manhattan skyline. She visualized the faces of those she often thought about—Billy, Rob, her mother, Rita, Joe Dillon. Of the five persons who'd been instrumental in her life, it seemed to her that only two had loved her totally and unconditionally: Rita and Joe Dillon. Rita's loyalty she understood, for she probably knew her better than anyone and had seen her good side as well as her bad.

It was Joe Dillon's persistence and constancy she couldn't comprehend. For the most part, he'd been exposed to her stiff, stubborn, worst self. Why had he put himself through such agony, especially since she had not given him one shred of encouragement? She had demanded so much of him and given so little of herself. Could she really have expected him to understand her reasons for resisting his loving overtures when she was only just beginning to weave through the complicated web of emotions herself? Was it too late for explanations, she wondered.

Her gaze traveled to her desk and the stack of mail she'd yet to scan. She was half-afraid to read his postcard. It was entirely possible that he'd written her off—and the end of his patience was postmarked a week ago.

A panicky feeling gripped her as she crossed from the window to the desk. Her hand actually shook as she picked up the postcard and read the message on the reverse side.

Ginny darlin',
It's been raining buckets for three days. Only one more shoot to go, but everything's been delayed due to the weather. Have a lot of time on my hands. I mostly spend it daydreaming of you. It's wishful thinking, I know, considering how you haven't written a word back to me. I suppose your silence is an answer in itself, but I keep hoping differently. To tell you the truth, I'm not all that anxious to return home. If it wasn't for leaving you in a lurch, I'd stay where I am. Modeling pays well, but I've about concluded that I'm more suited to sweating over a cotton crop than smiling for the camera. I should be coming into New York only a day or two behind the postcard. I don't expect you'll be waiting for me at the airport with open arms, but you can't blame a guy for hoping and trying.

All my love, J.D.

Her stomach tightened at his mention of quitting the campaign. "Stay loyal to me for a while longer, Joe Dillon," she murmured. "I do care, but there are so many things to sort out." She slipped the postcard into the pocket of her suit jacket and searched her desk for the checklist she and her creative team were to go over a final time.

God! She hoped she looked more together than she felt. She had to make the Don Sebastian label bigger than Guess or Jordache. Only by capturing the American fancy could Joe Dillon be released from his contract without causing much of a fluctuation in the market share. If everything held together for just a few more months, all parties involved would derive something positive from the joint venture.

Sebastian and Shapell would make a fortune. Virginia would get the credit and a partnership in the agency. Joe Dillon could retire from modeling with ample money to stake him in whatever future endeavor he chose to undertake. And the two of them would be free of professional constraints and able to give full reign to their private dreams and desires. Hopefully, they could strike a compromise about their future together and work out an arrangement by which they could both pursue their separate interests without either one feeling cheated or neglected by the other. Joe Dillon was an easygoing fellow—secure in himself. He'd understand that her career required a certain amount of dedication and her staying in New York. She'd certainly understand his reasons if he felt cramped and wanted to go South and grow cotton. After all, commuter romances were quite common these days.

Virginia smiled to herself at the appealing notion of spending weekends in the lazy-paced Delta. No phones, no pressure, just delicious peace and steamy passion. The mere thought of Joe Dillon's making love to her on a regular basis made her blood run hot and her heart beat faster. They would make up for being deprived of one another Monday through Friday by devoting themselves solely to each other every weekend until a more permanent solution could be worked out between them.

She reached for the intercom and buzzed Rita. "Do me a favor and find out when and what flight Joe Dillon is coming in on," she requested.

"You want me to arrange for a brass band, too?" Rita giggled.

"Just a limo." Virginia grinned broadly and clicked off.

CHAPTER THIRTEEN

THE CAREFULLY REHEARSED WORDS evaporated from Virginia's mind the instant she spied Claudia Shapell standing at the terminal gate. The client noticed her at exactly the same moment. Virginia considered turning around and acting as though she were searching for another gate, but scratched the idea a second later. Shapell had no way of knowing the real reason for her meeting Joe Dillon's flight. She'd most likely assume it was a customary courtesy she extended to her more valuable personnel. The best approach was to proceed as planned, Virginia decided.

"I had no idea you were picking Dillon up," the other woman said in way of a greeting when Virginia was within a few steps of her. "When we talked last he told me he didn't have a ride. So I thought I'd rescue him from a harrying taxi trip," she explained. Her smile was cool and her green eyes assessing as they took in every detail of Virginia's appearance.

"How nice of you. I'm afraid my motives for offering him a lift are more mercenary. I thought we might have a chance to talk shop during the ride across town." She checked her watch. "His flight should be arriving anytime. Should we flip a coin to see which of us does the honors?" She'd meant to sound glib, but instead, she came across as somewhat bitchy.

"Business always comes before pleasure." Shapell responded like a true tycoon. "But since I'm here, I'm sure you wouldn't begrudge me a minute or two with our overnight celebrity in order to welcome him back."

"Considering the staggering sum you pay the agency, I can hardly object." Virginia smiled sweetly.

Don Sebastian's partner considered her with a mixture of respect and amusement. "Actually, if these past few days are any indication, the money I pay Hanks and Udell is petty cash compared to what Sebastian Designs stands to gain. Already the other houses are worried. It's the buzz of the industry. The feedback I'm hearing from the teaser spots alone is cause enough to deem our debut in the States a triumph."

"It's too early to declare ourselves a winner, but the preliminary stats do reflect an even bigger and more immediate response than we'd anticipated." Virginia spoke like a pollster calling an election.

"Don't be so modest. We're a smash. And it's all due to your genius and Dillon's magnetism. We capitalize on him like McDonald's trades on their secret sauce. Beef burgers or beefcake, it's the same principle, isn't it?"

The woman definitely grated on Virginia. She wasn't about to legitimize the insulting comparison with a concurring response. Instead, she glanced toward the terminal door. The flight had arrived. Passengers were beginning to disembark. The crush of awaiting friends and relatives soon made the receiving area as big a bottleneck as the Van Wyck Expressway.

"Do you see him yet?" Claudia asked, stretching her neck and trying to peer over the head of travelers and welcomers.

Virginia caught a glimpse of his tall figure above the crowd. "There he is." She pointed him out to Shapell.

It was a dumb move. In the space of a blink, she was weaving and shoving her way toward him. Virginia's spirits sank as she saw Claudia fling her arms around Joe Dillon's neck and leave the rose imprint of her lips on his cheek. He looked appreciative to see a friendly face. Virginia had wanted to be the first person to welcome him home. She'd imagined him swinging her up into his arms and declaring how much he'd missed the sight of her. She'd wanted it to be an intimate reunion, or at least as intimate as it could be in the midst of a roomful of ogling strangers. Thanks to Shapell, she could scratch that idea, too.

"Damn," she muttered under her breath, staring daggers into Shapell's back.

It was then that J.D.'s eyes connected with hers. For a moment he thought his mind was playing a cruel trick. He no longer heard Claudia's chatter. All the noise, all the people faded from his consciousness as he started walking toward the mirage. It didn't vanish. She was really, really here. His thirsty eyes drank her in as he covered the distance to where she stood.

As much as she longed to kiss him hello, she knew she had to restrain herself in front of Claudia Shapell. She had to keep reminding herself to keep it low-key and businesslike. "Hello, J.D.," she greeted him, hoping he would read something into the familiar address. "You look fit and tan. Argentina must have agreed with you." She stuck out her hand.

"Yes, ma'am, it did." He gave her hand a squeeze and flashed her a wink on the qt.

"Is J.D. some sort of pet name you have for our boy?" Claudia had picked up on the familiarity.

Boy! Joe Dillon disliked the term intensely. Down South when people called a man "boy," it was generally meant in a derogatory sense. "My full name is Joe Dillon—J.D. for short. Miss Vandivere thought Dillon was simpler," he answered for her.

"I suppose it doesn't matter what we call you, so long as we get the name right on your check." Claudia pulled her designer sunglasses down from her hairline and squared them on the bridge of her nose. "I know you two have loads to discuss, so I won't intrude any longer. I'm hosting a small dinner party tonight in your honor, Dillon. Oh, don't scowl. I promise it'll be a simple affair. No photographers or press people. Just a few friends and one or two well-placed folk," she assured him with a tweak of his cheek. "Oh, and you're invited, too, Ms Vandivere," she said as an afterthought.

"Why, thank you. I'd love to come." Virginia pretended not to notice that she wasn't high on Claudia Shapell's guest list.

"Good. Then it's all settled. My place at eight. Dillon knows the way." Her tone implied that they were bosom pals, so to speak. In case Virginia might have missed the point, she pressed up against Joe Dillon and whispered in his ear before relinquishing him to the creative director.

Both she and Joe Dillon stood transfixed, and stared at Claudia Shapell's fashionably dressed figure until it faded from view. Finally they turned to each other, neither knowing exactly what to say or how to behave.

Virginia was the first to bridge the awkward silence. "I didn't know she would be here. I gave the excuse that we needed to talk shop during the ride across town. I hope you don't mind."

"Mind!" he hooted. "I've never been so glad to see anyone in my life."

She smiled and slanted him a gauging look. "I'd hope you'd say that. The excuse I gave wasn't a total lie, J.D. I do have a lot to discuss with you."

"I should have known." He smiled and glanced up, trying to decipher the overhead arrows that pointed the way to the baggage claim area.

"I've missed you," she said softly.

His eyes returned to her and he grinned boyishly. "Yeah? Then the postal service must've screwed up and all those letters you wrote me got sent to some other pining soul."

She looped her arm through his and began to lead him down the corridor. "I'll make you a deal. I'll give you a lift home if you'll give me a chance to explain things."

"So long as you don't try to back out of going to that shindig tonight. I got blisters tap-dancing from one end of Argentina to the other."

"Shapell came to the shoots?" Virginia knew nothing of her numerous trips. "You never mentioned it in your cards."

"I didn't want to waste precious space complaining about her."

The rose imprint of her lips still marked his cheek. Virginia took a tissue from her pocket and rubbed it off as they walked along. "I'm sorry I got you into this, Joe Dillon."

The regret he detected in her voice made him want to reassure her. "It's been a learning experience, Ginny darlin'. So far, my gentlemanly honor is still intact. It'll be okay. Like I told you once before, we backwoods type are a resourceful bunch." He laced his fingers in hers and flashed her that disarming grin of his.

She was counting heavily on his being able to evade a bedroom showdown until she came up with the boardroom strategy necessary to diffuse the explosive campaign. God! She hoped for both of their sakes that they would each succeed.

MOSTLY, they did talk business during the ride to Brooklyn Heights. J.D. had hoped for a few days' rest after returning from Argentina, but Virginia had other ideas, such as him doing a guest spot on a popular, early-morning radio show the very next day.

"I thought you said I wasn't to say a word or, in my case, drawl a word as the Don Sebastian man," he reminded her. "How do I do a radio spot and keep my mouth shut at the same time?"

"I underestimated your appeal when I made that provision. The women of America have embraced you, J.D., thanks to the pre-launch publicity we've done. Even the tabloids have picked up on your popularity. Just this week one of them published the results of a random poll they conducted of their female readership and you ranked fourth in their rating of the ten sexiest men. A couple of the others were Southern, too. Apparently it's in. Then again, you could speak pig latin and they wouldn't care."

He was unimpressed by the news of his becoming a national heartthrob, but he could see it had had an opposite effect on Virginia. She wasn't going to change her mind about the guest spot. So much for a day or two's respite from being the Don Sebastian man. He hid his disappointment.

Virginia was far less successful at masking her shock when the limo pulled up outside the rundown brownstone.

J.D.'s landlady, Mrs. Tuddy, was a trip with her forties' hairdo, her predilection for big band music and her ration books. The eccentric widow broke into tears when he presented her with the gift he'd brought back from Argentina especially for her. She loved tea but thought it was a luxury she could no longer afford since she had more vacancies than boarders. Joe Dillon remembered her fondness for the beverage and had packed enough tea to last the befuddled soul a year.

"It's a local blend called yerba maté," he explained to her. "They grow it in the northeast of Argentina and it's pretty tasty stuff."

"You're a doll." Mrs. Tuddy wiped her nose with a frayed hankie and then lit up a cigarette. "He reminds me of my dead husband," she told Virginia between puffs and sniffs. "He was always bringing me gifts. Sometimes he'd bring me stockings. They're so hard to get, you know. That's why I don't wear them anymore." She held up a bare, knobby leg as proof. Confidingly, she added, "You can paint a line up the back of your leg with your brow pencil and nobody much knows the difference. Well, I'll leave you two young people alone. There's some lemonade in the icebox and a fresh-baked angel food cake." A coughing spasm hit her, and she turned on the kitchen faucet to douse her half-finished cigarette under the water.

"Mr. Petrie decided to take my ration coupons down at the grocery store again," she informed J.D., dropping the soggy cigarette into the trash can. "He's such a funny man. One day he understands that everybody has to do their part in the war effort, the next day you have to argue with him about it. If it wasn't that I wanted the sugar for the angel food cake, I wouldn't have bothered with him. I don't think he's a Fascist. He's just cantankerous." Having deemed the local grocer no national threat, Mrs. Tuddy shuffled off through the swinging door, leaving Joe Dillon and Virginia alone.

The laughter Virginia had been trying to stifle broke from her as soon as the old woman was safely out of earshot. "Is she on furlough from Bellevue?"

J.D. grinned. "She's not as crackers as she seems. She just stood still while the world went by." He poured two glasses of lemonade from the pitcher. "The neighborhood folk just sort of humor her. People say her dead husband made his living on the black market. That's how come she has a trunk full of ration books in the basement. The grocer she mentioned knows she's strapped for funds and generally takes her ration coupons in place of payment. His wife isn't so charitable. When she's around he has to refuse. Mrs. Tuddy doesn't understand. She just thinks he's wishy-washy when it comes to patriotism."

J.D. was unaware of Virginia's getting up from the table and crossing to where he stood. It startled him when she clasped his face between her palms and pulled his mouth to hers. A groan escaped him and he gathered her into his arms, kissing her back with a need that poured from every fiber of his being. He was afraid to open his eyes. He'd done so much fantasizing lately. The thought occurred to him that maybe Mrs. Tuddy's condition was catching. Or maybe he was simply dreaming. What if he opened his eyes to discover he'd nodded off during the flight home and none of what had transpired was real? Virginia hadn't met him at the airport. They weren't in Mrs. Tuddy's kitchen. She wasn't in his arms. And he wasn't kissing her.

He blinked when she withdrew from his embrace.

"That was no oops, pardon-me kiss, J.D.," she told him, relieving him immensely. "I meant for it to happen." She cast him a tender smile, then returned to her place at the table.

Stunned by her sudden change of heart, he was at a loss as to how to react. "I swear, you change moods and directions more often than the wind," he uttered bewilderedly.

"I've come to some realizations while you were gone, Joe Dillon. I'm not sure I can explain myself but I want to try."

He collected the two glasses of lemonade, deposited them on the table, then turned a chair around, straddled it and gave her his undivided attention. "I've got all day, Ginny darlin'," he said in that deliciously appealing honey-glazed drawl.

And suddenly she was terribly self-conscious and a little apprehensive. "I, uh, don't know exactly where to begin," she stammered. Her throat felt dry. She hoisted the glass to her lips and took a swig of the tart lemonade.

He took her free hand in his and pressed it to his lips. "It'd be nice if you'd begin by telling me that my hopes weren't in vain and while I was away you discovered you do have some feelings for me," he murmured against her fingertips.

"It's true. I do," she answered honestly. "But things are more complicated between us. It's not a simple matter of just stating how we feel about each other."

"It's a damn good start." He succeeded in capturing her evasive eyes.

"Yes, well, there are reasons behind my reluctance to admit how I feel about you that need explaining. It's important that you understand me because it has a bearing on how we both act in the future."

Just her mention of a future together was enough for Joe Dillon, but he could see she was anxious to explain herself. "Okay." He released her hand, folded his arms across the top of his chair and donned a sober expression. "I can't say I see the connection, but if talking it out is what you want, then talk it out we will."

She couldn't help but smile. "I'm a complex person, J.D."

"Don't I know it," he put in.

She ignored his response. "At first I didn't realize why it was I fought so hard against the attraction I felt for you. I thought my reasons were exactly what I claimed them to be."

"The fact that you were the boss woman and I was contract labor and never the two should be cozy," he stated.

"That and the differences in our ages and backgrounds. Though those reasons were and are valid, they were also a convenient excuse to keep you at arm's length," she admitted. "The truth is, I was afraid to get involved with you."

Joe Dillon did not seem surprised by the disclosure. "Because of your bad marriage," he supplied.

"It goes much deeper than my ex-husband, Joe Dillon." She fixed her gaze on the lemonade glass and expelled a pent-up sigh. "Handsome men have been a thorn in my side for as long as I can remember. You see, I had an older brother. He was exceptionally good-looking, extremely bright and charming as hell. From the time we were kids, he was the one everybody noticed and made comments about. I just sort of blended with the wallpaper. My mother adored him, and always overlooked the mischief he got into. He had an uncanny knack for turning things around to his advantage—he'd either pull off some stupendous feat or simply butter her up until he was once again in her good graces. She'd always relent. I think she lived vicariously through her devil-may-care son. Me, well, I was like the bland food she prepared day after day—just another part of her ordinary existence."

Though she spoke about her childhood matter-of-factly, J.D. knew the hurt she'd experienced was still with her. It lurked just below the carefully controlled surface. He eased a hand over hers.

The supportive gesture gave her the courage to continue with the difficult admission. "Competing for the attention I thought my brother robbed me of became an obsession with me. Just once, I wanted to be first or better at something than him. I devoted my life to besting Billy. I couldn't get the A's first or be a gridiron hero, so I resolved that I would be a big success in business and the richer, more powerful of us two. I became single-minded in my purpose. My sole objective was to make my mother acknowledge that I was the child who deserved her attention and praise. Billy might've overshadowed me as a kid, but I was determined not to let him do it to me as an adult. So I kept driving myself. After a while it became second nature to me and I forgot what had originally started me on the fast track to success. I got so wrapped up in making a name for myself on Madison Avenue and putting fat deposits in my checking account, I wasn't aware of competing with Billy any longer."

"The football jersey you were wearing when I came to your apartment the night before I left, it was your brother's?" he guessed.

"Yes. Billy was an all-American at Notre Dame. He was a born athlete. The pros wanted him but mother begged him not to sign. She told him he'd do better— and be safer—accepting a position with a California-based company that had also made him an enticing offer." She shrugged and shook her head. "I always thought it ironic that he met his death on a routine business trip to Japan when the company plane suffered mechanical failure and crashed only a mile short of the runway."

"I'm sorry. I have brothers. Even though we bicker and scrap, I know it'd be a hard thing to deal with if I was to lose one," he offered lamely.

There was pain in her eyes when she finally raised her gaze to his. "Oh, it is hard, J.D.—harder than you can imagine. It's not just the grief. It's the guilt. The terrible, awful guilt at having been so jealous of my brother that I couldn't stop competing with him even after he was gone. I'm ashamed to admit it." Her voice broke and she hung her head.

Joe Dillon came to comfort her. Wordlessly he pulled her limp body from the chair and hugged her close.

She began to cry softly against his shoulder. "Sometimes I'm still jealous of him and I hate myself for it. I can't even make a visit home anymore without coming away resentful and angry. My mother has turned the house into a damn shrine. He's still all she can talk about."

He cradled her in his arms and gently swayed to and fro. "You're beating yourself up over something that happens more often than not when somebody we love passes on. Everybody has regrets—things we wish we'd have done differently—things we should've said while we had a chance. It's worse when a person's time is cut short without warning. There's no opportunity to set things straight and make our amends. If the truth be known, Ginny, I'll betcha your brother wishes he'd had an opportunity to square himself with you, too. I'm sure he wouldn't want to be to blame for what's standing between you and your mother now."

Her tears slowly subsided. "Maybe so," she answered pensively. "I hadn't really thought of it in that way." She removed the tissue from her pocket and dabbed her wet cheeks. "Some swell homecoming I've provided." She choked back the tears and focused on the mascara-stained tissue. "I'm sorry. I didn't mean to get off on a tangent. I'm sure you're wondering what all of this has to do with you."

He brushed back the wilted bangs that had fallen into her swollen eyes. "I've got a vague idea of the picture you're trying to paint. You associate good-looking men with trouble. First there was your brother, the charmer, and then your ex, the cheater.

But I'm neither of those things. What's more, before I came to New York nobody ever accused me of possessing fine looks. When I gaze in the mirror, all I see is a brown-eyed, sunbaked cotton picker. Nothing special. Just an ordinary Southern plow horse who's crazy in love with a high-strung Yankee thoroughbred."

She smiled weakly. "You should see yourself through my eyes. What you possess goes beyond mere good looks. You're a beautiful person, J.D."

He shook his head and stroked her cheek. "I swear, I can't figure you out, girl. I'm not real certain where things are leading or what to expect next. You keep changing the ground rules on me."

"Be patient with me, Joe Dillon. I do care for you and I want to be free to show you how much, but there are obstacles and obligations we can't ignore."

His arms encircled her waist and he pulled her to him with a forceful squeeze. "To hell with that," he pronounced. "For weeks all I've been able to think about was making love to you once more. I'm not in the mood to be jerked around. At the moment, I really don't give a damn about satisfying anybody else's need but our own." He bent his head to hers and claimed her mouth hungrily.

Her body melted into him. He tasted of lemonade and passion. One stolen afternoon together. What could it matter?

"I want you so badly. You don't know how much, Ginny," he told her in a ragged whisper, his hands slipping to her buttocks and compressing her hips to his groin. There was no mistaking the extent of his desire. "Come upstairs with me. Let's lock out the world for a few hours. God, girl! All I've had is a memory to keep me going. A man needs more. Give me a little something to hang on to in the weeks ahead," he implored her.

"What about Mrs. Tuddy?" was her breathless concern as his lips trailed the curve of her neck.

"She's napping this time of day. We can slip upstairs and she'll never know." He pressed a finger to his lips, took her by the hand and led the way through the hall, past the dozing landlady in the front room and up the flight of steps.

"Careful," he cautioned her in a hushed voice, pointing out a creaking spot on the stair steps and skipping it.

Virginia felt both foolish and excited at the prospect of sneaking around like a pair of children up to mischief.

Once inside Joe Dillon's room, she had second thoughts. It was small and stuffy and anything but romantic. She looked around, finding it unbelievable that he lived such a Spartan existence.

Joe Dillon opened a window, letting in a welcome breeze, and she sat down on the bed, trying to mask her preoccupation with his shabby living conditions. The room was clean but certainly not the Waldorf.

He joined her on the bed, casting a sideways look at her and smiling to himself at the prim expression on her face. "You're not impressed with my life-style," he ventured to say.

"Actually, no," she answered honestly. "I don't understand why you continue to stay here. It isn't as if you can't afford better." She allowed him to help her out of her jacket.

"Material things don't mean that much to me, Ginny. Besides, I felt I owed it to Mrs. Tuddy to stay on. She took me in and even lent me a toothbrush when I was down and out. I try to repay her kindness by doing odd jobs around the place whenever I can.'' He draped the jacket over the bed rail and turned back to her with a stubborn look. "Money doesn't change what I am. It won't ever. I was born of meager means and raised to believe in values that haven't a price tag. I'm a simple man who enjoys a simple life, Ginny darlin'. I'm thrifty with my savings, but generous to those I care about. I wouldn't expect you to live a life without security or comfort. But you've got to respect the fact that I come from sturdy country folk who prefer the basic pleasures to showy pretenses. I'm not ashamed of my roots and I don't want you to be.''

There was such conviction in the way he stated himself that she was deeply moved. "I've occasionally been ashamed of myself, J.D., but I doubt I could ever be of you.'' She wrapped her arms around his neck and slowly sank down on the lumpy mattress, taking him with her.

Nothing mattered any longer—not the drab surroundings, the drastic differences between them or the days ahead. The fact that they were in each other's arms and poised on the brink of making sweet, secret love was all that was important. Their lips met and their bodies fused. The outside street noises disappeared and she was hardly aware of any motion as Joe Dillon peeled off her blouse, skirt and stockings.

She would deal with the obstacles and obligations later. Not now. Not now.

Joe Dillon's hand grazed along her outer thigh, hiking her slip so that she could feel the sporadic cool breeze on her legs. His touch was smooth and hot in comparison. He did all the work. She didn't have to lift a finger as he removed the obstacles—first her slip, then her bra, and lastly, her panties. Her only obligation was to him—to make him happy, to convince him that she loved him wholly and truly, to satisfy a hunger that had grown to amazing proportions while he had been away from her. It was an obligation she gladly assumed, for she realized it could be many more weeks, maybe even months, before such a lovely moment was likely to occur again.

She had to tell him with her body what she had failed to say in so many words—that she loved him dearly. One stolen afternoon of making mad love on a lumpy mattress had to be enough for him to know that she'd entered into an unspoken commitment. It had to be enough to last them until they were free of the campaign.

Virginia Vandivere-Rice was the most creative she'd ever been throughout the afternoon. She was all woman. She did not think, speak or act like a Madison Avenue hypester. The only thing she was selling was herself. The only person in the world she wanted to please was her man.

Having to be quiet only served to heighten the sensuality between them. Everything became magnified—the smells coming from the corner bakery, the dampness of the river breeze, their own body heat. The nostalgic swing music playing on Mrs. Tuddy's old Victrola down below wafted up to the brownstone's rafters and mingled with the bed springs; telltale squeaking and her and Joe Dillon's muffled giggling. It was zany and wonderful.

Even more zany and wonderful was Joe Dillon's suggestion that she accompany him to the roof to see the view from his private terrace. Her protests were met with persistence.

"I'm sure it's a lovely view," she murmured lethargically. "But somehow the idea of getting dressed and climbing to the roof doesn't turn me on." She preferred to revel in the afterglow and not budge from his embrace.

"Okay, we won't bother with clothes." He untangled himself from her and dragged her reluctant body from the bed. Before she could stop him, he stripped off the top sheet and draped it around her shoulders.

"Are you crazy?" she said, laughing. "We can't go traipsing around on the roof in the buff."

"Sure we can." His eyes glinted as he wrapped the bed quilt around himself.

She collected the sheet around her naked length and tied it in a knot at the divide of her breasts. "It's threatening to rain, J.D. We could be struck by lightning and fried to a crisp."

"Will you quit making excuses? Come on," he coaxed her, taking her by the hand and tugging her toward a small door at the end of the hallway.

"Back in the boondocks they might not have ordinances covering such nonsense as this," she whispered. "Have you ever heard of something called indecent exposure?"

"Can't say as I have." He proceeded with the climb, pulling her balking figure behind him up the narrow staircase.

She tripped on the hem of the sheet, stumbling a step. His firm grip steadied her. Virginia was more intent on keeping a tight hold on the sheet. "Well, here in New York you can get arrested for what we're doing," she grumbled. "I can see the headlines now—

Don Sebastian Man Bares All on Brooklyn Rooftop.''

A whoosh of fresh air and daylight flooded into the cramped passageway as he flung back the door leading to the roof. He gave her a hand up to the flat surface above.

She brushed the hair from her eyes and adjusted the sheet, which had slipped down on her bosom.

"Well, what do you think? Was it worth the climb?" He spread his arms in a gesture for her to take in the panoramic view.

The bustling East River traffic and wharves, the arched spans of the Brooklyn Bridge, the Statue of Liberty, Governors Island and the towering Manhattan skyline were spread before her. She walked to within a few feet of the brownstone's edge and peered out over the kaleidoscope of history, mood and motion. "I always forget how magnificent a place New York is," she remarked.

He came up behind her, eased his arms around her sheet-clad body and drew her against him. "Yeah, it's a grand little spot, but I think the word *magnificent* applies more to you." He nestled a cheek in her hair. "Moody, magical and magnificent—that about covers you." He tightened his hold on her.

"I feel so special, J.D." She snuggled her head in the crook of his shoulder and sighed contentedly. "I wish we could stay on this rooftop forever. If only we could be like Mrs. Tuddy—forget about the daily grind and let the world's problems just pass us by."

Storm clouds rumbled overhead and a flash of lightning streaked across the pewter sky. His lips brushed across her bare shoulders. "I know," he agreed. "Up here I can breathe. Down there I get smothered."

She turned to face him. "Do you hate it here so much?"

He shrugged and tried to sugarcoat the truth. "You make it bearable."

Worry showed in her blue eyes. "You're not thinking of deserting me, are you?"

"Is it me personally or the opportunity I represent that you'd miss?"

"You're most important to me, but I won't lie and say the pending partnership in the firm doesn't matter." She smoothed her palms up his chest and locked her hands behind his neck. "I've worked hard and sacrificed a lot to get where I wanted to be. I'm nearly there, J.D. I can't just turn my back on everything when I'm so close to achieving the recognition I've always dreamed of. Please understand what this means to me and be patient awhile longer," she entreated. "We can have it all if we play it smart and bide our time."

Joe Dillon suspected that they had different notions of what "having it all" meant, but he didn't feel right about asking her to forsake a lifelong ambition inches short of realizing it. He kept hoping she'd see his side of things eventually. "I know it's a big thing to you to receive your due and I've got no qualms about doing what I can to make it happen for you."

"I knew you'd understand," was her relieved reply. She pressed closer and rose on her tiptoes to give him a grateful kiss.

He evaded her kiss with a backward step, untwining her hands from about his neck and folding them within his own. She could not mistake his earnestness once her gaze connected with his somber eyes. "I'd do most anything for you, Ginny darlin', short of giving over my self-respect. It's getting stickier and I don't want to get trapped in Claudia Shapell's bed like a bug in flypaper. There's only one woman I want to make love with and on that point I'm not compromising."

"You've done a good job avoiding the issue so far," she argued.

"So far. But I got a roomful of bribes that she calls bonus gifts. Sooner or later I figure she's going to want to make an exchange of sex for favors."

The wind picked up, ruffling the sheet and tousling her hair. His gaze dropped to the tantalizing portion of thigh exposed by the sudden gust. Big raindrops began to fall on the rooftop. Ever since he was a kid, he'd been stirred by stormy weather. It carried a certain tension that transferred itself to him.

"The campaign's going well. I think very soon I can get you out of your contract. A kiss goodbye is the closest thing to sex that Shapell will get from you." Virginia cast a wary glance up at the black squall clouds. "I told you it would rain on our parade," she said.

The rain began to come down steadier.

He reached for her, took her into his arms and playfully lifted her off her feet to swing her round and round. "I don't feel rain. Do you? Nothing but nothing is going to spoil our fun. I feel like making love," he shouted. "How about you, girl? I'll bet you've never tried it on a rooftop in the rain." Slowly, expressively, he eased her body down his hard length until their lips met. His kiss was as electric as the static lightning. With a tug on the makeshift knot, the sheet around her dropped to her feet. He molded her rain-slicked body to him, tangling his fingers in her wet hair.

"Your neighbors are getting an eyeful." Her voice was husky with desire and she trembled, not from the chill of the rain on her skin but from the hot friction they were creating. "What if they report us? We really could get arrested for this, J.D." As much as she feared the embarrassment, she honestly didn't want to stop.

"It'd be worth it," he rasped. Deftly he undid the quilt from about his hips, fixing it around her so that it cocooned them both.

He lifted her up, then placed his large hands under her buttocks, and she helped to evenly distribute her weight by clasping his neck and wrapping her legs around him.

Not only had Virginia never made love on a rooftop in the rain, she'd never made love in anything other than a horizontal position. It quickly became apparent to her that such was not the case with Joe Dillon. He handled it masterfully—quite literally holding her in the palms of his hands and controlling the tempo of their ardor.

Lusty passion in the gusting wind and pelting rain was another unforgettable experience—one she was sure she would take to her grave....

It was a wet-headed but thoroughly satisfied woman who sneaked past the dozing landlady and soundlessly let herself out of the brownstone sometime later. Though the Southern gentleman she'd left upstairs was the most exhausted he'd ever been, he lay in his bed with a broad smile plastered on his face.

At the click of the door, Mrs. Tuddy's eyes blinked open. It took her a few moments to clear her foggy head. After a bit she got up from her worn mohair chair, stretched her stiff bones and pulled back the curtain to take a peek at what was happening outside. The street was empty. Everybody was staying in out of the rain.

"Hmmph, days like these are good for only three things," she muttered, releasing the dusty curtain and reaching for the cigarette pack she carried in the pocket of her polka-dot housecoat. "Nappin', snackin' and . . ." She stuck an unfiltered Camel between her cracked lips, lit up and then shook her head amusedly. "Too damn old to engage in the other possibility. Memories will have to do you," she told herself. "Besides, at this stage of your life, a slice of angel food cake is almost as good."

CHAPTER FOURTEEN

CLAUDIA SHAPELL'S intimate little affair later that evening was only cozy in the sense that she cozied up to Joe Dillon the entire time. There were at least forty or fifty people on hand and the hostess was intent on showing off her invaluable asset—the Don Sebastian man. She took him by the arm to make introductions and stayed permanently attached to him throughout the livelong night. Outwardly he was polite and pleasant; inwardly he was fit to be tied.

For the most part, Virginia kept her distance, though there was a moment or two when she was strongly tempted to wrench Joe Dillon free from Claudia's clutches. Not only was the other woman half hanging out of her gold lamé ensemble, she was openly hanging all over J.D. Virginia caught the inviting looks she was giving him on the sly. She was treating him like her private possession and it made Virginia furious. Having to watch Claudia Shapell make subtle moves on the man who'd only hours ago made love to her was awful. She was miserable and jealous.

Joe Dillon looked just plain miserable.

Something had to be done. She knew his pride couldn't take much more and she wasn't too sure about her own. Frantically her mind searched for a way to diffuse the situation. Half a glass of champagne later, a solution struck her. She'd push up the promotion tour! It would take some hurried phone calls and a shuffling of dates, but nothing too terribly complicated. Rita would gladly put in the overtime to eliminate the problem of the stalking she-wolf.

During a rare moment when Claudia was cornered by a talkative guest and Joe Dillon was on his own at the buffet table, Virginia sidled over to him. She spoke in a low voice while pretending to contemplate the lavish spread. "I'm leaving in a few minutes. As soon as you can, make your excuses and meet me up at the top of the World Trade Center for a nightcap." Her lips extracted the roll of smoked salmon from a toothpick, then curved into a phony smile as Claudia approached them.

"You aren't mingling much, Virginia. You really should make the effort. There are several good business contacts on hand here tonight." Claudia actually attempted to feed Joe Dillon from her crystal plate. The idea of her spoon-feeding him beluga caviar made Virginia's stomach turn.

It had the same effect on J.D. He turned up his nose at the gray goo Claudia stuck in his face. "I'll pass on the fish eggs, if it's all the same to you."

"It's really very good. Try it at least," she insisted.

Virginia came to his rescue by distracting Claudia for a moment. "I hope you don't think me rude but I have a terrible headache," she lied. "I'm afraid I'm going to have to call it an evening."

"I understand completely." The hostess didn't seem at all upset by her announcement of an early departure. "I'm glad you could come on such short notice." She offered Virginia a condescending smile, then turned back toward Joe Dillon, once again looping her arm through his and leading him away into the thick of the party.

Virginia hated the whole scene. She wasn't impressed with Claudia Shapell's swank midtown co-op or the assortment of pseudosophisticates who'd gathered therein. They were treating Joe Dillon as an amusing novelty. And Claudia was by far the worst of them. By the time Virginia arrived in the lobby and requested the doorman to hail her a cab, her worry about Joe Dillon's future welfare had reached near-panicky proportions.

By the time he arrived in the bar atop the World Trade Center, she'd spent two wretched hours stewing over the worsening situation.

"How did you get free?"

"It wasn't easy." He downed the cognac as if it were snakebite serum. "I told her I had a bad case of jet lag."

Virginia sighed and then signaled the bartender for a refill. "I'm going to push up the promotion tour. I know you're exhausted from the Argentine shoots but it's the only thing I can think of to counteract her putting the moves on you. You'll do the radio spot and then catch a plane out of New York."

Joe Dillon said nothing until the bartender had served them and was busily occupied at the opposite end of the bar. "What good is that going to do?"

"It'll temporarily remove you from harm's way. She isn't likely to hopscotch across the country after you."

J.D. snorted and sampled the cognac again. "The hell she won't. She traveled to South America. What's to stop her from coming to Cincinnati or Miami?"

He was right, of course, but Virginia was in no mood to listen to logic. "I can cross her up by giving her a dummy schedule with juggled dates and the wrong sequence of cities. I'll also keep close tabs on her. If I think she's figured it out and is making plans to show up, I'll give you some forewarning and we'll keep you a jump ahead of her." She thought the strategy was sound.

J.D. wasn't as sure. "Even if we manage to outfox her, it'll only delay things awhile. Sooner or later she's going to quit pussyfootin' around and tell me exactly what she has in mind. Then what?"

"We'll deal with that when it becomes necessary," she hedged.

"When it becomes necessary," he parroted, shaking his head. "You're talking all around it, Ginny darlin'. The 'it' of it is me ending up in the sack with her. The 'when' of it is too damn close for comfort.

"Crudely put but probably accurate," she said, taking a sip of the cognac and grimacing at its burn as it slid down her throat.

"No probably about it," he replied flatly. "Like the saying goes, pretty soon she's going to make me an offer I can't refuse. You saw for yourself tonight. Things are coming to a head."

"I know it isn't easy for you, J.D. It's hard for me, too. I'm jealous as hell. But I have to try to set aside my personal feelings and do what I can to keep a lid on things until the campaign is solidly under way. Once Sebastian Designs has a firm grasp on the market share, we won't be confronted with as strong an opposition to your being replaced as we might otherwise encounter. It's a lot more likely that you'll be released from under contract without having to weather a nasty legal battle." She slanted a circumspect look at him to see if he was buying her theory.

His face was unreadable as he turned to gaze out the plate glass window at the city lights. "And everybody comes away happy, huh?"

There was a definite trace of cynicism in his tone. "Hopefully," she answered gaugingly.

"Yeah, well, maybe so, Ginny darlin'—" he shrugged and drained the snifter of the cognac "—but I've got my doubts."

"Why are you being such a pessimist?" She turned, too, and looked out at the highest view of New York.

"Because Claudia Shapell is nobody's fool. She knows she has me over a barrel, the same as she knows how much this account means to you. She'll play us against each other to get what she wants." He caught her chin between his thumb and forefinger and gently guided her eyes to his. "And if I still refuse to play house, it's a certainty one or both of us will get dumped. She'll see to it that we start mistrusting each other. Women like her are real good at fingering people's weaknesses and giving 'em a sharp poke when it'll hurt the most."

"What are you saying? It sounds to me as if you're afraid the feelings we have for each other aren't strong enough to bear the strain ahead."

"That's about the size of it," was his frank reply. "Hell, girl, yesterday I didn't even figure on us having a future together. I thought I was wasting my breath trying to convince you to give me a chance. We're making progress toward understanding what makes each other tick, but I'm not fool enough to believe we've struck the sort of bond it'd take to withstand Claudia Shapell's tugging at us from opposite ends."

He smoothed his thumb across her bottom lip. For the first time, she noticed the purplish half circles beneath his eyes. He looked tired, but handsome, nonetheless.

"Blind trust takes time—time we haven't got. There's more than mere miles separating us, Ginny darlin'. We're facing doubts—our own. Suppose you heard rumors to the effect that I'd actually gone through with bedding her on the road? What's the first thing you'd conclude?"

"I don't know." She purposely evaded the question.

"I do," he persisted. "You'd judge me in terms of your ex-husband. You'd assume the worst of me—figure I'd chosen my own self-interests over yours. You wouldn't even consider the fact that I might have prostituted myself for you. The thought wouldn't occur to you that maybe Claudia used you as leverage—that somehow she discovered how much you meant to me and traded on the fact by convincing me that you'd be the one to suffer the most if I refused her."

"For God's sake, Joe Dillon," she said scoffingly. "You're letting your imagination run wild. I really don't think she'd go to such lengths. You're giving her too much credit."

He grinned resignedly. "I've had more personal contact with her than you. I've got a hunch she'll do most anything if it suits her purposes."

"If you're trying to make me more shaky than I already am, you're succeeding. I need reassurances, J.D. Please tell me you won't do anything rash. Promise me you'll keep a cool head on the tour. I can work out a solution, but I've got to have time in which to do it."

She was trying desperately to blank out what she did not want to acknowledge—the fact that time was growing short and the fragile threads of their newly formed bond could easily come unwound, given the pressure Claudia Shapell might choose to exert in the near future.

J.D. tried once more to make her understand. He approached the problem from a different angle. "Put the shoe on the other foot. Pretend you're me in love with an adorable workaholic who's about to get what she's always wanted—a much-deserved partnership. You have to wonder where you stand in comparison to what has been the lady's sole desire. Suppose Claudia forces her to make a choice? Makes it clear to her that she can kiss any chance of a partnership goodbye if she sides with the complaints of contract labor? Or what if the important client suggests that it's in the creative director's best interest to deliver everything the client expects from the campaign, including making available the sexual services of a certain party on the payroll? She could insist that the ad boss use whatever influence she has over the backward Johnny Reb to convince him to go along."

"Do you really believe I would do such a thing?" She found it incredulous that he would question her motives.

"I'm only trying to get you to take into account the mind tricks Claudia Shapell can use against us. All she has to do is plant the seeds of doubt and then sit back and let us do the dirty work for her." He cupped her cheek in his work-toughened palm. "We each know what's in our own heart but we haven't the benefit of knowing for certain what's in the other's." His hand slid through her silky hair, then he eased her lips to his and brushed them with a testing kiss. "The thought of being separated from you makes me ache," he murmured. "But the fear of the damage our doubt can do twists like a knife in my gut. I don't want to lose you, Ginny darlin'. And I'm scared to death I might."

"You won't," she promised him, forgetting about the public surroundings and recklessly kissing him in full view of the packed bar. "I love you, Joe Dillon," she admitted when finally drawing back from the heat of the blazing kiss. "There, I've said it. Now you know what's in my heart."

He gave her an easy smile. A glimmer of amusement shone in his dark eyes. "You say it like someone declaring their intentions to run for Congress. You're not courting public favor, girl. You don't have to prove anything to me. Love isn't something that has to be said aloud. When it's there and it's right between two people, nothing needs to be put into words. You just know it's so."

"You don't believe me?" She was shocked by his reaction. "What will it take to convince you?"

"Time, Ginny darlin'. Time to grow close. Time to share. Time to be together like a man and woman should."

Her chin lifted stubbornly. "As I recall, it was you who professed to have fallen in love with me almost on sight. You claimed it was something a person instinctively knew."

"Yes, ma'am, I said that," he owned up. "And it was true to an extent. What I was referring to was the kind of love that starts things off. I knew right away that you were a woman I could grow to love more and more. What I'm talking about now is the deep, abiding love that lasts till death us do part. I'm talking marriage and children and a lifetime of commitment. Can you honestly tell me you're in a same frame of mind?''

The question startled her. *Marriage*—she'd tried it once and wasn't really good at it. *Children*—she'd entertained the idea of children a few isolated times in her life but not very seriously and certainly not lately. *Commitment*—funny, but at the mention of the word, she immediately thought of her work.

Honestly? No. She shook her head accordingly. She was beginning to feel a bit desperate about losing him and it showed.

He could see she was wrestling with the truth and her anxiousness over what the future held. "It's okay," he reassured her. "We're just at different places in our hearts and lives."

"You're way ahead of me. Will you wait to see if I can catch up?" She knew it was a lot to ask.

He did not answer her at first. Instead he reached into his coat pocket and withdrew a wide gold cuff bracelet. "It's a present I brought back from Argentina for you. I got so bamfoozled with what went on this afternoon I forgot to give it to you. Read the inscription inside."

She read it aloud. "To every thing there is a season, and a time to every purpose under the heaven."

"So long as there's hope, I'll wait for you, Ginny darlin'," he vowed softly.

Emotion welled in her throat as he took the bracelet from her trembling fingers and slipped it on her wrist.

"Stay with me tonight, Joe Dillon."

He wondered if he could ever refuse anything she asked of him.

CHAPTER FIFTEEN

JOE DILLON SAT in the broadcast booth of WKRA-FM, a set of earphones on his head and a microphone suspended in front of his face. He'd been assured by the radio station's manager that the interview would run only about twenty minutes and it would be "a piece of cake."

The fellow in the booth beside him was a popular local personality. His name was Guy Greco and he was king of the morning airwaves. He kept commuters and homebodies informed and entertained with a mélange of pop tunes, news, witty commentary, cash giveaways and general zaniness from 6 to 10 a.m., Monday through Friday, and he was a pro at eliciting the best and the worst responses from guests and callers alike. His show was appropriately called "Jabbin' and Jammin'" and was famous for "Take Your Best Jab," a segment where people could sound off about whatever or whomever irked them. Sometimes the guest interviewee was the target of the verbal stoning. Having little knowledge of the program's format—neither Claudia nor Virginia had wanted to scare him off— Joe Dillon hadn't any idea what he was letting himself in for.

"Here we go." The radio announcer took a swig from his coffee mug, swallowed quickly and then introduced Joe Dillon to the listening audience. "Well, so much for Madonna's new hit. It's a hot sound but I've got a real live hot body sitting in our studio and eager to talk to all those panting women who've been responsible for making the Sebastian look the newest fad. Don Johnson, take a hike! Jerry Lee Lewis, move over! It's a new generation. It's goodness, gracious, great *buns* of fire! Yes, like I promised, he's here, ladies. It's your chance to call in and talk to Dillon Mahue, the Don Sebastian man. But before I go to the phones, I want to chat with Dillon a bit and find out what it feels like to suddenly be singled out as one of the ten sexiest men in America today. And that's before the Don Sebastian line of clothing is even formally launched in the U.S. I guess what I really want to know is, why you and why not me?" he asked, chuckling.

J.D. was caught unprepared. He'd thought they were going to discuss the enthusiasm about the jeans, not his personal appeal. "I, uh, think it's the jeans the women are excited about," he stammered. "Mine just happens to be the body they're going to see in 'em."

Guy Greco wasn't about to let him off the hook so easily. "Designer jeans aren't what's turning women on, Dillon. Americans haven't even seen the ads yet. The phone lines are jammed because they're interested in you, thanks to all that savvy publicity the Don Sebastian people have been doing. Tell us something about yourself."

J.D. was really uncomfortable with the notion of giving particulars about himself. "Well, I'm a pretty ordinary person. Nothing special, really."

"I detect a Rhett Butler drawl." The radio announcer pounced on his accent.

"I come from Mississippi. A place called Cotton-mouth," J.D. answered.

"Never heard of it."

"Most folks haven't."

"So how did a Southern gent from a place no-body's heard of end up being the image bearer for an exclusive designer line? Was it a matter of being in the right place at the right time or what?" Guy asked, delving deeper.

"Yeah, I suppose you could say that. I was lucky," was J.D.'s abbreviated reply.

This character wasn't volunteering anything, Greco decided. He knew he'd better be inventive and draw him out or else the interview was going to bomb, and bomb big. "You seem genuinely surprised by the stir you've caused."

"I never expected it, and to be honest, I'm not real comfortable with all the hoopla yet. I'm glad there's so much excitement about the Sebastian look, but I'm not convinced it has anything to do with me person-ally."

Guy Greco gave up and went to the phones. "Talk to me, New York. You got something to say to the Don Sebastian man?"

"I sure do," an excited female voice on the other end responded. "Hi, Dillon," she greeted him.

"Hi there," he said warmly.

"I just wanted to tell you I think you're great look-ing and it's really a kick to hear your voice. I love your accent. It's sexy. Are you?"

Joe Dillon was taken back by the lady caller's bold-ness. "I don't know. It's not something a person can judge for themselves."

"You name the time and place and I'd be more than happy to give you an outside opinion. My name is Jennifer Kohl—K-O-H-L—and I'm in the phone book. Feel free to call *any*time."

It sounded like a serious offer. "Thanks. I'll keep it in mind," was his tactful reply.

"K-O-H-L," Guy Greco repeated. "I'm jotting it down, along with a a hundred or so other lecherous males in the greater New York area. Stay in touch, Jennifer. Call *any*time." He clicked to another call. "Talk to me, New York."

"Oh my God! I got through," a young woman squealed. "Oh, oh, can you hear me, Dillon?"

"They can probably hear you in New Jersey, sweetheart," Guy broke in. "I'm no doctor but it sounds as if you're hyperventilating. You want to take a second to breathe into a paper bag? We'll wait."

She giggled and went right on gasping and squealing. "He's so radical. I'm wild about him. Totally. I gotta tell him. Dillon, are you there?"

"I'm here," J.D. assured her.

"Oh my God! It's you. Oh my God!" She spoke a Valley Girl dialect with a Bronx accent. "I was at the airport yesterday. I saw you get into a limo. Like, you're even more gorgeous in person. I wanted an autograph from you but you were gone before I could get to you. Can I have one? Please, please, please," she begged him.

Luckily the station manager had prepared him for the inevitable autograph requests and had rehearsed him as to how to respond. "Sure. Leave your name and address with the station and I'll see to it that you get one," he promised her.

"I gotta ask something else," she yelped.

"Sure," Joe Dillon acquiesced.

"Are you, like, serious with anybody? There was a woman with you at the airport and it freaked me out. You can't be in a heavy romance. I'll die. Please say no."

J.D. paused.

Guy Greco immediately picked up the slack. "A mystery woman at the airport, eh? Hey, there may be hope for the rest of we hunks if you're unavailable goods. Please say yes," he kidded him.

J.D.'s decision to keep his personal life private had nothing to do with his image and everything to do with protecting Ginny's anonymity. "The lady was simply giving me a lift from the airport." Which was true. He did not elaborate.

Greco let the topic drop and picked up another call. "Talk to me, New York."

"Good morning, Guy. I feel so silly making this call. I'm a grandmother and haven't swooned over a man since Frank Sinatra. I had to tell your handsome young guest that my daughters and granddaughters think he's the berries and I must admit that my blood pressure rises every time I see his ads. I wondered if he has any plans to do something else in the future? How about TV or the movies?"

"How about it, Dillon?" Guy Greco asked him. "Do you want to be in the movies?"

"I'm no actor. What you see is pretty much what you get. I don't think there's much chance of me going Hollywood."

"Lots do it. Women everywhere fantasize about rubbing bodies with you. Maybe you're the next craze just waiting to happen," Greco suggested.

J.D. grinned lazily. "I can't sing, can't dance and can't act. By accident I fell in with some people who thought I wore a pair of jeans well. I slip 'em on like every other guy, but I get paid to do it. That's about it."

Guy Greco was wearing down—running out of provocative questions and patience. He went to the phone lines again. "Talk to me, New York."

"Yeah, Guy. I wanna take a jab at Mr. Buns," a gruff male voice said.

Guy Greco's spirits perked at the prospect of the program livening up. "Go ahead. Take your best jab," he prompted.

"Yeah, well, I just wanna say that I'm sick of hearing all these women having orgasms over this jerk. It really bugs me, the way they always gotta be making over some fancy schmancy schmuck like him and forgetting about us guys who bring the bacon home. My old lady spent a whole damn day and a chunk of my hard-earned money over at Bloomies last week on sissy jeans I wouldn't put on my butt. And you know why?" The irate caller did not pause for a reply. "So's she could drool over a life-size cardboard display of that creep. Tell me if that ain't crazy!"

"That's life, Mac." Guy Greco purposely egged on the agitated caller. "He gets the broads and you get the shaft."

What Joe Dillon was getting was the drift of how Guy Greco operated. He was like a pesky tick—a parasite that attached itself to a subject, then sucked it for all it was worth. J.D. waited for an opportune moment to jump in.

"Pretty boys like him make it hard for regular Joes like me. We ain't got time to buff our nails and style our hair just so. We're too busy busting our ass trying to pay for the bills our wives and girlfriends run up because they think we'll look better to 'em if we dress like him. Women don't appreciate what they got. They believe those ads being crammed down their throats. They want clones of his type and they treat the rest of us like we were lower than whale dung. Well, I got a flash for these gullible dames. They better start getting breathless over their own men 'steada working themselves into a frenzy over a cardboard Romeo like him. Their husbands and boyfriends are fed up with their drooling and their spending. As for Li'l Abner there, tell him to do us a big favor and take his sweet cheeks back to Dogpatch or wherever the hell he came from and get a real job.''

J.D. wasn't about to take any more of the man's abuse, but just as he started to speak up, Guy Greco cut him off.

"We got the message, pal. Thanks for calling in. Gee! We're all out of time. I know you're on a tight schedule, Dillon. I really appreciate your coming on 'Jabbin' and Jammin'' today and I wish you much success in the future. That's it for this segment but stay tuned, New York, because we're going to be giving away a thousand dollars—yesirree, that's right, a modest grand—to some lucky person whose birthday is the same date as the one I'll be announcing over the air in just a few short minutes. It could be you! Music, madness and *money*, it's all here on WKRA—the station *everyone* is listening to. But first, a public service announcement.''

He went to a commercial, pulling off the headset and smoothing back the five or six stray wisps of hair sprouting from the top of his bald head. "We got off to a slow start but generally I think it went pretty well," he remarked, sticking out his hand as J.D. stood up.

"You know what I think, Mr. Greco?" J.D. asked calmly.

"No, what?" he bit out.

"I think you're one of those people who like to cause a stink 'cause you get off on the aroma. You could've stopped that guy anytime, but instead you pushed his buttons to boost your ratings. Lower than whale dung doesn't even begin to describe how I view you." Joe Dillon stormed from the broadcasting booth, barreling through the door with such momentum that it hit the wall behind it and sprang back with repeated bangs.

The station manager hurried to catch up to him. "Mr. Mahue, hold on a sec, will you?" she huffed.

He stopped short and turned to glower at her.

"I'm sorry about the interview ending on such a sour note, but the Guy Greco show is an open format and—"

"As far as I'm concerned it was a real piece of work, not a piece of cake, ma'am." His dark eyes flashed.

The station manager had the decency to blush. "I truly am sorry. I'm sure you found the last caller offensive and I don't blame you. I stopped you before you left the building for two reasons, Mr. Mahue. To offer my apologies and to warn you about the crowd that has gathered out front of the station. You might want to take the service elevator to the basement garage and leave the back way."

The indignation melted from J.D.'s face and was replaced by a look of puzzlement. "What crowd? And what's it got to do with me?"

"Fans, Mr. Mahue. They've collected on the sidewalk and street, hoping to get a glimpse of you or an autograph as you leave the building. Surely you've been confronted with the situation before...." It was obvious from his expression that the situation, as she had so delicately put it, was a new experience for him.

"Not really," he admitted. "So what do I do now?"

"Where is your limo and driver?" she asked.

For the first time he grinned. "I don't travel in such high style. I took a cab over."

"You're kidding!" She found the notion incredible.

"No, ma'am," he replied, his face mirroring his earnestness.

"Perhaps you should consider changing your habits, Mr. Mahue. Emergency exits are an inevitable consequence of being in the spotlight. It's a little difficult to avoid utter chaos when you have to flag down a taxi in the midst of being swarmed by enthusiastic fans. Had I known you were without a limo, I'd have sent one for you. In any case, I'll make arrangements for a car and driver to come to the basement garage and return you home. It'll be my way of making amends. It's the least I can do."

J.D. thought it was a gracious gesture on her part. "I appreciate it."

"I'll just go make the call. The service elevator is all the way down this hall and to your right. It shouldn't be long before the car and driver arrive."

"Thanks," he bade her, moving accordingly with her directions and going to wait in the dank underground garage for a getaway car. He was too dazed to really grasp the sudden change in his life. Everything was moving too quickly. He was the same person, but nothing else was the same as when he'd left for Argentina. He needed quiet time and private space in order to reflect on the traumatic turn of events and collect himself.

When the car picked him up, he leaned back against the plush seat with a disheartened sigh. From behind the tinted windows, he passively observed the mob scene in front of the besieged building. Women in a variety of sizes, shapes and colors were assembled outside of the radio station, clamoring for the Don Sebastian man. They covered almost a city block and spilled out into the street. Police officers had been called to the disturbance and were in the process of trying to disperse the crowd.

"We want Dillon! We want Dillon! We want Dillon!" The chanting penetrated the interior of the supposedly soundproof limo. When they spied the sleek black sedan moving past them, the fans surged onto the street, stopping traffic as they held out pieces of paper for his autograph, blew him kisses and screamed proposals of every sort—from marriage to simply having sex, dinner or his child. It was madness. Wholesale insanity. Nuts!

He closed his glazed eyes, hoping the driver was good at what he did and would be able to maneuver the car through the tangle of people and traffic.

He kept telling himself it wasn't him the women were running after and shouting for. He was not the person they thought he was. His name wasn't Dillon Mahue. He was not one of the ten sexiest men in America today. He was just plain old J.D. from a place nobody ever heard of. Nothing special. Just a troubled guy who wanted out of the crazy mess he found himself in.

LATER THAT DAY, between packing and before he caught a plane out of New York, J.D. wrote a letter to his family back in Cottonmouth.

Dear Ma,

Sorry it's been so long between letters. I'm back from Argentina but getting ready to go on the road again. A promotional tour of some sort. I'm not sure what it's all about or what's expected of me, but I guess I'll find out soon enough.

I got your letter about a week ago. I was glad to hear everyone's doing fine. You asked about Cousin Mason. I never could track him down, but I've got a sneaking suspicion that I'll be hearing from him real soon because he's bound to be hearing of me since my picture is in the magazines and on television now.

It's crazy, Ma. Everybody's making a fuss over me. I don't know what I expected it to be like but I can tell you for sure I don't care much for it. I think I made a big mistake getting involved in the modeling business. It's too fast a life for me. But I've got to see it out for a while longer because of the reason I told you about earlier.

Speaking of which, things are moving pretty darn quickly in that area of my life, too. When I returned from South America, I found a different woman from the one I left. She says she did a lot of thinking about things while I was away and came to the conclusion that she loves me. God! I hope so, Ma, 'cause more than anything I want to marry this woman and spend the rest of my days with her. She's not ready for such a big step yet but maybe one day she'll have a change of heart about that, too. You'll like her, Ma. She's a special lady, same as you.

Don't worry so much about me. You raised us boys to be self-reliant and to use the good sense God gave us. I won't be swayed by the money or the fame. I know there are more important things to revere. I'm sending along a little money for the family. Buy yourself something real nice, Ma, and use the rest for whatever other needs y'all may have. I know you don't like taking it, but I got plenty and want to share it.

Give my best to the folks at home. I miss all of them, but especially you, Ma. Stay well and happy. I'll be in touch.

All my love, J.D.

He enclosed a cashier's check for ten thousand dollars, slipped the letter inside an envelope, addressed and sealed it, then put it in his pocket to mail on the way to the airport.

As he finished packing, his mind drifted from one thing to another. He imagined his mother's face when she read the amount of the check. She'd be stunned, then upset, but finally accepting of the gift. She'd know he wasn't trying to flaunt his success and that the money was meant as an expression of love. The modeling business he'd complained about did have one compensating feature—it afforded him an opportunity to subsidize those who were near and dear to him. Ginny was right about that much. She'd also warned him from the very beginning about the pres-

sures he'd encounter in the limelight. She hadn't min-
imized the impact it would have on his future privacy.
It was he who hadn't realized how much or how suddenly things would change.

He threw a few more pairs of socks into the suit-
case, zipped closed the lid and transferred the two
pieces of luggage from the bed to the door. That done,
he sat back down on the lumpy mattress, resting his
elbows on his knees and staring between his legs at the
scuff marks on the hardwood floor.

He was recalling a passage in a letter he'd received
from his mother while in Argentina—the part where
she'd responded to his telling her about Ginny and his
strong feelings for her.

> ...and though she sounds like a lovely person,
> there is something I feel obliged to point out to
> you. Once before you cared very much for a
> woman who was not of our kind. I'm not saying
> it's the same with your Ginny—only that there's
> a certain similarity. Be sure what attracts you to
> her, J.D. Be sure it is not the memory of a for-
> mer love—a wish to relive it, only with a differ-
> ent ending....

His mother hadn't expressed a sentiment that he,
himself, had not considered. He'd questioned his motives over and over again in Argentina, wondering why
he continued to relentlessly pursue Ginny when she'd
given little indication of any serious interest in him. In
fact, he'd asked himself over and over why he'd been
so strongly attracted to her in the first place. Was it the
memory of Ashley subconsciously at work inside of
him? Did she still haunt him? Was it her he saw in

Ginny? The questions still nagged at him. He shut his eyes and tried to be brutally honest as he examined his feelings.

And, as always, he came to the conclusion that he wasn't simply trying to relive a past romance. Yes, there was a similarity between the two women as far as general physical appearance and social standing, but their inner characters were vastly different. One had been spoiled and frivolous. He had been too infatuated as a starry-eyed youth to notice her flaws. The other was serious and strong-minded, but beneath the polished veneer she was sweet and shy, and he loved her truly and deeply as only a man who had grown sure of himself could.

He'd gotten it all straight in his head in Argentina. He knew he wanted Ginny for all the right reasons. He just wasn't sure if she wanted him. Her change of heart after his return came as a shock. Now he was having to deal with yet another jolt—the overwhelming reaction to the ads that had come out during his absence and transformed him into an overnight sex symbol.

His eyes open now, he webbed his fingers through his hair and just sat there in the late afternoon's marmalade light, trying to let it all soak in. He longed for the peacefulness he had known before becoming the Don Sebastian man. He longed to walk away from the glitz and notoriety and lead a simple man's life. But how could he do that and still remain loyal to the woman he loved?

The answer was obvious. He couldn't. Not yet. He had to go through with the tour.

He got up from the bed, picked up his bags and headed for the future, taking his worries with him like so much extra baggage. When, dammit, when would he be able to call it quits?

CHAPTER SIXTEEN

RITA AND VIRGINIA WORKED feverishly through the next day to set up a revised promotional tour schedule. Virginia hated letting Joe Dillon go, but it was a sacrifice she felt she had to make for his sake.

By noon the following day, Rita informed her that Claudia Shapell was holding on line one to speak with her. The agitated client wasted no time getting to the point. Virginia had barely said hello when Claudia inquired as to Joe Dillon's whereabouts.

"There's been a change in plans," Virginia informed her matter-of-factly. "We had to step up the tour. Dillon left last night to fulfill the scheduled appearances." Which was half a lie. The new arrangements did not require Joe Dillon to arrive at the first stopover until midweek. But Virginia hadn't wanted to take any chances.

"I'm just surprised by the rescheduling. Why wasn't I told?" Claudia demanded.

"I thought you were aware of the changes. I know you and Dillon speak often and I just assumed he had relayed the information to you." Virginia thought she sounded reasonably convincing.

"Perhaps I missed his call." Don Sebastian's partner was unsuccessful in masking her irritation.

"I could send a copy of the revised schedule over to your offices if you'd like," Virginia offered.

"Yes, do that. I want to be kept abreast of things," was the staccato reply.

"Certainly. You'll have it by the end of the day. Is there any other aspect of the campaign you'd care to discuss?" Virginia asked innocently.

"No, not at present. Good day, Ms Vandivere." The connection was abruptly severed.

Virginia smiled smugly. "And a good day to you, too." She hummed to herself as she replaced the receiver.

She buzzed for Rita to come into the office.

Her assistant did so immediately, more out of curiosity than conscientiousness. "She ees *muy* upset. What a shame," she said dryly, unable to hold back a grin.

"Yes, isn't it." Virginia savored the thought of Claudia Shapell's frustration. "I promised her a copy of the revised schedule by the end of the day. We have to work fast and be clever about it. We need to make small changes, just enough to mix her up but nothing too obvious or she may catch on to what we're doing."

"Don worry. We'll fudge it good. The most she will suspect ees that things got transposed in the rush of reprocessing." Rita beamed at the prospect of sending the woman off on a wild-goose chase.

"You're really enjoying yourself, aren't you?" Virginia sank into her chair, slipped off her heels and propped her stockinged feet on the desk. It was an unladylike thing to do but she was too pooped to care.

"Ees the pan calling the pot black," Rita returned, plopping into a chair herself.

"You mean the pot calling the kettle black," Virginia corrected her.

"Whatever." Rita dismissed her boss's penchant for exactness with a flick of a wrist. "I theenk maybe ees more than just tricking the witch that makes you all smiles today. Did we have a good time last night?" She pried without hesitation.

Virginia's grin broadened. "We had a wonderful night."

Rita nodded. Nothing more needed to be said on the subject.

"By the way—" Virginia recalled a promise she'd made to Joe Dillon "—I intend to take a few days off. I'll be out of the office from midweek until the following Monday."

"Good. Ees long overdue. Ees none of my business but are you maybe planning a trip to Miami?" Rita surmised that she intended to join Joe Dillon.

"I wish," Virginia answered wistfully. "I'm going home to take care of a matter that's also long overdue." Her expression suddenly sobered.

"You are going to speak with your mother about the business with your brother?"

"I'm going to attempt it. Joe Dillon thinks it's a problem I need to address. He told me how he'd drawn the wrong conclusions about why I hadn't written him while he was away in Argentina. He'd assumed the worst, solely because of a hurtful experience he'd suffered in the past. He suggested that I may be guilty of doing the same thing where my mother is concerned. Maybe he's right. I'm too close to the problem to be a good judge."

Rita was more interested in learning about the hurtful episode in Joe Dillon's past. "Some other woman did him dirty?" She fished for facts unashamedly.

"According to him it was a first love sort of thing," Virginia supplied. "She was from a wealthy Vicksburg family, out for a summer fling. They were young and foolish. He fell madly in love with her and he believed she felt the same. When the summer ended and she returned home, he wrote her faithfully. Many letters later, she finally sent a note back to him, saying it was fun but—"

"*Adiós,*" Rita put in.

"You've got the picture. I think he sincerely loved her and he perceived her rejection as a comment on his lack of refinement. He concluded that somehow he wasn't good enough for a woman of her class. When I didn't answer his postcards, he thought my reasons were the same—that I wasn't interested in pursuing a serious relationship with a man from humble roots. He says I look like her. I suppose he began to believe we shared more than eye color," she explained. "Anyway, he thought I might be making a similar mistake by assuming instead of discussing my preconceptions with the only one who can tell me whether or not they're valid. It's worth a shot, I guess." She didn't sound all that sure.

"You should do as Joe Dillon suggests." Rita wholeheartedly concurred with J.D.'s theory. "Go make peace with her. Don worry. I will handle things here."

"You'll know where I am and how to get in touch with me. I want you to call at the slightest inkling that

Shapell has picked up Joe Dillon's tracks.'' Virginia
was worried that she might not have ample time in
which to forewarn him.

"If I have any suspicion, I will call you right away,"
Rita promised, crossing her heart for good measure.

"Well, then, I guess it's settled." She sighed. "I'd
rather be boiled in oil than make this trip."

"Some decisions in life are not easy to make. You
don theenk you will be better off for it, but sometimes the opposite ees true. The hardest part ees not
knowing which to follow—your head or your heart."

"Ain't it the truth!"

INEZ VANDIVERE WAS completely stunned to have her
daughter show up on her doorstep in the middle of a
work week.

"Something's wrong," was the welcoming phrase
that greeted Virginia. "What is it? Aunt Caddie?"

Virginia quickly calmed her fears. "Everything's
fine. Aunt Caddie is well, as far as I know. I just decided to make a spur-of-the-moment visit home."

"Oh," was all her mother said in reply, motioning
for her to step inside. "You're letting the heat out and
the cool air in."

Her enthusiasm was overwhelming. It set the tone
for the remainder of the afternoon. After settling
herself in her old room, Virginia resorted to taking her
customary long walk in the woods behind the house.
It was her way of avoiding the frank talk she was not
yet ready to have with her mother. She wondered why
she was bothering. It wasn't very likely that her
mother would admit her partiality toward Billy. Huh!
That would be the day! Perfect and proper Inez Van-

divere admitting to a flaw in her character! Virginia could not remember a time when her mother had admitted even the slightest possibility that she could have formed a wrong opinion or be at fault.

At the end of her walk, Virginia pitched the stick she'd picked up along the way across the yard. "It's an exercise in futility," she muttered to herself. "But I'm not leaving without speaking my piece."

She felt better at having given herself the pep talk. Not a lot, but a little. She sucked in a deep breath of evening air and proceeded into the kitchen. Dinner was always at six o'clock. She could add precise to the list of definitives that applied to her mother. Perfect, proper and precise.

Inez set a tall glass of chalky liquid at Virginia's usual spot at the table. It looked disgustingly familiar. Just the thought of the grim stuff almost made her gag. Her mother used to insist that she and Billy drink skim milk two out of three meals a day. Once a habit was established by Inez, she never broke tradition. Virginia could decline to drink it, but the skim milk would remain next to her plate until the dishes were cleared. Mentally, she revised the list to include pigheaded as she pulled out a chair and took her place at the table.

The dinner conversation was as bland as the food. No frank talk, only small talk.

"How was the family reunion?" Virginia asked.

"Very nice," her mother answered. "How's the ad campaign going?"

"Really well," Virginia responded. "Pass the butter, please."

"You should drink your skim milk, Virginia. All the fuss being made about cholesterol these days only proves that I was right. Nutrition experts agree that skim milk is much better for a person."

"Maybe. But it's still gross."

"Suit yourself," Inez said between dainty chews of the boiled potatoes with parsley. "But you'll pay one day for those unhealthy dietary habits of yours. Mark my words. If stress doesn't cause you to have a heart attack, you'll suffer a stroke from the volumes of junk food you consume. It's loaded with fat and clogs your arteries and—"

Virginia cut her off abruptly. "I'll risk it, Mother."

Inez concentrated on cutting her grilled chicken breast into bite-size pieces.

Virginia silently revised the list once more. Perfect, proper, precise, pigheaded and pragmatic.

"I happened on some old photographs of you and Billy when I was cleaning out a hall closet a few days ago. I think they were taken that summer we went to Yellowstone. Do you remember the trip?"

It had started—the reminiscing. Virginia wanted to groan. "Mmm," was all she answered.

"Billy must've been thirteen or so. He was at that gangly stage. Would you like a dish of banana pudding?"

"Maybe later. So, has Aunt Caddie been to see you lately?" Virginia did her best to change the subject.

"She was here about three weeks ago. Did I tell you that she has a gentleman friend? He's a dentist. Retired, I think. He takes her to dinner from time to time."

"Really? That's great!" Virginia was excited by the unexpected news.

"What are you getting all worked up about? It's not as if they're having a romance or anything. They just go out to dinner together to break the monotony of eating alone." Inez found it absurd that her spinster sister-in-law was courting at an age when her peers were signing up to collect their social security benefits.

Virginia shoved aside her plate to rest an elbow on the table and put her chin in a palm. "Don't you ever get lonely, Mother?" she dared to ask.

The question took Inez by surprise. "I missed your father at first, but I adjusted. Having to raise two small children on my own kept me occupied. I don't believe in wallowing in self-pity."

Another *P* word. Her mother was also puritanical in her attitudes.

"You're in a strange mood," Inez commented, reaching for Virginia's plate and stacking it on top of her own.

She'd noticed. A breakthrough, at last.

"I get the impression there's something particular on your mind." Inez set the dishes and silverware in the sink, then returned to gather the tablecloth by the four corners and step out onto the porch to shake it out.

Virginia hesitated. Was it a good time to broach the touchy subject of Billy? Maybe she should give it a night. After all, she'd only just arrived. She didn't want to fight with her mother right off the bat. "Actually, there is something I'd like to talk with you about, but it can keep until tomorrow. Why don't you go sit down in the den and I'll clean up?" she offered as her mother came back inside.

"Thank you, dear. It is nearly time for my favorite radio talk show. You know, the one where people call in and give their opinions about topical issues. You wouldn't believe the nervy things people say on the air. Sometimes I get so mad at the sheer stupidity of some of the callers that I'm tempted to call in myself." Having folded and smoothed the tablecloth into a neat rectangle, Inez placed it away in a drawer.

"Why don't you?" Virginia stopped the drain, turned on the spigots and squirted some liquid detergent into the hot water.

"Oh, I couldn't. I'm not a public sort of person. I keep my opinions private."

Funny, Virginia thought sardonically. Inez had no trouble expressing her opinions about how her daughter conducted her life.

"If you're not sure where something goes, just leave it on the counter and I'll put it away later. Last time you did the dishes, I spent an entire week searching for my gravy ladle."

Inez disappeared through the swinging door. A second later Virginia heard her snap on the radio in the den.

"Oh, God! Who am I kidding?" she wondered aloud. Suds slopped everywhere as she took out her frustration on the pottery. "Walking on water would be an easier feat than getting through to her."

Once the dishes were done, Virginia bade her mother good-night and went upstairs to her room. It took her a while to fall asleep, mostly because she was disgusted with herself for falling into the same old pattern of retreating. "Ginny the Turtle," she mumbled, wadding the pillow beneath her head and squirming uncomfortably. "Tomorrow I do it, no matter what."

THE CONFRONTATION between mother and daughter happened the next evening. Virginia was waiting for an opening as they sat together in the den. There was another *P* word that applied to Inez—one that provided an excuse for Virginia to start World War Three. Predictable. Her mother could not resist dragging out the family album so that she could converse about her dead son.

Virginia said nothing for a bit as Inez flipped through the pages of photographs, pointing out small details and injecting trivia about Billy. When she could stand no more, she reached over, took the album out of her mother's hands and set it aside.

"What are you doing? I wasn't through looking." Inez was perplexed by her daughter's behavior.

"Did it ever occur to you, Mother, that you treat your two children in opposite ways?" Virginia fought to keep her temper in check and her tone civil.

"I haven't the foggiest idea what you mean." Inez regarded her with amazement. Virginia's temperamental outbursts were getting worse lately. It was probably the stress of her work, Inez reasoned. Perhaps she should suggest to her daughter that she investigate those transcendental meditation seminars discussed on the radio program the other night.

"What I mean, Mother, is that you treat Billy as if he were still alive and me as if I don't exist." There, she'd done it—finally said aloud what she'd been thinking for years!

Her mother instantly grew rigid. "That's a horrible thing to say to me. Besides which, it's totally untrue. What has gotten into you?"

"It is true." Virginia dared to differ. "You're obsessed with Billy. He's all you think about, speak about. He's the center of your life." She came to her feet and began to walk around the den, taking inventory of the scattered memorabilia. "Look around. You've turned the place into a shrine. Billy's diplomas, Billy's ribbons, Billy's portrait, Billy's trophies, Billy's bronzed baby shoes, Billy's Mother's Day card, team football pictures, scrapbooks. You even have a second-grade crayon drawing he made for you in a frame on the wall." She turned and faced her mother. "Where are my things, Mother? I won awards. I gave you Mother's Day cards. I made you crayon drawings. Anyone would think you only had one child." Having opened the floodgates, she could not stop the dammed-up emotion from rushing forth.

Inez was appalled to hear such bitterness spill from her daughter. Her mouth literally fell open. "That's utter nonsense," she sputtered. "You know perfectly well why I keep Billy's things about. It's all I have left of him. You, I can see and touch and communicate with. He's gone from me forever. I cannot believe you'd be so insensitive and petty." Inez's chin trembled and she gave her daughter an icy look.

Her mother's righteous indignation only made Virginia angrier. "It was no different when Billy was alive. He was the golden child—the one you paid attention to—the one you bragged about. Virginia?

Virginia who? You went through the motherly motions, but mostly I was invisible to you. Billy could get away with murder, but you were always critical of me. Why was that, Mother?'' she exploded.

"You're out of control, Virginia. I don't know what has gotten you in such a state but I certainly do not intend to sit here and listen to any more of your jealous rantings. I showed no partiality with my children. Never!'' was her emphatic reply as she got up from the sofa and headed for the stairs.

Something snapped inside of Virginia. She bolted past her mother, positioned herself at the bottom of the staircase and spread her arms to block Inez's way.

"You're right. But then, you're always right, aren't you? I am jealous—jealous as hell of Billy.'' She deliberately antagonized her mother.

Inez sucked in her breath. "Have you no respect for anyone? Why bring all this up now? I think it is unconscionable of you to try and pick a quarrel with the dead.''

"I just don't understand. What did I do wrong? Or maybe a better question is what did Billy do right? Did he know some magic formula to make himself shine in your eyes? Or was it more a matter of a secret chemistry between the two of you?'' Virginia knew she was pushing it, but she'd already gone way past the point of no return. Besides, she was sick of retreating. She actually wanted an all-out confrontation.

"What are you suggesting?'' Her mother's face blanched and she stepped back, aghast.

"I'm not implying anything kinky, Mother. But there was something special between you two. You favored him for some reason. Why?'' Virginia persisted.

Confusion clouded Inez's eyes. "What is it you want me to say? It wasn't a matter of my favoring Billy. It was just that we got along better than you and I did. That I won't deny. Maybe it had something to do with his being more like me. Our natures were similar. You were always so serious and introverted."

"Wrong, Mother," Virginia snapped. "You may have convinced yourself that was the reason but it's simply not true. Billy wasn't like you at all. He was passionate and fun loving, disorganized and reckless. All the things you aren't. I was the one most like you. Miss Good-Goody, nose-to-the-grindstone Virginia. Heiress to her mother's perfect, proper, precise, pigheaded, pragmatic, predictably passive genes." Suddenly, what she was saying registered. She'd accidentally stumbled onto a hidden truth. The proof was written all over her mother's face. "That's it, isn't it?" she pressed. "I reminded you too much of yourself. Billy was what you wished to be. I was the dull reflection of what you were and would always be."

"I will not listen to another word of this craziness." Her mother pushed away her outstretched arms and started to march past her up the stairs.

Virginia stood aside but made the fatal mistake of injecting one last, cruel observation. "It seems I've inherited all of your worst traits, including my jealous nature. I busted my butt for years trying to impress you, hoping to extract one small word of praise, but I could have saved myself the trouble. If I'd won the Nobel prize, you'd never have acknowledged it. You didn't want me to succeed at anything because then you'd be forced to admit that you were alone in your dullness—a dispassionate, disgruntled, boring person, stuck in a rut. Now I realize that you were jealous of the opportunities I seized and you missed.''

Inez's hand cracked across Virginia's cheek. "You're as mistaken as you are impudent. I'll expect an apology in the morning or you can leave my house for good." Hurt and livid with anger, she could not bear another second of being in her daughter's presence. She turned her back on Virginia and went up to her room.

Virginia flinched at the slam of the bedroom door. She rubbed her smarting cheek, then sat down on the bottom step and cradled her head in her hands. She didn't feel relieved at having finally said her piece; she just felt miserable.

SLEEP WAS AN IMPOSSIBILITY that night. Virginia was too restless to stay in her small bedroom. At 1 a.m. she gave up and went down to the kitchen to have a toddy, thinking it might help relax her. When she flicked on the light switch, she discovered her mother seated at the table.

Neither looked directly at the other or said anything for a moment.

Finally Virginia broke the silence. "You can't sleep either, huh?"

"It's not unusual for me. I often wake up at this hour." Inez made an effort to act casual about sitting and brooding in the dark. "I fix myself a cup of warm milk and then go on back to bed."

Warm *skim* milk, Virginia mused to herself. She tucked a stray hair behind an ear and surveyed her mother. She looked drawn and old in the harsh yellow light. Grief had taken its toll on her. Inez hadn't been herself since losing her son. Virginia felt a pang of guilt at having put her through another ordeal. Right or wrong, good or bad, she was her mother, for God's sake. The woman hadn't had an easy life—so many years alone doing the best she could to make ends meet. It occurred to Virginia to wonder why she had dwelled on what her mother hadn't done rather than what she had done. An enormous sense of compassion washed over her as she gazed at her mother's wilted figure.

"Instead of having warm milk, why don't I fix us a cappuccino?" she blurted.

"Does that have liquor in it?" Inez was baffled. Suddenly her daughter was in a much more amiable mood.

"Well, normally it doesn't, but I do add a little for flavor. Come on, Mother," she said coaxingly, coming to Inez's chair, kneeling down and tugging on the tie of her chenille bathrobe. "Let's shake things up a bit. Do something out of the ordinary. What's wrong with a couple of bland dames like us adding a bit of spice once in a while?" She smiled tenderly at her.

Inez knew Virginia was trying, in a roundabout way, to make amends. She remembered that even as a little girl her daughter had had trouble expressing her innermost feelings. In that respect, she most certainly was her mother's daughter. "We haven't the necessary ingredients," her practical self answered.

"Oh, yes we do." Virginia bounced up to get the bottle of orange liqueur she'd stashed at the back of the pantry. "I brought it with me," she explained, brandishing a pint of spirits. "I knew you'd disapprove, so I hid it."

"Very sneaky, Virginia." Such a stunt was more like Billy than Virginia. It seemed there were facets of her daughter's personality that had somehow escaped her notice. To some degree, Virginia's complaints about the lack of attention were justified. If only it wasn't necessary to say so aloud. Inez dreaded the thought. But it was necessary. It was something she owed her daughter—the unvarnished truth.

"We'll compromise by mixing a dab of my liqueur with your skim milk. All right?"

"I suppose so," her mother agreed.

They exchanged no more words while Virginia prepared the cappuccino. They both used the quiet time to focus their thoughts.

It was Inez who initiated conversation once Virginia sat down at the table. "It's tasty," she said of the cappuccino.

"Healthy, too." Virginia grinned nervously and sipped from her cup. "At least, that's what I tell myself."

"I shouldn't have slapped you." Inez did not look at her daughter. Instead, she stared at the artificial flower arrangement in the middle of the table.

"I provoked you." Virginia put down her cup and, with a tenuous stretch of her fingertips, eased a hand over her mother's. "I'm sorry for the hateful things I said to you. A lot has been building up inside of me, and when it exploded, it came out all wrong."

Inez sighed and leaned back in her chair. "Not *all* wrong, Virginia," she said tiredly. "I've done a lot of thinking about what you said and there is some truth in it. I suppose I did show partiality, but not for the reasons you accused me of."

Her mother paused for a reflective moment, trying to collect herself before going on. "You were right in saying that you are most like me. But I didn't consciously recognize that, and it played no part in my favoring Billy. He was special to me because he reminded me of your father. It was hard for me to lose a husband I adored when he was so young. I missed him terribly. Without even realizing what I was doing, I somehow came to view Billy as a replacement. It was as if my heart were divided into thirds—there was a section for your father, one for Billy and one for you. I was truly unaware of Billy's gradually taking over the spot reserved for your father until he occupied two-thirds of my affection and you only a third. It wasn't right, my doting on him like I did. But you must believe that I didn't do it intentionally. Billy didn't understand it any more than you did. That's not to say that he didn't take advantage of my blind spot. He did. But it was me who let him."

Virginia was stunned. Her mother had finally admitted a flaw. She'd expected to feel a sense of satisfaction but it didn't happen. She only felt sorry for having made her mother undergo yet another painful experience. The soul-searching she'd done on her daughter's behalf must have been pure torture.

"I never meant to hurt you, Mother. I'm not trying to take Billy's place with you. I just wanted to hear from your lips that you loved and were proud of me, too."

Inez lifted her teary eyes and engaged the searching gaze of her daughter. "Oh, my dear..." Her heart ached to reassure Virginia. There was such yearning in her daughter's voice and on her sweet face. "I take so much pride in you. How could I not? You have grown into a lovely, capable and caring woman."

Virginia broke into tears at hearing the words.

Inez opened her arms to her. Virginia slid out of her chair, crouched beside her mother and buried her head in her lap.

"Shhh, dear, don't cry." Inez smoothed back her daughter's hair and bent to kiss her forehead.

Virginia hugged her around the waist. "I'm so sorry about being jealous of Billy. I love and miss him, too. Do you think he forgives me?"

"Of course he does. I never told you about a long-distance conversation I had with Billy shortly before his accident. He was in one of his rare serious frames of mind. He told me he regretted the way the two of you had drifted apart. His exact words were, 'I should've been there more for Gin.' Though I tried to tell him it was a natural result of both of you growing up and going in your separate directions, he kept insisting it was more than that. He mentioned having been too wrapped up in his own life to give much thought about what was happening in yours. He admitted that he'd purposely avoided returning your phone calls or looking you up when he flew into New York because to him you were still the pesky kid sister and a royal pain. When you quit making the effort to stay in touch, he realized he'd shut you out and felt guilty about it."

"Really?" Virginia reared back and looked anxiously up at her mother.

"Really," her mother reassured her. "'I sorta miss her' is how he put it at the end of our conversation. Then he told me he planned to set things straight between the two of you, first chance he got. But you and I both know how he was. I'm sure he meant to do as he'd said, but Billy could be easily distracted and wasn't very good at following through on his intentions. If I know my son, he's wondering the same thing in heaven as you are on earth. I'm sure he's asking himself, 'Do you think she forgives me?'"

Inez clasped Virginia's face between her palms and smiled knowingly. "If I know my daughter, the answer is 'Of course she does.'"

"God! I feel so much better." Virginia snuggled her head in her mother's soft lap once more.

"I'm glad." Love for her daughter—a silent longing to make up for the unintentional hurt she'd caused her—made Inez's throat constrict and her eyes brim. Her knees swayed in a rocking motion as she rendered soothing pats to Virginia's back—very appropriate, since, in a fashion, she was fulfilling a leftover childhood wish for her daughter. It was as if time had regressed and Virginia was once again her vulnerable baby girl.

"I love you, Mother." Virginia's heart pounded. She squeezed her eyes shut and pressed a cheek closer against her mother's legs.

"I love you, too, dear."

Virginia thought about the inscription inside the gold bracelet Joe Dillon had given her. *To every thing there is a season, and a time to every purpose under the heaven.*

Inez thought about her two children and how, from this day forward, she must never again allow one to eclipse the space of the other in her heart.

CHAPTER SEVENTEEN

INEZ AWAKENED BEFORE VIRGINIA. A bowl of oat bran flakes, raisin toast and freshly squeezed orange juice were set at her daughter's spot at the table by the time she arrived downstairs.

Virginia made no protest when her mother poured the skim milk over the flakes. "Thanks," was her only comment.

Inez brought her cup of coffee to the table and sat down to keep her daughter company while she ate.

"It looks nice outside. Which would you rather do first? Tend to the flower garden or go to the cemetery?" It was Saturday, after all—the day Inez set aside to place fresh flowers at her son's grave.

"Neither."

"But you always go..."

"I know, but it's not written in stone. I thought we might take a look at the new mall in town. We could shop and then have lunch at that quaint little country inn we ate at once before."

Virginia was touched by her mother's desire to spend quality time with her. She was making a point by foregoing her weekly trek to the cemetery. Her suggesting a girls' day out was more special to Virginia than any gift she'd ever given her.

"I'd like that." She smiled warmly across the table at her mother. "But are you sure? I really don't mind if you want to stop by the cemetery on the way."

"No, Virginia," her mother answered firmly. "You did me a favor when you took me to account about my preoccupation with Billy. There comes a time when the grieving must end. Billy will always claim his rightful place in my heart, but no more than his fair share of a mother's devotion."

Virginia nodded and swallowed a spoonful of bran flakes. "Have there been any calls for me this morning?" she remembered to ask.

"No. Are you expecting one?"

"Just business. I'm trying to keep tabs on a promotional tour under way for the new campaign," she explained.

"So, it's going well for you," her mother surmised.

"Things are going better than well, Mother." Virginia deliberated only for a moment, then decided she couldn't keep the news about Joe Dillon to herself. "Personally as well as professionally," she hinted.

"Oh . . ." Inez couldn't help but notice the glow on her daughter's face. "Is this your roundabout way of telling me that there's a new man in your life?"

Virginia grinned widely. "He's not someone you would expect me to be attracted to, Mother. I tried hard not to be, but he was persistent, thank goodness."

Inez had never seen Virginia quite so animated. It was plain to see that she was really taken with her new beau. "He means a lot to you, then?"

"Yes, Mother, he does. I know you'd given up hope, but I've actually fallen in love again." She drank down her juice.

"Well, it certainly happened quickly, unless it's another well-kept secret you've been guarding. Tell me something about him."

"He's from Mississippi." She got up and brought the coffeepot to the table, pouring herself a cup and refilling her mother's as she related details about Joe Dillon. "He's not what one would call polished, at least not in the same way as the slick breed of males I deal with daily. He's plainspoken but extremely gracious in his manner."

"Mmm, a Southerner..." Her mother was having difficulty digesting the fact. "I don't know why, but the thought never crossed my mind that you'd be interested in anyone who wasn't—" she searched for the proper phrase "what do you call them nowadays? Movers and seekers or something like that."

"Shakers—movers and shakers." As Virginia updated Inez's vocabulary she opened a packet of artificial sweetener, emptied the white powder into her cup and let it dissolve in the black coffee. "Maybe that's what makes him so special—the fact that he's so incredibly different from any man I've ever known. Very warm and sensitive. Unmaterialistic. Genuine and steadfast."

"All fine qualities," Inez agreed. "But surely he has one or two small failings...."

Virginia lowered her gaze, brought the coffee cup to her lips and half mumbled, "Did I mention that he's younger than me?"

"How much younger?"

"Nearly ten years."

"Goodness!" Inez took a second to absorb the shock. "Such an age difference," she uttered thoughtfully.

"I know. It sounds like a lot, but if you knew him it would hardly seem significant. He's a solid person. In many ways he's more mature than men twice his age. He's in touch with his feelings and knows exactly what he wants out of life. One of the things I appreciate most about him is his common sense. Actually, it was he who convinced me to come talk to you about Billy and all the mixed-up feelings I had welling around inside of me. He said I owed it to myself and to you to find out once and for all if my childhood hang-ups were legitimate. Of course, I don't think he meant for me to get so radical about it." She grinned sheepishly at her mother over the edge of her cup.

"I like him already. And if he knows you as well as you say, no doubt he allowed for the possibility of your blowing up. You do have a tendency to explode under pressure, Virginia—a trait you inherited from your father, not me."

Virginia let the remark pass without comment.

Inez pried a bit deeper. "What does your young man do for a living?"

"At the moment, he's under contract to Sebastian Designs. He's the model representing a new line of jeans being launched in the States. Hanks and Udell is handling the account, so technically he works for me."

"Oh, dear. Another looker. I would have thought you had learned your lesson." Everything had been going well until the mention of Joe Dillon's modeling career. Concern brewed in Inez's eyes.

"I thought the same thing at first but, believe me, Mother, J.D.'s nothing like Rob. He's not impressed with himself and he dislikes being in the limelight."

"Then why did he take the job?"

"I talked him into it." A picture of the day she'd interviewed Joe Dillon flashed before her eyes. She was remembering how she'd considered him then as opposed to how she considered him now. She'd thought of him as raw material with potential—not as a flesh and blood man with feelings. So much had happened in between. She was not the same person any longer. Funny, but she hadn't realized before what a big transformation had taken place within her. In the short space of a few months, her whole outlook had changed—she'd become less compulsive, less narcissistic. She'd failed to notice what an influence he had had on her. What else had slipped her attention, she wondered. Had Joe Dillon changed, too? Was her influence on him a good or bad thing?

"What is his normal line of work?" Her mother's voice broke in on her musing.

Here came the tricky part—trying to tell her mother that the man she loved picked cotton. Virginia chose her words carefully. "He, uh, prefers working the land. Before modeling, he grew cotton in the Delta."

"A farmer!" Inez stared at her daughter disbelievingly.

"What's wrong with that?" Virginia instantly became defensive.

Inez could not contain herself. An amused smile formed on her lips, then broadened into a wide grin and escalated into laughter. "The idea of you being in love with a man who tills dirt instead of trading stocks is funny, Ginny. Really funny. If someone would've asked me if I thought it was possible, I would've said never in a million years." Another seizure of chuckles overtook Inez.

Virginia could not remember her mother ever laughing so hard at anything. "Well, I fail to see the humor in it. Working the land is a time-honored profession."

Aware that her daughter was truly vexed by her reaction, Inez regained control of herself. "Yes, of course it is. I'm sorry. It's only the notion of you giving up the power lunches to relocate in the cotton fields that tickles me. You have to admit, it's a totally un-you life-style."

"I don't plan to work the fields with him, Mother," Virginia said impatiently. "J.D. and I haven't yet discussed the direction our relationship will take once the campaign is over, but I'm sure we'll come up with a compromise. I've given it some thought. One solution could be to commute on weekends."

Her mother's lighthearted mood vanished. The laugh brackets around her mouth disappeared and her forehead puckered. "For a relationship to work, it takes a day-to-day commitment, Virginia. You can't just fly in and out of a man's arms."

"Couples do it all the time, Mother," Virginia argued.

"Maybe so, but I certainly have my doubts about such an arrangement working out on a long-term basis. It may be convenient, but it's hardly cementing."

"You and Joe Dillon should get along famously. He has all these old-fashioned ideas, too. He has a thing about gentlemanly honor and earning his way."

"There's nothing wrong with adhering to old-fashioned principles. In fact, I think it's commendable. If you ask me, it's the lack of higher values that has caused the world to be in such a sorry state to-day.''

"Well, sometimes a person can be too principled for his own good. It borders on being stubborn.''

Inez pursed her lips, wondering if she should venture an opinion about something she only suspected. She decided to speak her mind. "Something in the way you're behaving makes me suspect that there's a conflict at work inside of you, my dear." She held up a hand at Virginia's attempt to deny what had yet to be established. "I'm not going to lecture you, Virginia, but I am going to inject a word of caution. Don't ever try to sway a man from his principles, because, even though he may go along to appease you in the beginning, it'll drive a wedge between the two of you in the end."

Virginia's only response was to shrug. It was food for thought.

"When do you think I'll have an opportunity to meet this young man of yours?" Her mother wisely chose not to pursue the touchy issue any further.

"Soon, Mother."

"I once knew a family of Dillons. It was years ago, of course. They were from Missouri, I believe. Probably no relation," she speculated aloud.

Virginia was amused by the fact that her mother had made the same wrongful assumption as she had. "Dillon is his middle name, Mother. In the South, people often combine first and middle names, so that they sound like one. His full name is Joe Dillon Ma-hue. J.D. is a nickname."

"Oh, I see," her mother said dully. It'd take some time for her to assimilate all the new information that had been thrust upon her so suddenly.

The telephone jangled. Inez went to answer it. When she returned she looked puzzled. "That was a man from the telephone company, checking to be sure my service was restored. Cable problems, he said."

"Did he say how long the line's been down?" An uneasy feeling began to coil in Virginia's solar plexus.

"Since yesterday sometime."

"I have to call my office." Virginia dashed to the phone and punched the appropriate buttons.

Her mother looked dumbfounded. "Goodness, dear. You'd think it was a 911 emergency," she said reprovingly.

"It may be." Virginia paced to and fro, stretching the long cord its full length. "Rita, it's me," she said brusquely. "I know. I know. I didn't realize until now that the phone line's been down here since yesterday."

Virginia listened for a moment, her face reflecting the bad news Rita imparted. As of yesterday afternoon, Rita had been getting the runaround from Claudia Shapell's secretary. Rita had kept trying to get a trace on Shapell, but her New York Office was guarding the information like some CIA dossier. When Rita was unable to get in touch with Virginia, she'd taken it upon herself to check with the Argentine offices. She'd spoken to Don Sebastian personally. He'd professed to be as much in the dark as to the whereabouts of his partner as was Rita.

"You shouldn't have called him, of all people," Virginia fussed. "Speak English. I can't—" She twisted the phone cord around her fingers and shifted her eyes to the ceiling. "I'm sorry. I didn't mean to criticize you. You did what you thought best and there's probably no harm done. We might be over-reacting. Maybe she's up to nothing more than a long weekend in the Hamptons. Keep trying to get a line on her. I won't be back in the city until late tonight. If you find out anything you can either get in touch with me here or leave a message on my recorder at home." There was another short pause as Rita chattered away on the other end of the line. "Okay...mmm...fine, fine," Virginia humored her. "Mellow out, Rita. We don't have to file a missing persons report just yet. Oh, and, Rita—don't call Don Sebastian again, no matter what." She hung up the phone and stood motionless, trying to gather her wits.

"Trouble at the office?" Her mother wore a wary expression, as if she half expected Virginia to cancel their plans.

"Nothing that won't keep," she told her, praying it was so. "We're not going to let it spoil our day together." She mustered a convincing smile. "Maybe we'll find a fabulous boutique. I'll buy you something special to wear when you come to New York to see that play we've yet to take in."

Inez was touched by the sweet offer. "I don't want you squandering your hard-earned money on me, dear. Of course, I suppose my wardrobe is a little out-dated. It's been a long while since I had any desire to venture beyond these four walls. Maybe it is high time I took steps to get out of my rut. You're absolutely right," she declared with a decisive nod of her head. "I've been hibernating in the country for far too long. A trip to New York would be a nice way to reenter the world."

"Good. Then it's settled. Today, the shopping mall in town—next week, the Big Apple." Virginia gave her a gentle nudge toward the kitchen door. "Go get ready. Time's a-wastin'."

Virginia did not realize how true a statement it was, especially where she was concerned. For she was not yet aware that Claudia Shapell was in Miami with Joe Dillon and their luck had just run dry.

It WAS NEARLY TEN O'CLOCK at night when Joe Dillon stopped at the hotel's front desk to check on his messages. The night clerk handed him a pink slip with Rita Mundo's name and the number for the agency written on it.

"Thanks." Joe Dillon took a step toward the elevator.

"There's a lady waiting to see you. She's been here quite a while," the clerk informed him.

Joe Dillon cast a glance about the lobby. "Where is she?"

"She told me to tell you she'd be waiting in the bar, sir."

"Which way is that?"

"Straight ahead and to your left, sir."

Joe Dillon struck out in the direction the clerk had pointed him in. He had a bad feeling about who his visitor was. He hoped it was Ginny surprising him, but he had a sneaky suspicion such was not the case. Ginny would've known he'd be antsy about an unannounced visitor. She'd have left her name at the desk. He could hear the music coming from the bar. His heart quickened as he stepped into the dimly lit interior and cast a look down the row of bar stools.

A haze of smoke hung heavily in the air. He couldn't see very well. His eyes moved cautiously around the room. His worst nightmare materialized from the smoky shadows. She was sitting in a booth in the rear.

"Dillon," her voice beckoned him. "Here I am." She raised a hand and motioned for him to come join her.

He thought about turning around and making a mad dash for the elevators but just as quickly discounted the notion. She'd only follow him. At least they were surrounded by people in the bar and Claudia would have to keep herself reasonably in check.

"Surprised to see me?" She tossed back her head and shot him a flirtatious grin.

He was unsure whether she was being cutesy or coy. He decided to give her a safe answer. "A little." He slid into the booth and met her gaze levelly.

"I had a bit of a problem tracking you down. Somebody over at the ad agency does sloppy work. According to the tour schedule I was given, you're supposed to be in Atlanta."

"Well, then, one of us is in the wrong city." He shrugged off the mix-up. "How'd you find me?"

"Process of elimination." She plucked one of the two giant olives from the tiny plastic sword floating in her martini and popped it into her mouth. "When I discovered that you weren't where you were supposed to be, I called each hotel on the list until I found the one at which you were registered. It was an inconvenience, but here I am." There was no mistaking the suggestive note in her tone as she rolled the olive around on her tongue.

"Yeah, here you are," was his unenthusiastic reply. The cocktail waitress approached Joe Dillon, asking what he'd like to drink. "Nothing, thanks. I'm not staying."

Claudia pulled off a jade earring. The gem glittered in the candlelight as she sat twisting it between her fingers and studying him. "Are you expected somewhere else?"

"No. I'm just tuckered, is all."

She hoisted the martini to her lips. "I didn't travel all this way to watch you yawn, Dillon." She definitely sounded peeved.

"Sorry. If I had known you were coming, I'd have rested up."

Her expression was unreadable behind the upturned long-stemmed glass, but he felt the distinct press of her knee against his own under the table. "It's noisy in here," she complained. "We can't talk. Let's go up to your room." She set aside the empty martini glass and reached into her purse for one of her many credit cards.

"I don't think that's a good idea, Claudia. People might get the wrong idea." He knew it was a flimsy excuse but it was the only thing that sprang to mind. Claudia Shapell didn't give a damn what a bunch of strangers might assume. Her fashionable name was not at risk in Miami.

"You're a darling to want to protect my pristine reputation, but I hardly think we're apt to bump into anyone we know."

He looked worried. She noticed as she laid the credit card on top of the check and signaled the cocktail waitress. "Relax, Dillon." Her voice was silky and slightly amused. ''We've been working you too hard. You're a bundle of nerves.''

She had that much right, J.D. thought to himself. How in the hell was he going to get rid of her? He couldn't think straight. He couldn't suggest dinner or dancing because he'd only moments ago told her he was dead on his feet.

It seemed only a second or two had passed before the tab was settled and Claudia was walking ahead of him out of the bar. He lagged behind her, still trying to come up with a plausible reason why she should not accompany him to his fifteenth-floor suite.

She was chatting about the hotel's art deco design. Her words all ran together in his head.

''What floor?'' she asked him upon reaching the elevators in the lobby.

Joe Dillon was lost in thought and uncommunicative.

She touched his arm and drew him inside the elevator, asking him again on what floor his room was located.

''Fifteen,'' he answered, looking straight ahead as the doors slowly closed. He felt smothered. His fingers went to his tie. He loosened it and undid the top button of his shirt. Claudia was talking about a Palm Beach acquaintance of hers. Nothing she said made any sense to him. He was intent on only one thing— figuring out a way to get free of her. It didn't look likely that he would succeed.

They arrived at the fifteenth floor. He took his sweet time walking to the door designated Suite 1502.

''Oh, I don't believe what I did,'' Claudia exclaimed, opening up her handbag and riffling through it.

Midway removing the key from his pocket, Joe Dillon let it slide back inside to mingle with the change. "What's wrong?"

"I left my earring on the table in the bar. How stupid of me. It's very expensive. Would you be a sweetheart and run back downstairs to get it for me?"

Any excuse to stall. "Sure," he said obligingly, striking out for the elevator again.

He'd only gone a few feet when she called to him. "The key, Dillon. I don't want to stand out here in the hallway till you return."

He had no choice but to toss her the key.

On the way back down to the lobby, he came up with a device by which to elude her. He'd have the night switchboard operator place a call to Virginia with instructions to ring him in his room when the call went through. He'd pretend it was a relation in Mississippi and talk a blue streak until Claudia got disgusted enough to leave. Yeah, that might just work. He felt somewhat relieved at having come up with a measure by which to perhaps outfox the fox.

The earring was still on the table, near the ashtray—precisely where she had planted it.

WHEN JOE DILLON ARRIVED back at his room, the door was slightly ajar. The interior was dark, except for a cone of light spilling from the bathroom. "Claudia?" he called out nervously.

She emerged from the bathroom, wearing nothing but a white towel.

His fingers clenched the earring. It didn't take a genius to figure out he'd been set up.

"You don't mind if I borrow a towel, do you?" she asked. The kittenish tone she'd adopted sounded totally out of character and downright silly.

"I guess not. You planning on taking a bath?" There was a detectable edge to his voice.

She undid the clip from her hair and shook her unnaturally blond tresses. "Maybe later." His uncooperativeness was making her grow impatient with him. Her cajoling mood evaporated—replaced by an almost condescending change in attitude. She walked straight to the bed and folded back the spread. "Spare me the dumb country boy act, Dillon. It's not that I haven't found it charming, but it's wearing thin."

He watched, eerily fascinated by her purposeful motions and blasé inflection. She flung back the sheet and rearranged the pillows.

"You've known since the beginning that I was attracted to you. We've been playing a seductive game, you and I." She eased herself onto the sheets, stretching sexily. "It's been fun, but the object of the game is for us to eventually act out our sexual fantasy." She rolled onto her side, cradled her head in her hand and crooked a finger at him.

The moment he'd dreaded had arrived. The ultimatum had been delivered. The towel split, exposing the fantasy she was offering him. He had but two recourses: accept it or reject it.

He stayed where he was. His silence intrigued her.

She sat up, tilting her head and gazing at him through half-hooded eyes. "Don't tell me you haven't done this before," she taunted him.

"Would it matter?"

"No, not at all. Take off your clothes, Dillon. I want to see beforehand if you're all I imagined."

"Put yours back on, Claudia. Because whatever you've been imagining in that scheming head of yours isn't going to happen." Joe Dillon finally moved. He walked away, not toward her—marching into the bathroom, gathering up her personal things and then dumping them unceremoniously on the bed at her feet.

"I don't think you understand the rules of our game." One corner of her mouth twisted into a crooked smile as her painted toes twiddled with her satin-and-lace undergarments. "Let me put it to you bluntly. You were a nobody before Don Sebastian Designs and you can just as easily be returned to your previous existence if I so choose. It can be done in a flick of the fingers." She snapped hers to demonstrate her point. Her voice dropped to a cold, totally emotionless pitch. "Either you come through in the sack or you're going to be one unhappy bumpkin. Do I make myself clear?"

"Yes, ma'am, perfectly clear." His back molars gnashed together. He was sorely tempted to pick her up and toss her out into the hallway buck naked.

"Well, then?"

"Your threats don't mean beans to me, Claudia. I don't give two hoots about the money or being the Don Sebastian man. In fact, I was looking for a way to get out of my contract. You'll be saving me the trouble."

"Oh, really," she shrieked, shooting from the bed and shimmying into her lacy bikinis. "Well, you can go to hell!" She jiggled into her bra and threw on her blouse. "Now that I know how much you want out of your contract, I'll do everything in my power to hold you to it—every single, miserable day of it. What's more," she spat out, jerking on her skirt and stuffing her stockings into her purse, "I'm going to stay on your ass constantly. Oh, yes, count on it." She flung back her head and shot him a murderous look. "Then, after I've drained the last drop of sweat and spirit from you, when you're of no further use to me, I'm going to see to it that a nasty rumor begins to circulate about you. Something to the effect of how the Don Sebastian hunk can't cut it between the sheets."

"Are you all finished?" He hoped so, because he wasn't in the mood to take any more of her crap.

His calm demeanor only served to infuriate her more. She grabbed a shoe and hurled it at his head.

He ducked and it hit the door with a splintering whack. It was a standoff for a breathless moment as the two of them stood glaring at one another. Each was thinking in terms of a *B*-word and applying it to the other.

"Bastard!" she hissed.

His good upbringing prevailed. He did not resort to name-calling, though it took amazing restraint on his part to retain a gentlemanly posture. He walked over, picked up her shoe and flung open the suite door. "Take your offer and your shoe and get out."

As she stormed past him, she snatched the shoe from his hand and set the tone for any future dealings between them. "I make a much better lover than I do an enemy. You'll regret tonight. It's a promise."

Sometime during the night, it occurred to Joe Dillon to wonder why the switchboard operator had not placed the call to Virginia as he had requested her to do. He switched on the light and checked to see if the phone was working properly. It was then that he discovered it had been unplugged, and he knew Claudia must have done it to ensure that they weren't disturbed....

THERE WAS A MESSAGE from Rita on Virginia's answering machine when she arrived home Saturday night.

"Ees me. Eet ees Friday night. I traced Shapell. She ees in Miami. I called Joe Dillon's room and guess who answered? I hung up. I don know what else to do. Call me at home in the morning."

Neither Virginia nor Joe Dillon got much sleep that night. She kept wondering about what had transpired between him and Claudia Shapell in Miami on Friday night. He knew for certain and was deeply worried about the consequences of it.

CHAPTER EIGHTEEN

IT WAS TOWARD MONDAY'S END when Joe Dillon finally showed up at the agency. Virginia and Rita were engaged in deep discussion and unaware of his presence in the office doorway. They were both talking at once—each throwing out suggestions as to where next to concentrate their search efforts for him and what should be done about the logjam of scheduled appearances.

"Save yourselves the trouble, ladies." Two pairs of eyes traveled in his direction.

"J.D.! We've been trying to locate you—all day yesterday and today. Where have you been?" Virginia was up out of the chair and across the room in a blink.

"In an airport lounge, mostly." He looked awful, Virginia thought—haggard and unshaven and minus his usual easy smile.

Something in his eyes when they connected with hers caused her to stop in her tracks. "You could've at least called me. I've been sick with worry. When you were a no-show at Lomans, I didn't know what to think. Dammit, J.D. The store was expecting you to put in an appearance. They advertised the event. Nearly two hundred women crammed into the men's department expecting to get a glimpse of you. The manager had a near riot on his hands after announcing that you were unavoidably detained and your appearance had to be canceled. Lomans is a big chain. You just don't tick off important retailers."

J.D. offered no excuses. Ticked off didn't even begin to describe how *he* felt. He walked past her and slumped into a chair with a sideways look in Rita's direction.

She offered him a sympathetic smile. Virginia was in one of her frazzled states. Stress had a way of turning her into a one-woman firing squad. Rita considered asking him if he wanted a blindfold or a last cigarette.

"I'm sorry about Lomans. I guess I should've contacted somebody and told them what was going on."

"What exactly is going on, J.D.?" Virginia went back to her desk and assumed her director's chair. To J.D., she looked as crisp as he felt wilted. She was wearing a svelte Chanel-style suit, while he was dressed in jeans, a T-shirt and high-top tennis shoes. She was jittery; he was grim.

"All I know is what Rita and the desk clerk told me," she went on. "Rita informed me that Claudia Shapell answered the phone in your suite late Friday night, then the desk clerk told me that you checked out of the hotel early Sunday morning."

"I theenk now ees a good time for me to make myself scarce." Rita could see that Joe Dillon was uncomfortable with the idea of spilling the story in front of her. True confessions were hard enough without an audience.

He slanted her a grateful look as she got to her feet.

"She ees worked up with worry over you. Don take it personally." Her hand rested on his shoulder a lingering second before she beat a hasty retreat.

He could feel Virginia's eyes boring holes through him. He shifted his weight in the chair and stretched out his cramped legs. "It's over, Ginny. She made her demands known and I refused. It got ugly between us. She tried to bully me with threats and I told her to go bump a stump. It's as simple as that."

Simple as that! Was he kidding? Virginia couldn't believe he was taking an act of Armageddon so matter-of-factly. "I need facts, J.D. You can't just waltz in here and calmly inform me that it's over. What sort of threats did she make?"

"First she said if I didn't shape up and do what she wanted, she'd send me back to my previous existence with a snap of her fingers. When I told her I didn't give a damn about being the Don Sebastian man and had been wanting out of my contract for a while, she did an about-face and vowed she'd hold me to every miserable day of it. I think her exact words were 'I'm going to stay on your ass constantly.'" J.D. imparted the facts as casually as if he were reciting a grocery list. He seemed disgusted but certainly not as upset as she was.

"Well, it's not totally unexpected. It could be worse, I suppose. Since she knows where you stand, I doubt she'll press the issue anymore." The gears of Virginia's mind were whirling, computing the odds of salvaging the campaign while keeping J.D.'s pride intact. "After a little time has passed, I can maybe smooth things over with her." She didn't realize she was speculating aloud.

Joe Dillon couldn't believe what he was hearing. What in the hell was she talking about? *Smooth things over... It could be worse....* "I'm through with it, Ginny," he said bluntly. "I wash my hands of her and the campaign. The only reason I've stuck it out for as long as I have is because of you. But no more, girl. I don't want to smooth anything over. Leave it alone." He'd been fighting to hold his anger in check but it was gradually beginning to seep to the surface. Ginny's minimizing everything had the same effect as pouring gasoline on a fire.

"You know how much is at stake, J.D. I realize that you're upset by her come-ons but I think you're overreacting just a little." The thought of losing the Sebastian account had her crazy. She could see the partnership slipping away. So she rationalized, not even realizing that she was acting in typical compulsive personality fashion, saying or doing whatever it took to get her way. She did feel somewhat disembodied, however. It was as if someone else were saying the words. They were coming from her mouth but another person was speaking them. Someone she once knew—someone who existed in the B.J.D.—before Joe Dillon.

"We're talking heated words, not body heat, Joe Dillon. She'll cool off when she considers the situation carefully. She's a businesswoman first. She won't allow her personal feelings to—"

"I won't have an affair with her so you can have an affair with glory," he boomed back. "I'm getting a picture of you, Ginny, and it isn't real flattering."

She sat straighter in her chair and set her chin obstinately. "What's that remark supposed to mean?"

A jaw muscle twitched as he leaned forward a bit. He braced his forearms on his knees and matched her steely look. "It means I don't understand you. It means I've got a sickening feeling in the pit of my stomach that a partnership matters more to you than my self-respect. And what that means, Ginny, is that one of us is going to have to back down or else you and I are going to have a parting of the ways. I love you, but I don't like you much right at the moment."

His words stung her. How could he say such hateful things? Was he too dense to realize that she was only trying to spare him from a horrible ordeal? She was doing it as much for him as for herself. If he tried to walk out on his contract, Shapell would hire a hotshot lawyer skilled in a hundred and one ways to keep him indentured to Sebastian Designs. His manly assets would legally, if not physically, be hers. What purpose would a nasty and costly court battle serve, except to drag everyone connected with it through the mud?

"I knew it would come down to this sooner or later. Well, like it or not, I am your boss and I do have a say about matters that affect this agency." She fought to quell the quiver in her voice. "And I'm cautioning you strongly against doing anything that might result in embarrassing my firm."

He stared at her unblinkingly. There loomed a long, aching silence before he regained himself sufficiently to answer her. "*Your* firm," he said. "Did I miss your graduation party?"

"It was a figure of speech." She found his sarcasm unbecoming.

He cast a glance about her office—for the first time taking a good hard look at the posters displayed on the walls. Catchy slogans, slick sell jobs, was that all she was about? God! He hoped not, but he was no longer so sure. He slumped back against the chair and expelled a deep sigh.

It was evident to her that conflicting emotions were churning inside him, but she mistakenly believed it was the pros and cons of waging an expensive lawsuit that he was wrestling with. "The idea of taking legal action is a bad one, J.D. Your chances of getting out of your contract are better if you let me handle things my way."

"Before I came in here, I wasn't sure about going public with my complaint. I knew there'd be some who'd snicker at the notion of me claiming to be sexually harassed on the job, a lot who'd find it peculiar that a man would be offended by such an offer and even crazier to turn it down. Listening to you tell me the reasons I shouldn't go through with it, though, has helped me make up my mind. I can't go along with what you want this time, Ginny. In your own way, you're as demanding and as ruthless as she is. A person's dignity doesn't matter to you people." He smiled ruefully and dropped his gaze to the marble paperweight on her desk. "When push comes to shove, you're as hard inside as that slab of polished rock."

Her heart lurched in her chest. "J.D., please let's not talk about our differences when we're both tired and edgy. Believe it or not, I really am just trying to protect you from a sophisticated world you don't understand. You can't win a sexual harassment suit. You have no proof. No previous accusations have been

leveled at her. It's your word against that of a re-
spected businesswoman who wields influence and has
highly placed contacts in the city. Who do you think
they'll believe?''

He pushed himself up out of the chair and squared
his shoulders. ''You may be right. I may lose in court,
but I won't have any trouble looking in a mirror in the
mornings. And maybe I can spare some other unsus-
pecting fool from meeting the same end as me. He'll
read my story in the papers and think twice about
being fast-talked into easy money.''

Her legs felt wobbly as she followed his lead and
stood up—not just physically, but also for what she
believed to be the only sensible course of action. ''You
say you love me, Joe Dillon....''

''I do, Ginny darlin'.'' His soft-spoken drawl was
like a caress.

''Then, I beg of you, don't go through with your
plans to take Shapell to task in a courtroom. Think of
us—the damage it will do to our future relationship if
you put me in the middle of your fight.''

He gazed at her through bottomless brown eyes,
then reached across the desk, took her hand and
brought it to his lips. ''I guess you'll have to choose
sides, Ginny darlin'. I'll try not to hold hard feelings
if it happens that your loyalties don't lie with me.'' He
squeezed her fingertips before releasing her hand.

Her vision clouded and her mouth trembled as he
walked toward the door without a backward glance.
''You're either too stupid or too stubborn to see beyond that foolish pride of yours. You're screwing
everything up for us and for what? A chance to make
a social statement? You Southerners have a real talent

for championing lost causes. Slavery. Segregation. And now some passé code of gentlemanly honor.''

He halted at the door and turned around to face her. ''I *care* about honor. Stubborn I may be, but I'm no stupid hick. You know, it's only beginning to dawn on me how alike you and Claudia Shapell really are. You're a businesswoman first, last and always. You don't allow your personal feelings to get in the way of cutting a deal. You're going to make some lucky agency a terrific partner.''

''Damn you, Joe Dillon,'' she shouted hysterically as he strode out the door. Her pride smarted from the blow he'd dealt her. She shook uncontrollably as tears spilled down her cheeks.

Rita poked her head around the door. ''Ees everything okay with you?''

Virginia couldn't answer her. She stood paralyzed and crying in her prestigious Madison Avenue office, surrounded by the glass-framed testaments to her genius.

Virginia Vandivere-Rice was one smart executive—an adwoman extraordinaire—but she was a dismal failure at love. Only one person's opinion of her truly counted and she'd lost his respect. Losing an account was nothing in comparison. Joe Dillon was all that really mattered. She knew it now. She'd accused him of not being able to see beyond his foolish pride. God! Why couldn't she have seen beyond her blind ambition a few minutes ago?

''I just made the biggest mistake of my life,'' she gasped between sobs. ''He put my interests above his own and I repaid him by doing just the opposite.'' She stared at Rita through red-glazed eyes. "How do I make it right again?" she choked.

"You don need me to tell you. You know what you must do."

An inner voice seconded Rita's words. *Yes, I know what has to be done.* A determined calm settled over her as she sank into her chair and pressed her palms to her eyes until the tears subsided. She was responsible for the jam Joe Dillon was in. She was supposed to be a creative thinker. For once she'd use her talent unselfishly. Somehow, some way, she was going to free Joe Dillon from the trap she'd set for him.

A thought struck her. "Come sit down, Rita."

Rita knew the look. Something was jelling inside her boss's head. "Ayyy! I don theenk I am going to like this conversation," she said warily.

"Yes, you will." Virginia's spirits rose a tiny bit. "I want to hear your impressions of Don Sebastian. That's all."

Her tone was too cajoling. Rita was on her guard. "Why you want to know about him?"

"I'll tell you my reasons after you give me the lowdown on him."

"First, can you maybe order us dinner?" Rita bargained. "I theenk better on a full stomach."

"Chinese, okay?" Virginia would have taken her to Lutèce in order to bribe the information from her.

"Be sure they throw in lots of hot mustard." Rita knew she had an advantage and had no qualms about pressing it.

"Anything else? Extra fortune cookies, perhaps?" Virginia picked up the phone and began to dial the number for the Cantonese restaurant around the corner.

"Tell them to be sure and make the fortunes good ones."

"You're a shameless opportunist, Rita."

"I know. Ees because of my first husband. He was a penny pusher."

"You mean penny-pincher."

"Whatever." Rita was more interested in food than quibbling.

CLAUDIA SHAPELL HAD AGREED to meet Virginia in her office late the next day. She showed up ten minutes late and was in a foul humor.

"You said it was urgent we meet. It had better be. So let's get down to it, shall we? What's so important that we couldn't postpone discussing it?" She did not even bother to take a chair. She stationed herself at the window, presenting her miffed profile.

"Joe Dillon wants to call it quits and he says that you're the reason." Virginia wasted no time "getting down to it."

Claudia's face betrayed nothing of what she was thinking or feeling. She focused on the street below. "What else does he say?"

"That you have been coming on to him since the onset of the campaign. He contends that you made your intentions to have sex with him official in Miami. He also claims that he refused and you threatened him. Is any of it true?"

Claudia dug into her purse, pulled out a gold case and extracted a thin brown cigar. She lit up, blew a plume of smoke through her nostrils, then asked, "Have you an ashtray around here?"

Virginia handed her one. Claudia stayed at her post by the window, balancing the ashtray in a palm, her lips drawn in a tight line—neither admitting nor denying the accusation.

"I need to know," Virginia pressed her.

"Why? Are you concerned or merely curious?" Claudia snapped.

"Actually, both." Virginia played it casual. She didn't want Shapell to think that she was making a moral judgment. "Already the campaign is in trouble. Joe Dillon failed to make several scheduled appearances. Of course, that's the least of our worries. If he should decide to go public with his complaint, it would certainly make things messy."

"Has he said he intends to make a stink?" Claudia's voice took on an icy tone.

"In no uncertain terms." Virginia noticed a slight narrowing of the other woman's eyes.

Claudia took a last drag from the cigar and then ground it out in the ashtray. Her gaze panned to Virginia. "He's bluffing," she spat.

"I think not. He wants out of his contract—one way or the other. In my opinion, it would be better to release and replace him rather than risk a nasty lawsuit that will drag all of us through the mud," Virginia ventured.

"No way! He stays. I won't be blackmailed. If it's a dirty legal fight he wants, then that's exactly what he'll get. Let him take me to court. He can't prove a damn thing."

"You're sure? More than just your reputation is at stake," Virginia reminded her.

A wicked gleam sparked in the woman's eyes. "Do you think me a fool, Ms Vandivere? I don't take unnecessary risks."

"According to Joe Dillon, you do." Virginia hoped to rattle her.

"Well, I say differently," Claudia retorted.

Virginia was getting nowhere with the woman. It was time to switch tactics. "Fine. Well, then, we'll proceed on the assumption that what can't be proven doesn't exist." She forced a smile. "You know, Claudia, I have to be honest and tell you that a part of me is disappointed."

Her change in attitude caught the other woman off balance. "About what?"

"Oh, I know it's awful of me, but I was almost hoping Joe Dillon's accusations were true. The idea of the male chromosomes being on the opposite end of the crap they've been dishing out to us for years amused me."

Claudia's interest was piqued. She came and sat down, depositing the ashtray on top of Virginia's desk and then crossing her shapely legs. "What do you mean, exactly?"

Virginia gave her a pointed look. "I mean, I found the idea of turning the tables on the good old boys appealing. I'm sure you must have encountered some of the same indignities I did when working your way up through their ranks—off-color jokes, slips of the hand, breathing down your neck at the watercooler, suggestive remarks. Male hormones are always running on overtime. You know what I'm talking about."

Virginia treated Shapell like a sorority sister who'd gone through the same initiation rite.

"Oh, yes. I've endured my share of pawing and propositions. Amazing creatures, men. When they're aroused, all the blood drains from their head. Their brain cells are temporarily dead. It's the only explanation for the incredible risks they take with their careers. It's no wonder we're gaining on them. When you consider that a goodly portion of the male work force is at intermittent intervals brain-dead because they're all trying to score with the females in their respective offices or plants, it's a hell of an incentive to hang in there. While they're busy flirting with anything in a skirt, or are incommunicado because they're running around arranging for hotel rooms in which to get a quickie or a nooner, we're scoring in the boardrooms and taking over the assembly lines. It serves the bastards right for taking too much for granted."

"It's not enough, though," Virginia mused aloud. "Each of them should know what it feels like to be treated like a sex object—to be passed over for a promotion, not because he lacked in ability but because he said no to a superior with the power to nix his chances. It happened to me. It happens every day to scores of other women. Recently there have been reported cases of the reverse, but it's never anyone you know and you can't really be sure of the facts. Just once, I wish I had personal knowledge of—or maybe I should say, the personal satisfaction of—knowing at least one of the smug S.O.B.'s got a taste of the sexist baloney we've been swallowing."

Claudia's glossed lips curved at the corners, setting in a decidedly devilish grin. "My, aren't we vindictive? Well, since we're of a like mind and similar nature, let me make your day. Dillon's accusations are true. It's a shame you couldn't have witnessed the scene for yourself. You would have enjoyed it."

"I'm sure I would have," Virginia said, playing along.

"I will deny it ever occurred, of course. I think I'll find having legal intercourse with him infinitely more satisfying than physical intercourse." Claudia laughed at the prospect.

Virginia's nails dugs into the flesh of her palms. She had to remind herself how critical it was to Joe Dillon's future that she not betray her true feelings.

Claudia glanced at her wristwatch. "I'd love to fill you in on all the humorous details but I'm expected at an art exhibit in less than an hour. It's a showing of Marces Preven. Are you familiar with his work?"

"Afraid not." An art happening was the last thing on Virginia's mind.

"He's quite good." Claudia took a compact from her purse and quickly inspected her makeup. "On canvas and in bed." She clicked shut the compact and dropped it back in her purse. "I'll expect you to keep me posted as to Dillon's intentions. You might tell him it would be a big mistake to pursue legal channels."

"I already have," Virginia said truthfully.

"Then do so again," was Claudia's last word on the subject.

Virginia followed Claudia as far as Rita's desk. She wanted to make certain the woman did not return unexpectedly. Once she was sure the coast was clear, she went back to her desk to retrieve a small rectangular object from under the clutter of paperwork.

A faint click resounded as her thumb flicked the black button to the off position.

"Gotcha!" A pleased smile curled on Virginia's lips as she opened a drawer and placed the tape recorder inside.

The jangle of Rita's bracelets heralded her return from the ladies' room. "So? What happened?" She was near bursting with curiosity.

"Ms Shapell was most cooperative."

Rita expelled a relieved sigh. "I was a nervous wreck."

"Me, too," Virginia confessed. "Let's get on with it. Place the necessary calls. One to Don Sebastian, one to Joe Dillon."

"Don you want to tell Joe Dillon the good news yourself?"

"No, not yet. Just convey my message the way we rehearsed it. Tell him I want to meet with him in my office, the day after tomorrow, and to come with an open mind. Be sure to pass along to him that it's a request, not a demand."

Rita nodded. She was looking forward to talking to Don Sebastian again. He had a charming manner over the phone. This time she'd try to keep it short. Ginny was going to have a fit when she got a look at this month's long-distance bill.

CHAPTER NINETEEN

JOE DILLON DID NOT KNOW what to expect from the upcoming meeting with Ginny. A part of him figured she was going to try once more to dissuade him from bringing suit against Sebastian Designs; another part of him hoped she would have had a change of heart. In any case, he had to keep the appointment, if only as an excuse to be near her again.

He hated what was happening between them—the mistrust, the prideful standoff. He wished with all his heart it could be different. But then, he had to remind himself that wishful thinking was a bad habit of his— a way of not facing the truth. And the truth of the matter was, he and Ginny could not bridge the gap that Claudia Shapell had gouged between them. The past two days had been hellish for him. He didn't know how he was going to live without Ginny. Worse yet, he didn't know how he could live with himself if he gave in to her.

These were the thoughts that swirled in his head as he rode the elevator up to Ginny's office. He was functioning on autopilot. He smiled at Rita out of sheer reflex action as she escorted him inside. His eyes immediately went to Ginny, almost missing the distinguished-looking gentleman already seated in the room.

"Good. You came," Virginia said in relief. "There's someone I wanted you to meet." Her gaze traveled to Don Sebastian as she simultaneously motioned for Joe Dillon to take a chair. "You'll recognize the name. Don Sebastian, may I introduce to you your ambassador in the States, Joe Dillon Mahue."

The silver-haired gentleman stood. "It is a pleasure." He spoke with a rich Spanish accent.

J.D. looked bewildered. "Likewise" was the best he could manage.

When the two men were seated, Virginia explained the circumstances to J.D. "I called Don Sebastian and asked him to come here so that we could try to settle the problem that has arisen. I took the liberty of filling him in on the details, J.D."

"I was shocked to hear of your complaint against my partner," Don Sebastian interjected. "It is a most serious allegation."

"Yes, sir, I know it is." Joe Dillon squared his chin. "But I also happen to think that a man's self-respect is a serious matter."

"I agree." Don Sebastian nodded thoughtfully. "Please do not misunderstand me, Señor Mahue. I am not here to try to influence your decision. I have come because I am interested in learning the truth. If my partner has done these things you claim, I will take action myself. Of this, you can be sure."

"Which is precisely why I asked you gentlemen to join me today," Virginia broke in. Her gaze came to rest on J.D. "I have proof of Claudia Shapell's harassment."

Joe Dillon sat stunned. "How could you? We were alone when—"

"She and I had a conversation about sexism—in general and in particular—a few days ago. I taped it." Virginia withdrew the tape recorder from the drawer and set it on her desk. She looked to Don Sebastian. "When Mr. Sebastian and I first talked of this matter, he said he could do nothing unless the claim could be substantiated. So I tricked Ms Shapell into confiding in me what really took place."

Virginia switched on the recorder and let the tape speak for itself. When it was done, both men wore a disgusted expression.

Don Sebastian was the first to speak. "I do not know what to say. It is a terrible blow to be deceived by someone you think you know so well." He turned to Joe Dillon with an apologetic look. "I am sorry, Señor Mahue. I hope you understand that I knew nothing of my partner's scheming. A man's honor is most important to an Argentine. You have my guarantee that I will confront my partner and she will answer for her despicable actions. If she does not agree to stop her exploitive practices at once, I will sever our partnership and expose her shameful conduct. Those in the design world will shun her because of the black name she gives our business. She knows I will do it, the same as she knows I will be monitoring her every move until I am satisfied she can be trusted. Even so, I do not feel it is enough to censure the guilty. Please, you must allow me to make restitution to you for the injury you have suffered."

Joe Dillon could see the fury in the elder man's eyes. "I can see that you're a man of honor, Mr. Sebastian. I only want two things from you—a release from my contract and your word that whoever represents your line in the future doesn't get the same kind of sexist treatment."

Don Sebastian considered his terms carefully. "I will of course honor both your requests, but I humbly ask you to reconsider and remain as my ambassador."

Joe Dillon grinned for the very first time. "I'm no model, Mr. Sebastian. I made a mistake when I signed on. I miss working the land. I realized how much when I was in your fine country. I've got plans to return to Argentina. As a matter of fact, I've already put money down on some rich acreage up near Paraná River."

It was the first time Virginia had heard of such a purchase. The news hit her with a jolt.

"My own *estancias* is in the pampas. One day I will retire there. But first I will marry. It would be too lonely a life without a woman to brighten the long days and warm the cold nights."

"My sentiments exactly, Don Sebastian." Mischief twinkled in Joe Dillon's eyes as he shot a look in Virginia's direction.

"Will you choose to marry a woman of my country or one from your own?" It seemed a logical question to Don Sebastian. Since Joe Dillon had already invested in the land, he assumed he would wed very soon.

Virginia wanted to scream. The two of them had forgotten all about the original purpose for her bringing them together. It wasn't to discuss Joe Dillon's marriage prospects.

She cleared her throat to get their attention.

Don Sebastian had the decency to look embarrassed. "Please forgive me, Miss Vandivere. You are busy and we should talk of matters of immediate concern.''

"That's quite all right. I just want to make sure that the three of us are in agreement as to how to deal with the situation,'' she said primly.

Don Sebastian and Joe Dillon exchanged shrugs. Neither understood what more needed to be said.

"We have each other's word, Ginny.''

Incredible! She'd knocked herself out and they summed up the whole ordeal as requiring nothing more than a five-minute huddle in order to get their signals straight.

"There will have to be adjustments made in the campaign, of course,'' Don Sebastian put forth. "I leave the decision of a replacement in your capable hands.''

Virginia sat back and contemplated them both for a moment. "Someone else at Hanks and Udell will be handling your account, Don Sebastian. I'm resigning my position,'' she announced.

Joe Dillon was staggered by the news. He stared at her uncomprehendingly. "But why, Ginny?'' His voice registered the alarm he felt at hearing she intended to give up her dream of a partnership.

"Because if you're determined to go to Argentina, then so am I.'' She was almost as shocked as Joe Dillon at what had spilled from her lips. She'd given a good deal of thought over the past two days to what would truly make her happy, but she hadn't definitely decided the future direction her life would take until a moment ago. When he'd mentioned buying property in Argentina, she knew he was serious about starting anew on another continent. She knew then and there that she had to go with him. A life in New York would be meaningless without him. She wanted and was ready for the deep and abiding kind of commitment he'd once talked about.

A roaring silence filled the room. Don Sebastian realized the meeting had suddenly turned personal. "Perhaps you two young people would like a little privacy?"

Neither one responded. Their attention was riveted on each other.

Don Sebastian's departure went unnoticed.

"God! Say *something*, J.D." Virginia's heart was pounding wildly. She feared he no longer wanted her with him.

"You'd be giving up a lot, Ginny. I don't feel right about asking it of you."

"You didn't ask. I volunteered. Can't you please forgive me for being such an ass? Don't you love me still, J.D.?" Her bottom lip began to tremble. She was shriveling up inside—scared to death she'd done too little too late.

In a flash he was out of his chair, around the desk and kissing her soundly. "I'll be loving you to the grave and beyond, girl," he vowed.

He pulled her up into his arms, embracing her so tightly he squeezed the breath from her. "It'll be a good life, Ginny darlin'. I saved most of my earnings. It's not exactly a fortune but it's enough to stake us to a dream or two. We're going to build an empire together in Argentina. Hell! We'll build two empires. Cotton and advertising. How's that strike your fancy, Mrs. Mahue?"

"I've been a bad influence on you," she said worriedly. "What happened to the unmaterialistic man who wanted nothing more than the simple pleasures out of life?"

Joe Dillon cupped her face between his hands, tilting back her head and holding her gaze. "He also wants to give the woman he loves any and everything her heart desires."

She linked her arms about his waist and gazed up at him with adoring eyes. "It's not necessary. I'm embracing all I'll ever desire right at this moment. I love you so much, J.D."

A knowing smile curved his lips. "You'd grow restless with the simple life after a while. I figure I need to provide an outlet for that ambitious nature of yours. Carving out a kingdom in South America ought to keep you challenged for the next fifty years."

"At least," she said, laughing. "I'm game for whatever makes you happy, so long as we work in the time to produce three or four heirs to the Mahue name and fortune."

"Oh, that's the easy part." He grinned down at her, then winked. "And the best part."

VIRGINIA WAS PACKING UP a few last personal items in her office when Julie Dobeckie came in.

"I can't believe it. I mean, I heard it a week ago, but it still isn't registering." The young woman walked around the desk, trailing her fingertips over the polished surface.

"Well, as you can see, it's true." Virginia took down a framed poster from the wall and set it on the floor.

"How can you do it? You're my idol. All I've ever thought about, dreamed about, was being in your place one day. You've got everything I want. Prestige, power, the respect of your male peers, not to mention a big fat salary." Julie's hand reverently stroked the rolled edge of the leather director's chair. "Why would a woman who has so much going for her chuck a brilliant career for a man? It's crazy." She rested her elbows on the back of the chair and cradled her chin in her hands.

Virginia took down the last framed poster and turned to her with a patient smile. "Once I would've thought the exact same thing. Yes, I've enjoyed the due that comes with success. I worked hard for it and I deserved it. But you know what, Julie?"

"What?"

"I'm not addicted to it anymore. Men have had a longer time to be comfortable with success and power. Women have no role models, so they're still trying find their legs and strike a workable balance. I'm not giving up my career. I'm only fine-tuning it so that I can combine it with a personal life."

"Oh, so you're planning to stay in the ad game in Argentina?"

"Yes, but on a smaller scale. I intend to open my own agency when I'm ready." Virginia could see that Julie was itching to try on her chair for size. She stacked a few boxes in a corner, then collected her purse from a shelf in the closet.

"Have you any idea who your replacement will be?" the eager beaver asked.

"No," Virginia answered, walking over and extending her hand to Julie.

"I hope everything works out for you, Ms Vandivere. I learned a lot from you."

"I hope so, Julie. If women are to ever get ahead, the ones who are the pioneers must give those who come behind a helping hand."

"I'll try to remember that." Julie gave her a winning smile before releasing her hand.

Virginia crossed to the opened door, then paused and turned back to Julie with a half smile. "You know that old saying about being careful what you wish for because you might just get it?"

"Yeah," Julie said warily.

"Well, I probably shouldn't mention this, but I recommended you for my job."

"Really?! But why? I mean, there are others who are a lot more seasoned than me."

"Because you're good. Now all you have to do is prove it. Good luck." Virginia walked out the door—the door that still bore her name and title: Virginia Vandivere-Rice, Creative Director. She was trading them in for a new name and title—Ginny Mahue, wife and entrepreneur. It sounded good. It sounded right.

"Gee! Thanks! I mean, thanks a bunch! Wow! I don't believe it." Julie's elated gibberish floated out the opened doorway.

"What's with her?" Rita asked.

"I told her I recommended her for my job. She thinks I did her a favor." Virginia shot Rita a wink.

"Ayyy! Now I know I am going to retire early. I theenk maybe I will come to Argentina for a visit."

"That'll be nice. J.D. will love it."

"I'll try to come by," Rita said dryly.

"Come by? Don't be silly. You'll stay with us, of course."

"But I have already told Don Sebastian I would stay at his *estancias*." Rita grinned slyly.

"You devil, you!" Virginia laughed out loud. "Could he be a likely candidate for husband number four?"

"He ees-sss hot stuff. And you have to admit, Mundo knows men." Rita's shoulders shimmied and she rolled her dark eyes.

Virginia smiled, remembering how it had all begun....

Harlequin Superromance®

COMING NEXT MONTH

#402 PRECIOUS THINGS • Lynda Ward
Amanda and Mark Wexler lived charmed lives, complete
with a thriving antiques business and a showpiece of a
home in Portland, Oregon. And then it was discovered that
the baby Amanda was carrying had Down's syndrome.
Suddenly their marriage seemed as fragile as one of the
antiques in their showroom. Rising above this development
would require more giving and caring than either had
ever known . . .

#403 BODY AND SOUL • Janice Kaiser
For the five years Derek Gordon's wife had been in a coma,
he'd been tortured by one question: when does a marriage
die if there's been no death but the marriage itself? Poetess
Lara Serenov's friendship provided the caring and
compassion he needed during a difficult time. But one day
compassion turned to passion and Derek found himself
tormented by a whole new series of questions. . . .

#404 WEST OF THE SUN • Lynn Erickson
To Ben Tanner, Julie Hayden's heart seemed as hard and
parched as her drought-stricken ranch. But then Ben and
Julie discovered a mysterious valley. Under the magical
influence of the land Julie began to blossom again, while
Ben himself rediscovered the meaning of love
and wonder. . . .

#405 PRIZE PASSAGE • Dawn Stewardson
Psychologist Holly Russell wished there were more places
to hide aboard the cruise ship *Taurus*. Then at least she
could avoid Mac McCloy and maybe her hormones and her
heart would stop racing each other. She hoped they would
because Holly already *had* a fiancé—a perfect man, chosen
by exact scientific criteria.

Have You Ever Wondered If You Could Write A Harlequin Novel?

Here's great news—Harlequin is offering a series of cassette tapes to help you do just that. Written by Harlequin editors, these tapes give practical advice on how to make your characters—and your story—come alive. There's a tape for each contemporary romance series Harlequin publishes.

Mail order only

All sales final

This April, don't miss Harlequin's new Award of
Excellence title from

Award of
Excellence

elusive as the unicorn

*When Eve Eden discovered that Adam
Gardener, successful art entrepreneur, was
searching for the legendary English artist, The
Unicorn, she nervously shied away. The Unicorn's
true identity hit too close to home....*

*Besides, Eve was rattled by Adam's
mesmerizing presence, especially in the light
of the ridiculous coincidence of their names—
and his determination to take advantage of it!
But Eve was already engaged to marry her
longtime friend, Paul.*

*Yet Eve found herself troubled by the different
choices Adam and Paul presented. If only the
answer to her dilemma didn't keep eluding her....*

HP1258-1

The Adventurer
JAYNE ANN KRENTZ

Remember THE PIRATE (Temptation #287), the first book of Jayne Ann Krentz's exciting trilogy Ladies and Legends? Next month Jayne brings us another powerful romance, THE ADVENTURER (Temptation #293), in which Kate, Sarah and Margaret — three long-time friends featured in THE PIRATE — meet again.

A contemporary version of a great romantic myth, THE ADVENTURER tells of Sarah Fleetwood's search for long-lost treasure and for love. Only when she meets her modern-day knight-errant Gideon Trace will Sarah know she's found the path to fortune and eternal bliss....

THE ADVENTURER — available in April 1990! And in June, look for THE COWBOY (Temptation #302), the third book of this enthralling trilogy.
